# STONEMOOR HOUSE

# STONEMOOR HOUSE

## Kay Stephens

This first world edition published in Great Britain 1995 by
SEVERN HOUSE PUBLISHERS LTD of
9–15 High Street, Sutton, Surrey SM1 1DF.
First published in the USA 1995 by
SEVERN HOUSE PUBLISHERS INC of
595 Madison Avenue, New York, NY 10022.

British Library Cataloguing in Publication Data
Stephens, Kay
  Stonemoor House
  I. Title
  823.914 [F]

  ISBN 0-7278-4768-6

All situations in this publication are fictitious and
any resemblance to living persons is purely coincidental.

Typeset by Hewer Text Composition Services, Edinburgh.
Printed and bound in Great Britain by
Hartnolls Ltd, Bodmin, Cornwall.

# Chapter One

Steeling herself to go out there, Pamela stood by the window watching. Their weary faces transformed now, smiling as light-heartedly as the children they were encouraging, the other women seemed to have shed the war's anguish overnight since VJ Day.

Mothers and grandmothers, aunts and older sisters, they had adopted celebration as naturally as their good frocks, cherished since 1940 and protected now by pinafores. They ran in and out of houses, through yards, up and down white- or yellow-stoned steps, their energy newly restored. Replenishing the tables that stretched halfway along the street, they brought plates of sandwiches, buns and biscuits, jellies, fruit, and custard. Everything was for the youngsters, these jabbering Yorkshire kids who now seemed assured of a decent future.

Pamela had sworn she couldn't endure the street party jollification. One thing only had changed her mind. The look her mother had given her. She had grown to expect the challenge that lay behind the sympathy in those familiar blue eyes; the look that said "Don't give in, don't be soft, love."

Mildred Baker was anything but soft; Pamela could never complain her mother expected more of others than of herself. Widowed when a factory accident killed the father Pamela remembered with lingering affection, Mildred had raised two young boys as well, and cheerfully, bringing them through the war years unaided while Pamela herself was in the WAAF. Tom and Ian were a credit to her now, twelve and fourteen, fun yet with a serious side. The three of them had grown up aware that Mum almost made up for a missing father.

Inhaling deeply in an effort for self-control, Pamela willed herself to walk towards the door. She need only smile, that was all, give her mother reassurance that her daughter had inherited a measure, at least, of her own native grit. And there had been a concession, willingly made: Mildred Baker's word that none of the neighbours would be told, not until after tomorrow. These two days were declared a holiday, after all, for national rejoicing.

Even her brothers didn't know; that also had been on Pamela's insistence. They were excited – about this party, and the bonfires that would follow. She hadn't the heart to burden either Tom or Ian. Tom, although the younger of the pair, was the more thoughtful, would want to share her pain. This wasn't the right time. And as for Ian, he'd always been closer to her, reminding her as he did of the father she had idolised. Ian had suffered badly, all those years ago, through being just old enough to understand what that factory accident meant to their family. She didn't want to bring that sort of distress back into his eyes, the brown of sherry.

Her own eyes gazed back from the pockmarked mirror on the wall by the door, blue irises nearly obscured by lids heavy from lack of sleep, shadows beneath them. Otherwise, she hardly looked any different. Her dark gold hair had been curled last night, wound around pipecleaners, just like every night. As if there still was a reason for making the best of herself. Nothing had been said, but Pamela had known her mother approved. She'd never let herself go either, had she? Memory resurrected Mildred's visit to the woman next door for a home shampoo and set,

2

before going to the undertaker's all those years ago. At the time, Pamela had believed that unnatural. She'd long since recognised it as one aid to facing the unacceptable.

Always clean and tidy, that was Mildred Baker. Today, as Pamela walked towards her she registered that her mother also generally managed to be smiling. How anyone achieved that, she really couldn't imagine.

"What wants doing?" Pam heard herself asking, addressing not only her mother but the group of housewives congregated behind one of the long sides of the table.

Peggy Kemp from across the street answered.

"Hallo, love. Well, it's the tea we're waiting on. Her next door to me has borrowed a big teapot, she's inside filling it up again now."

"Happen I could help to pour," Pamela suggested, yearning for something to occupy her hands.

"We'd be glad if you would," said her mother. "Your young wrists'll be stronger nor ours, and yon pot's right heavy."

The woman was emerging with the tea, nearly staggering as she carefully negotiated the steps to her yard.

Pamela ran across the grey setts to meet her. "I'm coming to give you a hand."

Filling beakers, cups and the occasional half-pint pot, Pamela hurried back and forth between the table and the blackened sandstone wall where tea was dispensed. Many of the children hadn't seen her since she'd returned to Halifax, and gave her a grin or spared her a word amid chattering with their contemporaries. Being with the youngsters made Pamela feel a bit better, as if her face might not be set permanently in a look of despair. You couldn't frown with them, nobody could, not while they were squabbling over buns, or laughing into their jellies. Pamela herself nearly laughed, watching a lad carefully retrieve jelly that had slithered off his plate then go dashing indoors to rinse the grit off the wobbling red mound.

They were a grand bunch of kids, united perhaps by the war which, if it hadn't brought much bombing to the town, had produced uniform deprivation. The worst shortage, of their menfolk, had drawn everybody together. And the few dads whose health or age had made them unfit for service had taken other children to their hearts. They had helped out, patching up well-worn toys, teaching skills with battered bicycles, sharing rare wartime treats.

Today the tinies who didn't possess older siblings were tended just the same, and maybe with more patience, by boys and girls alike who enjoyed a mothering role.

"Don't it do your heart good to see 'em?" one mother asked, smiling at Pam. "It's the kids that count, you know, in the end. And we've got a champion lot here, bless 'em."

When Pamela agreed, the woman smiled again. "I daresay that's what you'll be thinking of, now the war's finally over – a family. Have you heard yet when your hubby's due home?"

Pamela shook her head, moved away, became very busy tying the hair ribbon of a tiny girl in a dress hastily made out of a Union Jack.

The child's mother was watching as she collected up empty plates. "Getting your hand in, are you?" she laughed, nudging Pamela's ribs. "You lot that haven't had bairns yet will be making up for lost time, soon as you're together again. When is he coming home, love?"

Evading similar questions became an obsession, while Pamela tried to fill her mind with tasks: small mouths that had to be wiped, and noses; toddlers to be escorted to lavatories. When eventually the women began clearing

4

away the dirty dishes, she took several piles of them into her mother's kitchen, closed the outer door with a thankful sigh.

Mildred Baker bustled in five minutes later. "There, you look a lot better. I knew it was no good shutting yourself away, brooding. It's allus best to keep going with summat. And to mix with folk. You'll not find it nearly so hard next time you meet any of 'em."

No? wondered Pamela. Not when they'll all have heard by then – will be bound to come out with all their advice, their homilies, *sympathy*? One kind word, and she'd go to pieces; two, and she'd never pull herself together again.

"Why don't you put your feet up, Mum? I'll see to these. You've been hard at it all day. And for weeks beforehand, if I know you, baking stuff and so on."

"Aye, well – we knew peace were on its way, didn't we? Had to be prepared."

"So why don't you have a sit down?"

"If you're sure you're all right."

Her mother's iron-grey head was nodding as she dozed in the chair when Pamela finally went through to the living room.

"I've put our stuff away, Mum. I've left other folk's stacked on the kitchen table. It's going to take days for everybody to sort out what's their own."

Mildred nodded. "Time you had a bit of a rest an' all, isn't it?"

"Didn't I say? I'm going out, just for a while, with Dorothy." It was a lie, but she needed to get away, ached to be on her own with this fact that she alone must learn to accept.

"That's right. It'll do you good. You'll happen see the lads, a gang of them's touring the bonfires. The one in the next street were lit afore I came in, I could smell it from

5

here. Are you going down into town? There'll be dancing in front of the Town Hall, I reckon . . ."

And nobody to dance with, ever.

"See you later, Mum. Ta-ra."

The sky was darkening above the slate roofs of the rows of back-to-back houses. Pamela called goodnight to the folk putting away tables that had been placed end to end along her street. Across Parkinson Lane she spotted their Ian and Tom, faces aglow with excitement, nearly as bright as the flames beginning to devour the pile of timber which some white-haired man was lighting. With a group of lads her brothers were laughing, shrieking, carefree. So light-hearted they seemed younger than their years.

How will I tell them? she thought, how drain their happiness?

From the street end she could see Beacon Hill, justifying its name with a blaze that challenged the bonfires now appearing on countless sites all about her. There would be other beacons too, she supposed, signalling peace across her beloved Yorkshire hills.

Groups of people were hurrying down Parkinson Lane, smiling and talking, heading towards the town centre celebrations.

Pamela turned in the opposite direction, walking briskly, her head down. She'd no desire to talk to anyone, old friend or neighbour. Past silent mills she hastened, terraces and larger semi-detached houses, and she did not glance their way.

The familiarity of years took her up Warley Road and into West View Park. She followed a path now barely visible, merely a paler stripe between stretches of lawn as the night gathered around her. And then there she stood, gazing out from the top of the stone steps where she'd played so often as a youngster.

About and before her ranged the hills, sentinel over the commerce in these valleys of the industrial West Riding. Her favourite place. And lit now with more bonfires flaring at intervals throughout the landscape. Voices carried on drifts of woodsmoke, and laughter, rejoicing.

Pamela swallowed, tears filled her eyes, but she was still too stricken to weep. And dared not let go in case she lost control completely. "Oh, Jim," she sighed, slowly shaking her head.

The news had come yesterday, while she was at the airfield packing to come on leave.

A drunken motorist had finished what Hitler's Luftwaffe had attempted last year – by speeding into Jim's motorbike to crush the head still scarred from the night his fighter crash-landed.

Her own CO had extended her leave indefinitely on compassionate grounds. Arriving home, her mother had held her. Everyone, when they heard, would be just as sympathetic. Nothing could help.

What would she do? With her life – in the immediate future, long term? They had had such plans. Ever since VE Day they'd been planning again. They had worked together before the war, even before they married. It wasn't big, as businesses went, but it had been their own. She had always had a bit of a flair for decorating, had met Jim years ago when, doing up her bedroom, she had been defeated by papering the ceiling.

He'd teased her a bit, but had done a good job, and had talked a lot while he worked, dispensing professional advice along with getting to know her. She had been delighted when Jim asked her to join his firm; even doing the books when she'd rather have been revamping someone's house hadn't really mattered. Gradually, though, he had let her share the actual decorating, and

7

she had believed she'd found the work to fill the rest of her life.

And now she was on her own. Her feelings were too raw for even thinking about the business. How could she carry on? She would be twenty-seven next birthday: life stretched before her, an unending succession of fruitless days which must be endured.

Unable to bear the view, or anything resembling beauty, Pamela turned away. Leaving the park, she headed back through streets of stone houses where lights shone out from windows proclaiming the joy of release from that everlasting blackout. Passing the end of her own street, and not yet ready for facing her bed and the night, she continued downhill.

Walking swiftly, ignoring the crowds hastening in the same direction, Pam reached Bull Green. She hesitated at last, pondering, staring as yet more folk poured from every road at the wide intersection. Where could she go? Shaking her head over this new lack of purpose, she followed everyone else, numbly, aware only of her desire to walk away from everything.

Surrounded by north country voices, Pam emerged in Southgate and paused again to stare incredulously at the mass of dancing citizens stretching as far as she could see towards the town hall steps.

Over the roadway setts, stumbling on pavement edges, the entire population of Halifax seemed to be dancing. Letting go, letting down their hair, letting victory envelope them.

She had expected to feel more alone, to feel more sharply the emptiness of loss. Somehow, though, she now felt hardly anything. All emotion was dulled by this scene, as unreal as her life with no Jim to return to Yorkshire.

"Pamela! Just the person I wanted to see . . ."

The voice a foot or so behind her head had made her jump. She swung round to meet smiling brown eyes beneath a policeman's helmet.

"Hallo, Roger," she said dejectedly.

"Is Jim home as well?" he asked, searching the nearby throng for his old schoolfriend. "I've heard summat that could be useful to you both. Came across a store of decorating stuff t'other day. Belonged to an old chap who died during the war after a long illness. His widow's not bothered so long as she gets shot of it and makes a bob or two. I have all the details at home, I'll call round with them. There's masses of wallpaper, and plenty of distemper and gloss paint. They've been stored right well, an' all, most of it's going to be all right."

"Thank you, Roger, but . . ." Pam began awkwardly, then stopped, and willed herself to cease being so silly about not telling folk.

"I just know it'd be the very thing to start you off again. With decorating materials likely to be in short supply for ages."

Pamela nodded, swallowed. "I really appreciate you thinking of us, love. It's just – well, I don't know now whatever I shall be doing. Jim – Jim won't be coming home, you see. He was killed, on the road, an accident . . ."

"Oh, God! Oh, no, Pamela . . . When – when was this?"

"Day before yesterday. I heard while I was packing to come on leave."

"Eh, I am sorry! I don't know what to say. Me and Jim were like brothers ever since we were in the Infants together."

"I know."

"Whatever will you do, lass?"

9

"Eh, I don't know. It was all we thought of, getting demobbed, starting the business up again. It's all I know, Roger . . ."

"You were damned good, as well. Especially at working out colour schemes and that. You could still do that, I suppose . . . Why don't we have a talk? I'll come round sometime when I'm off duty. You are stopping with your mother?"

Roger was trying to look at his watch without appearing offhand with her. And then the town hall clock struck the quarter.

"Afraid I've got to meet up with my sergeant now. But I will see you afore so long. Take care, mind."

Why, Pam thought savagely, why take care? When there was nothing to look forward to any longer, no point to this existence. Grimly, she sighed and turned her back on the revellers.

The pungent smell of woodsmoke was stronger than before, wafting to her on the night air, stinging eyes and throat as she trudged uphill, against the flow of excited families, away from the town centre.

Passing the People's Park, she all but choked on a sob trapped inside her. They had walked around its paths so often, she and Jim, had sat listening to the band on Sunday afternoons. Jim was a fanatic about brass bands, had been so proud when they had performed on this bandstand. And then there were all the times while they were courting and had lingered together in the pavilion here to kiss in its limited privacy.

Nothing would ever be the same. No matter what she attempted now, her life was a casualty.

Pamela listened two days later while Roger Jenkins read over the list of decorating materials that he had discovered. She never had liked waste: it would be a terrible shame if all this stuff were not put to good use. During their last leave together Jim had been bemoaning the fact that any such new materials might only be allocated for repairing war-damaged property. If he could have survived, he would have been highly delighted to learn of all this stock.

Determined not to make everybody miserable about her own loss, Pamela asked how Roger was.

"I'm all right," he assured her with a smile. "Not bad at all."

He certainly looked well, the police force evidently suited him. At least there were some things that she could still feel glad about. Roger had joined the RAF at the same time as Jim, but that hadn't lasted. The rigours of training had caused a recurrence of his childhood asthma, in a massive attack. A short stay in hospital had been followed by his discharge on medical grounds before he saw any active service.

Pamela had gathered that once his doctor back home had the asthma under control, Roger had approached the police force about working with them. They had been glad to weigh against his health, taking on a young man when so many of his contemporaries were being conscripted into the forces.

"Have you managed to keep the band together?" she enquired.

"Just about – not that we get to play so often, these days. We rely heavily on the chaps that're retiring age. Sometimes, lads that are on leave join us for one night. I'm afraid there's only me and another fellow around the same age now. You might remember him, he had polio when he was a kid, that's why he's remained in civvies."

Pamela couldn't make a decision about those decorating materials. She felt torn today, her old enthusiasm

11

for renovating people's houses providing her with mind pictures of how these precious items might be used, compelling her to visualise how good it would be to work again at this job that she had loved.

But her love for Jim had been the greater, and prevented her from contemplating restarting the firm without him.

"I just don't know," she told Roger. "Happen I might be able to think a bit straighter after the funeral."

In the event, the funeral reduced her to such a rigid mass of strain that she could hardly think at all. Jim's mother, widowed long ago like her own, seemed shrunken by grief. Pamela could only grasp the fragile shoulder and watch over the little woman who remained huddled so pathetically on her knees throughout the church service. Her own brothers caused her nearly as much concern. As soon as they were told, both Ian and Tom had insisted that they wished to attend the funeral. Pamela had been touched, glad that they remembered Jim for his interest in everything they did. On the day, though, she felt racked by the sight of tears that neither lad was mature enough to contain.

She herself would not weep, or not until she was quite alone. Despite the days that had elapsed since her return to Halifax, she was still afraid that once she let go she would never cease weeping. And that would never do, she could only rely on herself to somehow find enough stamina for surviving.

The emotion Pamela needed to release had not emerged by the time she was heading back to the airforce base in Kent. But here, at least, she would find some means of occupying the hours that felt so unremittingly empty. Her CO welcomed her back briskly, if with a reminder that she might have extended her compassionate leave.

Pam smiled wanly. "Thanks, but I'm better here really.

12

For the time being, any road. But I'll be grateful if I'm allowed to get away when there's things to see to – Jim's affairs, and all that."

The officer nodded. "No problem there. And what of the future, Sergeant Canning? If you need to take early release from service, I'll see what I can arrange. You were in business, weren't you?"

"Before the war, aye. Don't know what I want now."

"No. Well – early days yet. Just come to me if I can help."

Everyone was being kind, but there was little easing of the pain brought on by the first news of Jim's death. Pamela was beginning to feel afraid that the rest of her life would be blackened by this appalling loss.

This dread was still with her when she returned to Halifax to deal with Jim's finances. Roger Jenkins was the other executor, and when he'd phoned to say Jim's solicitor was ready to see them again, had offered to meet her at the station.

"How are you, love?" Roger asked, stepping forward at the barrier to take her case. He was in civvies today and the neat trilby he'd raised had reminded her that Roger always was a snappy dresser.

When he removed his good gaberdine raincoat in the solicitor's office, she noticed that his suit, although prewar, was beautifully pressed. His brown hair was neatly parted.

Suddenly, Pamela caught herself wondering if she was observing all this about Roger as a defence against examining her feelings. Certainly, today she was experiencing no more than the sensation of unreality which had epitomised her life these past several weeks.

The fact that Jim had made a will before going to war seemed to simplify everything that must be done. Pamela was relieved to sit back and listen while Roger and the solicitor examined the finer points of her husband's modest estate. She was glad his mother was to receive an amount which ought to augment the pension already paid to her, enabling her to stay on in her terraced house.

To Pamela herself there would come little cash, which was no more than she'd anticipated, but there was the bulk of his personal possessions. The only exception to this bequest was the stipulation that Roger should inherit his prized saxophone.

Roger's delight made Pam thankful their good friend was being rewarded for his assistance.

She was still feeling glad about this when the solicitor began outlining Jim's hopes regarding the company that they had run together. She had given little thought to its featuring in the will. With both of them going off to the war, they had ended the lease on their tiny shop and had got rid of many items of equipment. On paper, though, Jim expressed the wish that it should be restored to a viable business, with Pamela in charge.

"I'll have to think about that," she admitted gravely. "I'm sorry, but this has all been such a shock. I hardly know what I'm doing now, never mind in the future."

The solicitor hadn't sounded very understanding, but Roger made up for that as they sat in the bus taking them to her mother's.

"Don't let anyone hassle you, love. Jim wouldn't have wanted that. He was probably just mentioning the business to make it clear that he didn't want anybody but you to start it up again."

"Happen so. But the fact remains that he seemed to expect me to carry on where we left off. Trouble is, Roger, I don't believe I have it in me."

"You did some good work before the war, Pam."

She smiled slightly. "Thanks. Jim had taught me most

14

of what he'd learned when he was apprenticed. Even how to tackle ceilings! D'you remember how he used to love telling how he'd had to paper the one in that tiny bedroom of mine, because I couldn't manage it?"

"And I always thought you had more flair than he had for colour schemes," Roger persisted.

"Aye, well – he'd learned his trade in the days when everybody wanted all their woodwork graining. And wallpaper had to be serviceable, and not show the dirt. He'd not been allowed to use much imagination."

"While you could, and did. If you wanted, you know, you could go in for this in a big way. Launch out into proper interior design, not just stick to a bit of painting and decorating."

Pamela remained unconvinced, but she invited Roger in nevertheless when they reached the end of her mother's street.

Roger declined. "If you don't mind, I'd rather be on my way."

"You're not on duty later today, are you?" asked Pam, feeling awkward now about the time he had spent with her at the solicitor's.

"No, love, nowt like that. Just somebody I promised to see."

While she stood on the street corner thanking Roger for all he had done Pamela quelled a ridiculous feeling that he was being secretive about where he was going. Why should he tell her, after all? she thought as she turned away. He had been Jim's friend really, and was being extremely good to her now, but neither of those facts meant he owed her any explanations.

Her mother emerged from the kitchen as soon as Pamela opened the door that led straight into the living room.

"How did you get on, Pam love? Was it all straight-forward?"

"Most of it, aye. Jim's left his mother enough for her to manage on, thank goodness. And Roger's to have his saxophone, he's suited to death about that."

"Oh, I see." Mildred Baker looked crestfallen.

"What's up, Mum? I'm pleased for Roger to have it. He couldn't have been more helpful to me since this happened."

"Aye, I know. Take no notice."

"Only . . .?"

Her mother sighed as she went back into the kitchen. "I were being proper daft, I suppose, but I were hoping it might have come to our Ian. Jim knew he were getting fond of band music . . ."

"But Ian's never learned to play, Mother. It took you all your time to pay for his piano lessons. Now Roger could be as good as Jim himself was, once he has his own instrument to practise on."

"Aye, I daresay." Only Roger could have saved up for a sax long before this if he'd really wanted one, thought Mildred. And now our Ian doesn't stand a chance. I'll never be able to give him anything like that.

Laying aside that particular care, Mildred glanced at her daughter who had followed her and was leaning against the draining board. "Shall I put the kettle on? You're looking right peaky, love."

"I'll see to it. You're busy with your baking. I could certainly use a cuppa, I'm a bit shaken up. Jim put a clause in the will suggesting that I carry on the business."

"Well, he would, wouldn't he? He'd not want anybody else fancying they could muscle in on it."

"But how can I, Mum? On my own . . .?"

"That's up to you, of course. But I'd have thought you'd

16

have been relieved to have that all sorted out. It'd give you a bit of security."

"Happen. And maybe it'd just be one big worry."

"Eh, love – you're still right down, aren't you? I wish I knew how to help. But I do understand, you know. I had to manage after I lost your dad, remember. And on nowt more than taking in folk's washing and ironing."

Pamela's smile was rueful. "I have a feeling that I'd be glad if that were all that's expected of me!"

The blue eyes so like her own narrowed. "Get away with you. That's no sort of talk. It just shows how bad you've taken all this. Sit down, lass, I'll see to that tea. What you need is a good looking after . . ."

Being looked after, though, wasn't the solution for Pamela. She recognised during the next couple of days what she had begun to suspect on her first visit following Jim's accident. Her mother's sympathy, however well-meant, threatened to reduce her to a state where she was willing to be taken over. A few hours of comforting and Mildred Baker's warmth, and Pam began believing that she might just go to pieces. I believe I prefer it when she's warning me not to be soft, she thought.


During the following Sunday afternoon someone knocked at the door. Going to answer it, Pam found Roger Jenkins on their yellow-stoned steps.

"Glad I've caught you still at home, love," he began, brown eyes smiling. "Coming for a walk with me?"

Pamela hesitated for only a moment. "Aye – go on. Just come in and wait while I tell my mum, and get a coat." These West Riding autumns were too chilly for going without, even when it was as sunny as today.

"Where are you taking me then?" she asked as they set out along the street.

17

"Just for a bit of a walk. Knowing you, you'll not have been so far since I saw you t'other day."

Pamela grinned sideways at him. "I did venture out to the corner shop yesterday. Still, this is nice. I do appreciate it, Roger."

He began talking about his job, not something he did very often, but Pam had always found police work interesting. Listening to his account of a case that had been brought to court recently, Pamela realised that the Roger who dealt with villains was very different from the gentle individual she had known for years as Jim's friend.

They were heading in the general direction of Savile Park – 'the moor' to local folk. Pam was surprised when Roger suddenly took off down a narrow street. At the far end he stopped in front of a couple of lock-up garages. He was feeling in his pocket for a key.

"Couldn't let you go back without taking a look," he said.

Pamela sighed as he inserted the key in a padlock.

The garage seemed very dry inside, even fairly warm. She noticed that somebody had put up boarding to insulate its thin walls. Shelves along the two longest sides were neatly stacked with cans of paint and varnish. Three trestle pasting tables held roll upon roll of wallpaper.

"You've got a cheek, you beggar!" Pam exclaimed ruefully. "Bringing me here without a word. You should have said, you know."

"And you wouldn't have come. I'm not apologising, love. I wanted you to see all this stuff, so's you know what you're considering."

"What makes you think I'm considering owt?" she asked, though her tone had softened slightly. "I've said

18

already I think taking on the work Jim and I did together would be too much for me."

"You allus were too modest. Just look at this lot. And the old chap's widow only wants fifty pounds or so."

Pamela gave him another sideways glance. "If I hear of anybody in the trade who's interested I'll pass on the word."

"You know that isn't what I intended."

"Aye – well . . . Jim always said you were very persuasive. Afraid that'll cut no ice with me."

"There's some beautiful papers here, though, much better quality than you'll find for many a long month even now the war's behind us."

Pamela consented to examine two or three rolls, and admitted privately that she couldn't argue with Roger's evaluation of the wallpaper. When they emerged she thanked him for making sure that she saw what was being offered. "But I don't want you to go on about it, love, please," she added. "I've got to take my time over making my mind up."

When she arrived back home Pamela noticed immediately her mother's unaccustomed air of excitement.

"I've got news for you," Mildred exclaimed before her daughter had hung up her coat. "Our Elsie's been round, sends her love . . ."

"That's nice."

"Well, listen then – your Cousin Charlie's on his way home. That Japanese POW camp he was in was one of the first to be liberated by the Allies."

"That's good, Mum. I'm very pleased. And how is he? Has Auntie Elsie heard?"

"He's better than a lot of 'em, by all accounts. Undernourished, mainly. Oh – and he's got summat wrong with one of his feet, can't walk properly. He's going to need a lot of feeding up."

19

"I wonder how his mother will cope," said Pam.

"I was coming to that. You know how our Elsie's never been so well herself since the TB got to her bones. Actually, I've said I'll have Charlie here for a bit."

"Mum! Haven't you enough on with the two lads?"

"Eh, bless you, they're neither of them any bother now. And it'll be handy for Elsie to see him whenever she wants, being only a couple of streets away."

"Oh, aye. She'll be here many a time, cadging cups of tea."

"Don't you think that's rather unkind, Pamela? You know our Elsie's allus been delicate . . ."

"I know she's allus taken advantage of you, Mum. It's time somebody protected you from your own good nature. Any road, where are you going to put Charlie? It isn't as if we had a bedroom to spare."

"He can have mine while you're still in the WAAF, can't he? And I'll sleep in yours. When he's a bit better he'll happen manage to get up to the attic if I put him up there with the lads."

"How about sending him home once he improves that much?" enquired Pamela drily. But she hugged her mother, overcome by recognition of the need Mildred Baker had always had to care for folk.

Returning to the WAAF, Pamela spent the long train journey wondering if she really belonged anywhere. She felt quite uncomfortable at home, these days; conscious that no one really knew how to react to her bereavement. Any more than she understood how to deal with the awkwardness her loss had created in her family. Maybe she should settle for a peacetime service career. There was a lot to be said for the stringent routine and for having one's mind occupied by matters that weren't generated by oneself. Her mother would have

20

a bedroom spare for Cousin Charles. And she herself, with a steady income and few needs on which to lash out, might manage to save for the saxophone young Ian coveted.

# Chapter Two

Snowflakes fluttered down beyond windows which still retained the lattice of adhesive tape that had protected against the blast which could shatter them.

"I didn't really think it would come to this, you know," Pamela said, smiling towards her commanding officer for the last time. "When I came back here I'd almost decided to stay on in the WAAF."

"But you'll find it satisfying in civvy street, I'm sure, continuing the work begun with your husband."

"Well, at least I know by now that I've got to give it a try. I suppose that's an improvement on the way I felt before."

"You'd suffered an appalling shock, a badly timed one as well, just as everybody else was beginning look to the future."

"Well – don't be surprised if I eventually come to you asking to be taken on again!"

"I would be surprised, very. You underestimate yourself, my dear. Please bear in mind that I've said so."

They had given her a good send-off here in Kent. The mess had resounded with the party laid on by her colleagues, they'd even invited over some of the personnel from another air base in Surrey where she had begun her service. Pamela had been warmed by discovering that quite a few people there still remembered her.

She was going to miss them all, she reminded herself

while checking her billet for any property that she might have mislaid. In fact, one of the worst things about her civilian job would be working on her own, and she'd be obliged to do that, at least until she proved she could get the business onto a viable footing again.

Roger had offered to help, pointing out very swiftly that the way he worked shifts would often leave him free to give her a hand. Pam knew that she couldn't let him, that she wouldn't. Whether this venture succeeded or not, she must not become beholden to anyone.

"You've a stubborn streak in you," her mother had remarked after listening to these sentiments. "And it isn't always very attractive."

Pamela had smiled. "No, but happen it'll ensure I make a go of things on my own."

As soon as she had made the decision, she had poured every scrap of energy into setting up the firm again. While her senior officer was twisting a few arms in order to obtain her early demobilisation, Pam had spent all her free time planning ahead. During a hasty trip to Halifax she had contacted Roger and had gone with him to offer for all the decorating materials that he had shown her.

The elderly widow would have settled cheerfully for the fifty pounds already mentioned; Pam had given her sixty, and had come away feeling they both could be content with the deal. She had also offered a sum for monthly rental of the garage itself. It would serve while she looked around for premises of her own. There wasn't a square inch to spare at home, these days.

Cousin Charlie was installed in the biggest bedroom from which he emerged only to sit listlessly in the living room. So far as Pamela could tell, he experienced no sense of relief over having been repatriated ahead of lots of men. She could sympathise with her Aunt Elsie's assumption that Charles had had to batten down all his emotions in order to survive imprisonment by the Japanese, but she couldn't help wishing he would now try to show some signs of wanting to return to life.

"I'd never admit as much to anybody but you," Pam had confided to her friend Dorothy during that brief visit to Halifax; "but he gets up my back the way he won't even contribute owt to the conversation."

"Happen he's out of practice," Dorothy had suggested. "We don't know what them places were really like. It might have made him turn in on himself. Or the chaps could have run out of summat to say."

"I'm being rotten, aren't I, picking on him?" Pamela had said. "Oh, Dot – is it just me? My subconscious? Do I resent Charlie surviving when Jim didn't?"

"Nay, love, you're not that sort. I suppose your nerves are still a bit raw, all our nerves are."

Dorothy had promised, though, that once Pamela was home for good she would resume her old habit of dropping in at the Baker household.

"Don't hang on to your mum yet, but I might turn up with a few buns from time to time." Dorothy had left her munitions work to return to serving in a confectioner's. Despite continued rationing, broken cakes and misshapen buns still came out of the ovens, some so badly damaged that they could not be sold.

Pamela had grinned. "If they don't make Charlie take notice, I daresay you will! That dark pageboy is so glamorous. I wish I'd kept my hair longer like you. Though I suppose I'll be glad it's as short as this when I keep having to wash paint out of it."

"You could grow it again once you're out of the WAAF. I'll show you how I used to tie mine up out of the way when I was among all that machinery," Dorothy had promised, inspecting her friend's corn-coloured waves. "I do hope these next few weeks pass quickly," she'd exclaimed. "I can't wait to have you back in Halifax for good."

It was Dorothy who picked her up at the station when that day finally came. Always ready to work to earn herself extra money, Dorothy was skilled with her sewing machine. Even during the war she had remade clothes and curtains for people and had turned worn sheets with their sides to the middle. Peacetime had brought the longing for fresh appearances, both on folk's backs and in their homes, and Dorothy had cashed in on the need for more renovations. The result was a little prewar motor car for which even the limited availability of petrol could never dampen her enthusiasm.

"We're going to have some grand times," she assured Pamela as she helped stow her luggage. "We could even take that cousin of yours out for a drive at weekends since he can't walk so far."

"Wait till you see what he's like before you make any rash promises," Pamela cautioned. "I love our Charlie dearly, but he could do with a cracker behind him nowadays."

Strangely, however, Cousin Charles seemed to improve that very afternoon. Dorothy breezed in, just as she had years ago, pausing only to hug Pamela's mother before dashing in and out of the house and unloading the car. The bustle evidently had attracted Charlie who had been resting. After his halting progress down the stairs, he opened the door at their foot and limped into the room.

"You're back then, Pamela," he remarked, nodding in her direction before turning to stare at Dorothy.

"Did you know my friend Dorothy Stubbs before the war?" Pamela asked him as she began to introduce them.

"Can't think that I did, I'd not have forgotten her,"

26

Charlie replied, smiling towards Dorothy's hazel eyes which were glinting from a face with dainty features and a frame of glossy black hair.

"I can tell you've had a bad time," said Dorothy, extending a hand for his. "We'll have to see what we can do to pull you round again. You don't want to spend every day sitting about in front of t'fire; you need some fresh scenery for a start."

"And how am I going to get that?" Charles demanded sharply. "I'm still as weak as the proverbial kitten. You must have heard how long it took me just to come downstairs."

"I know, love, you must find it very frustrating," Dorothy began.

"He does that, poor chap," Mildred put in, her blue eyes anxious.

"Well, then," continued Dorothy briskly. "Take a look outside. Not bad, my little car, is it? Want to think about coming for a ride one of these days?"

"Eh, that'd be fair grand. Champion!"

"We'll say Sunday, if you like." Beaming, Dorothy turned to Pamela. "You can come an' all if you want, get reacquainted with our lovely countryside."

In the event, Pamela did not accompany her cousin and Dorothy. She had spent the week going through all the stock that she had bought, listing items and doing a separate schedule of other materials that she would need. Sunday, she would devote to planning the advertisement that she must insert in the *Halifax Courier*. She had found the copy for one of the original adverts worded by Jim which, with minor alterations, would announce that she was back in business.

"I'm going to be hard put to it to cope with the paperwork once I get really started," she remarked during tea. "I'll be missing out on jobs while I'm keeping that side up to date."

"Not necessarily," said Dorothy smiling. They were all sitting round Mildred Baker's large table. "You want to get your Charlie, here, to do your invoicing and so on. He's just promised to do mine for my bits of sewing jobs."

"Would you, Charlie? Could you, do you reckon?" All Pamela could recall of her cousin's prewar job was that he'd been a plumber.

"Did my own books, didn't I? How else do you suppose I got the brass coming in?"

Pamela grinned. "You've got yourself a job then, as of now. We'll have to work out how much I can pay you. Won't be a big amount at first, I'm afraid, but . . ."

"Don't talk daft, lass. I don't want your money. Your mother's been unstinting looking after me, hasn't she? I'll be glad to give a bit back. And more than thankful to have summat to keep me occupied."

"Right then, you can help me get organised. I shall have to have a look round, find out if anybody else has supplies of decorating materials, and what's the best value. I can make rough notes while I'm out, get you to sort them afterwards."

Pamela's feelings were very mixed during those early days as she went about Halifax and surrounding towns looking for the items she would need.

She'd always had few illusions about her home town which had too many factories, mills and narrow streets to have any pretentions of beauty. Certain areas, though, did offer magnificent views of wooded slopes and moorland, reminding her of the ease with which she could reach the more attractive parts of the West Riding. Travelling home by bus from Huddersfield she seemed to see with fresh eyes the breadth of countryside viewed from the top of the Ainleys. At this height, her world appeared to be spread before her, the hills stretching towards the far distance suggesting so much space that signs of industry grew insignificant.

Returning another day from Leeds, she relished once more the glimpses of Shibden valley where trees were unfolding their leaves to the spring sunlight.

Always, however, she became filled with sadness because there was no Jim now to share this love of the Yorkshire countryside. And the evidence of springtime made her realise how time was passing, without her finding any means of accepting his death. Some days she felt as if she would never bear the permanent absence of this quiet man who had been the centre of her world.

On one such day Pamela was returning to her mother's weighed down with the difficulties of restarting the business on her own. The advertisement in the *Halifax Courier* had been disappointingly situated near the foot of a page and had brought no enquiries. Jim would have been sure whether the expense of a second advert was justified, today she herself felt unsure of everything.

Pamela could hardly manage a smile when Roger hailed her from across the street. "I've just come from your mother's, left a message for you to contact me."

"You'd better come in with me now, tell me what it's about, that's if you can spare the time?"

"Sure. I'm not on duty till six."

"So, what's all this then?" Pamela asked while her mother went to put the kettle on.

"Did your advert bring in any work?" Roger enquired.

"Not a scrap. Mind you, did you see where they'd stuck it?"

Roger nodded. "Happen that won't matter too much now. I've heard of something that could be really big – a whole house interior to be redecorated . . ."

"Really? Where's that, love?"

"A bit of a way out, that's the only drawback – up Cragg Vale."

Pamela grinned. "Well, at least buses run there. I take it they do still run out that way?"

"Aye, so far as I know. A bit beyond my beat, is Cragg Vale."

"So who's this person who wants the house doing up?"

"Just a minute –" Roger felt in a couple of pockets before locating the note he had made. "Had to write his name down. Andre Malinowski."

"What is he then – Polish? Mum tells me there's a lot of Poles settling round Halifax. Latvians and Lithuanians an' all."

"Not sure what nationality he is, I could hardly ask the fellow. He's an education chap, mind. Speaks English very well."

"That's something. I wouldn't fancy struggling to communicate with somebody who didn't. How did you come across him then?"

"The first time, he came into the station to ask directions. He'd just driven up to Yorkshire. Then I bumped into him again t'other day, asked how he was getting on, like. That was when he told me what a nice house he'd bought, but that it all needed doing up."

"And did you mention me, Roger? Is he expecting to hear from me?"

"I told him what you were doing, naturally. If you want, I could borrow a car, run you out there to see him . . ."

Pamela was about to thank Roger and decline, but then she thought about Cragg Vale and how it stretched for miles out towards Blackstone Edge, one of the bleaker moors of the West Riding. Maybe this wasn't the occasion for asserting her independence.

"Thanks," she said. "I'd be ever so grateful."

"When would suit you, Pamela? We'd have to go on spec, I'm afraid. If he has a telephone, Andre didn't give me the number."

"I'd be able to see just where it was and what sort of a house, even if he happened to be out. As far as I'm concerned, it'd better be as soon as you can make it. My demob gratuity's dwindling already."

"Tomorrow then? Morning, if you can, that way I shan't be watching the time for going on shift."

Roger's friend Leslie Rivers was driving the prewar Ford when they picked Pamela up next morning.

"You remember Leslie, don't you, Pamela?" Roger said. "Used to play in the band we had."

Pamela wasn't sure that she did recall meeting the slender, fair-haired young man, but smiled in his direction, saying "Hallo" cheerfully as she got into the car.

"This is ever so good of you," she began as they set out through King Cross then took off along Burnley Road.

Leslie laughed. "Eh, that's all right. I'm well up on my work, so it's grand to have a bit of an outing."

"What's your job, these days, Leslie?"

"Same as always, tailoring. Got my own business now, I was kept busy making uniforms during the war."

Roger leaned over from the front passenger seat to talk to her. "We thought we'd drop you off at this house, then make our way to the Hinchliffe Arms. It can't be far away, we'll have a drink, happen a bite to eat. We'll pick you up again, of course. This Andre chap will have some idea how long showing you round should take."

Pamela was very thankful that she hadn't come here alone when they took the Cragg Vale road out of Mytholmroyd and drove on and on past the turn off for the pub, and into increasingly desolate terrain. They had passed through lovely countryside after first leaving the

31

main road, with hills rising gently from meadows so green that she rather envied a party of girl guides heading back to their campsite. Now, though, homesteads were more widely spaced with evidence on the steeper slopes to either side that fields and woods were giving way to moorland.

"I'm certain I haven't missed it," Roger asserted, consulting the directions he'd been given. "Stonemoor House, it's called."

"What's this on the left?" said Leslie.

"You're right," Roger exclaimed.

They were off now up a grassy lane which, without its edging drystone walls, would have been indistinguishable from the surrounding scrubby hillside. Then all at once Stonemoor House was before them, as solid as if it had grown from a rocky outcrop.

"I say that's rather special," Leslie remarked. "Wouldn't mind that myself."

"A bit remote, isn't it?" said Pamela.

Leslie laughed. "All the better," he said, nudging Roger.

Sensing that they were visualising a convenient place for entertaining any girls they were dating, Pamela said nothing more.

And the door of the house was opening, allowing her scarcely any time in which to admire the porticoed entrance and the stone pediment which rose from above large second-storey windows.

Roger was out of the car already and shaking hands with their host, a man whose broad shoulders gave the impression that he was big. In fact, when Pamela reached his side she discovered he was only slightly taller than her five foot eight inches.

It was the way Andre was dressed, however, which really captured her attention. He was wearing immaculately tailored slacks and a shirt that appeared to be knitted

32

in silk, with a circular collar fitting perfectly up to his neck. Both were startlingly white, so unusual here in the heart of Yorkshire, that Pamela had to quell an exclamation.

Andre's grasp was firm on her hand while Roger introduced them, and the grey eyes gazing back from beneath rather heavy brows seemed acutely assessing. The voice greeting her in English as careful as his appearance was deep, quite pleasing.

Rather disconcerted by both Andre's manner and his attire, Pamela found she was only barely conscious that Roger was preparing to leave now, enquiring how long a tour of the house might take.

Andre shrugged, looked questioningly at Pamela. "There are five bedrooms, two bathrooms. And several rooms on this ground floor. How long do you suppose, Mrs Canning?"

"We shall need to discuss your ideas after I've got the feel of the house. Shall we say an hour?"

Andre turned to Roger. "You must return whenever you wish. I shall be happy to extend to you my hospitality."

Hearing Leslie and Roger drive away, Pamela was forced to contain her sudden uneasiness. Although perfectly polite, Andre's welcome had conveyed a stiffness which could mean her unannounced arrival was awkward for him. She imagined his wife might be preparing a midday meal, maybe even waiting for guests to join them.

"I hope this isn't inconvenient," she began as he turned from closing the door. "I mean – well, I hope your wife won't be put out . . ."

"My wife is dead," he told her flatly.

"Oh, I am sorry," said Pamela swiftly. She was about to add that she also was widowed, but Andre was shaking his head dismissively.

33

"Let us proceed," he suggested sharply, his squarish face expressionless.

For the first time, Pamela gazed carefully around the large entrance hall. She had judged the house to be early nineteenth century, and it was constructed in good Yorkshire stone to withstand hostile elements. The interior promised to be splendid, with wooden panelling here and a wide staircase enhanced by an intricate ironwork balustrade, its handrail of mahogany.

The panelling, although seeming to be original, had suffered from overpainting in a heavy brown which had cracked and flaked. Pamela itched to begin swotting up on techniques and commence restoration.

Andre opened the door of the nearest room and motioned that she should precede him. "Did Constable Jenkins tell you my requirements?" he asked suddenly. "I want everything to be white, throughout the house."

"Oh, but that might not be right," Pamela began, thinking of the woodwork she had seen already and how it should be restored as near as possible to its natural colour. And this room in which she stood was, if anything, more demanding of sympathetic treatment.

"Are you questioning my taste?" he asked, though his manner was rather less arrogant than the actual words.

Reminding herself that she was here because she needed work, Pamela smiled. "No, of course I'm not. It's just – well, you have such a beautiful home, and it looks to me as if its decor is really quite valuable as well."

"If extremely delapidated and dirty!" Andre exclaimed, with the first glimmer of humour.

"I won't say another word till I've seen every room," Pamela promised, smiling. "Then we'll sit down and have a nice long talk."

Having learned his priority though, she was beginning to feel afraid that there might be no means of reaching

34

agreement over what she should do. This room, for instance, was staggering. Beyond the evident many years' neglect, was something which she had never expected to be privileged to see in her native West Riding.

The wall covering was badly faded, but it looked very much like an original design from the period of the house itself. She hurried towards the nearest wall to examine one of the decorated panels outlined in a pattern incorporating sphinx heads and scarabs.

"Were the people you bought the place from French?" she enquired over her shoulder, still scrutinising the wall.

"No, they were as English as yourself," Andre told her, coming to her side. "Why did you think that they might be?"

"It's just rather strange, that's all. Maybe it hadn't been in their family long, anyway. Do you know if it had?"

He shook his head as Pamela turned towards him.

"I didn't expect to find this over here, that's all," she continued. "I've seen similar decoration only once before, in a French chateau, a year or two before the war." She moved on to inspect the next panel which was enhanced by palm trees and lotus plants.

"I believed it appeared more Egyptian than French," Andre began.

Pamela beamed at him. "That's just it," she exclaimed. "This is in the Egyptian style. It was popular in France following Napoleon's Egyptian campaign. I've never thought that anybody would have adopted it over here."

"Are you an authority on the history of design?"

She laughed. "Anything but! I'm just interested – mainly in how fashions change and develop."

Andre nodded as though he understood.

"Perhaps you should show me the rest of the house," Pamela suggested, disturbed by what she had seen so far, and hoping for some rooms at least which might be more suited to her usual kind of work.

The next room contained more furniture than the odd items in the one that they had left. Pamela saw at once that Andre possessed a taste for antiques, and evidently the wherewithal to indulge this liking. Again, though, it was the walls that drew her notice and they echoed the styling that she had already examined.

"Is every room like this?"

He shook his head. "Only the two. The others on this ground floor have wallpaper, all very discoloured."

Pam found this was so. From its ornate pattern she took it to be Victorian or later. "That certainly must come off," she remarked, but glanced towards the tall sash windows whose narrow glazing bars and frames seemed to confirm her judgement of the period of the house. "You're going to have to be careful here, though, or the whole effect could be ruined."

"In what way ruined?"

"Well, by introducing a scheme too modern for the place."

The kitchen was next, and bore evidence of updating in the nineteen-twenties. Having lost all feel of its origins, there seemed little in here that could be spoiled by further renovation.

"Now this is one room where you could use as much white as you wanted."

Andre merely shrugged, and indicated that they should inspect the upper storey.

Here also, each room was decorated in accordance with ideas long since abandoned as old-fashioned.

"Why do you not like my concept of having all the walls in white?" Andre demanded.

He sounded most defensive. Pamela was dying to ask him why he was so obsessive about white, but decided

36

playing for time in which to alter his ideas would be more diplomatic. She kept silent, therefore, until the rest of the house had been examined and they went back downstairs to sit on rosewood chairs which she felt sure were Regency period. Willing herself not to picture how well they would look in a room restored as she advocated, she steeled herself for what she feared would be a refusal to engage her.

"It is unfortunate that you have difficulty in accepting my ideas concerning refurbishment," Andre began. "I have sensed that you would work thoroughly, and take pride in what you were doing."

"I always try," said Pam, not without a touch of asperity. She didn't think much of his implying that she was at fault for not concurring with him. "And I haven't said I would refuse to carry out your wishes. Only that I believe you should consider having something more in keeping with the period of your home."

He contemplated this for two or three minutes. "Might I suggest that you tackle one room initially? In the white that I have set my heart on. If that is to my satisfaction, we could then discuss what should be done with regard to the rest of the house . . ."

It was far less than the extensive commission for which Pamela had hoped. But it was more work than she'd found to date anywhere else. And it would provide a toe in the door, the opportunity for her to try and influence Andre's notions.

"Yes, why not," she said brightly. "Providing we can agree on a price. I'll put an estimate in the post for that one room. If you show me the one you have in mind, I'll make a few calculations."

"It will have to be a bedroom. I really cannot continue to sleep in such dismal surroundings."

"Not quite what I hoped for," Pam admitted when Roger and Leslie picked her up. "Unfortunately, he's got ideas that don't coincide with what would look right in a house as old as that."

"A waste of time then?" Leslie suggested sympathetically.

"Well, not entirely." She told them how she had arranged to estimate for decorating one bedroom. "At least, they're all large rooms so it could be worth my while. And there's a slight hope that I'll get him round to my way of thinking."

When they had dropped her off at home, Pamela went indoors to find Cousin Charles beaming at her.

"I've got a message for you, Pam. A woman called round just after you'd left. She wants her living room decorated."

"Had she come far?" she asked, concerned that her being out could have cost her a job.

He shook his head as he handed across a slip of paper taken from behind one of the spotted china dogs on the mantelpiece. "Nobbut round the corner, in Highfield Place. She said she'd be in the rest of t'day."

"Alice Wilson, don't recall the name. But I'll go and see her straight away. Where's Mum, have you all had your dinner?"

"Long since, aye. She had to go to the school, summat to do with Ian."

"He's not had an accident or owt, has he?"

"Don't think so. It sounded more like he were in a bit of bother."

"I hope you're wrong! Mum has enough on without him playing up. Any road, I'll just go and see what this woman wants. If you're hungry when I get back I'll make us a bit of a biting-on."

Pamela was delighted to learn that Mrs Wilson remembered work which she and Jim had done for them before the war.

"As soon as I saw your advert in *The Courier* I said to my husband that you were the one I was going to have. That's if you can fit us in."

Pamela grinned. "Don't tell more than a dozen, but it's only this morning that I've taken down details for my first estimate since leaving the WAAF."

"We're in luck then, that's good. Well, you can see what's to be done. I'd like a beigy sort of shade for the paintwork, especially for the built-in cupboards."

Like many of the local houses, next to the fireplace the room had large double cupboards set above drawers. In a dark grained wood as they were at present, they tended to dominate.

"And do you want wallpaper on the walls, or distemper like you've got now?"

"It'll have to be distemper again, I'm afraid, we can't run to owt more expensive. We'd do it ourselves if my hubby didn't work nights. We've got two-year-old twins, you see, and they're always into everything when he's about, won't leave him alone. That's the trouble when you've only one big room and a bit of scullery, isn't it?"

Pamela smiled. "Just as well, for my sake, eh? Anyway, I'll do you an estimate and pop it through the door later on."

"When can you start?"

"As soon as you want. This room won't take me so long. And the other work I'm hoping to get is up Cragg Vale. It'll be a day or two before he receives my estimate and makes his mind up. There won't be much of a delay if he does want me to go ahead."

"It is just you on your own then? Somebody in the fish shop was saying that was how things are."

"That's right. Until I begin making enough to set on somebody to give me a hand."

And that, thought Pamela hurrying back home, is the

way things look like remaining in the foreseeable future. The prospect of employing someone seemed like bliss but far distant.

Turning the corner of her own street, she noticed her mother walking through their yard to the door as if she carried the world on the shoulders hunched inside her fawn raincoat. Don't let it be bad news about our Ian, Pam prayed silently. They all had more than enough to cope with just now. But Ian, who in so many ways reminded Pamela of her father, could turn just as difficult as their dad had been agreeable.

# Chapter Three

Pamela became very glad that she had obtained these two opportunities for work. They all needed something to cheer them up. As soon as she had followed her mother indoors that day she had learned that Ian had been seriously reprimanded by the headmaster.

"It's him and another lad that's in bother," Mildred told her grimly before she even began removing her coat. "What do you think? They've only been buying demob shoes cheap off chaps that have come out of the forces, then they're selling them down the bottom end of town somewhere."

Pamela caught their Charlie's eye and was compelled to smother her own brief amusement. It wasn't funny, not at all. Even though she couldn't help feeling the boys had been quite enterprising.

"It was one of the teachers who spotted them and reported to the head. He's given them a right ticking off. Before he sent for me and the other lad's father. They say we must keep an eye on them now. How do you do that, though, with boys of fourteen? They come and go more or less as they like, you can't keep 'em inside the house, can you?"

"Hardly," Pamela agreed. "Especially when they go off to school first thing in a morning and you don't set eyes on them till teatime. Did you see our Ian while you were there? Has he taken it to heart?"

Mildred shook her head. "Never saw him, the headmaster and their form teacher wanted a quiet word with us, that was all. He advised watching the lads from now on, rather than reprimanding them at home. I think he's rather afraid that if too much attention is given to this they might end up enjoying the bit of notoriety."

"Eh, I don't think Ian would," Charlie observed.

Mildred sniffed. "No, well – I never thought he'd get up to something like this, did I?"

Certainly, when Ian and his brother came in from school, he appeared to have been subdued by the ticking off. Even their Tom couldn't get a smile out of him.

"I don't know what's up with him," he said, when Ian went out to the lavatory. "I asked him if he'd been told off at school, but he wouldn't say owt."

Pamela was relieved when she got a quick response to her estimate for the work to be done in Highfield Place. Alice Wilson's husband called round on his way to the factory that night with the request that Pam should commence the job as soon as possible.

"I'll come in the morning. Did your wife explain that I'm going to try and get this completed before I begin on a big job that's lined up? And I'll work as quietly as I can, I know you have to get your sleep during the day."

Mr Wilson grinned. "Eh, bless you, love, it'll be all right. Ever since our two little lasses were born I've had to sleep with earplugs in."

Beginning on an actual job gave Pamela's morale a boost. If only she could attract more business, she might manage to survive. Ever since Jim's death, she had been willing herself not to dwell on the old days, and nor on the hopes they had formed. After so long away from painting and decorating, she would need to concentrate now until she had got back into her routine. She felt thankful that she was starting with something ordinary like this, rather than in Stonemoor House where even the more modest rooms seemed daunting.

Here, in the house which closely resembled the one where she had grown up, the whole feel of the place was so familiar that she had no real qualms about tackling its redecoration. The basic layout was the same, with its cupboards at right angles to the window, and adjoining the combined cooking range and firegrate. The latter was very like her mother's of cast iron and steel, and set within a red tiled surround. Beginning to strip down the woodwork of the doors to enable her to use the lighter shade requested, Pamela felt quite contented.

The twins, Mandy and Melanie looked angelic but were full of mischievous energy. Evidently, their mother already had their measure. As soon as she arrived Pamela had laughed, seeing how they both had on the reins they wore when out walking. And both were anchored by them to the legs of the New World cooker.

"It's about the only thing that's too heavy for them to shift," Alice Wilson explained. "And if I don't fasten them into the scullery somehow they'll be running in and out and getting under your feet."

After the few minutes' fuss and excitement when Pamela arrived, the girls settled happily to playing with the toys that surrounded them. She was glad to be among such cheery company, yet at the same time she felt a yearning gnawing into her. Even though the fiercest agony of her grief had eased a little since the day of the street party, she still found it hard to accept that Jim would never be around to give her the family they had planned together.

Three days after beginning at the Wilsons' house, Pamela realised she was enjoying work again and was thankful that it kept her mind away from the shortcomings in the rest of her life. She had laboured quite slowly on preparing the woodwork and was rewarded by the satisfaction of seeing that the initial coats of the new shade were going on very nicely. While they dried ready for the next layer of paint, she would start on the walls. The Wilsons had chosen an attractive shade of peach which lent warmth to the room without losing any lightness.

Among the brushes that she had purchased in the job lot of materials were several in pure bristle which had never been used. One was exceptionally wide, ideal for these walls, and of far better quality than any obtainable since the war.

Pamela had been glad to have new brushes. Their good condition was essential for producing a decent job, yet brushes were one of the few things that had caused arguments in the old days. Perhaps because she had been so determined to please, Pam herself had always been meticulous about cleaning each brush after use. Jim had generally claimed he was too busy, and she had come to recognise that he found every other task more interesting. For a time, she had cleaned each brush he discarded along with her own. Finally, however, she had rebelled. These days, she would have cleaned up after him gladly, just to have him around.

"I've got some nice decorative corners that I can let you have cheap," she told Mrs Wilson when the first coat was on the walls. "Just a few leaves in autumn colours, they are, arranged into a right angle. They look ever so nice if they're placed, say, a foot from the top corner of the wall. And they stop it seeming so plain."

Alice Wilson smiled. "I'd like to have a look, if you don't mind. Only I'll show you what I have got to go on one wall."

She went to the sideboard and brought out a pair of pictures edged in black passe-partout. One of a crinoline lady and the other of a gaudily dressed gentleman, they were fashioned in brightly coloured silver paper against a black background.

"Very colourful," said Pamela, hoping her expression didn't reveal that they were not to her taste.

She was beginning to realise that her own taste had changed considerably since the time before the war when her horizons had rarely widened to include visits beyond the West Riding, and only the once across to France.

I'd love to travel more, she thought suddenly, even to work away from home for a while. When Europe eventually settled itself as peace grew more firmly established, she would like to see beautiful cities that still remained. It was early days yet, they were only in the late spring of 1946, but she could even picture herself helping to restore interiors of buildings that had been substantially destroyed.

I'd have the time now for learning more, she reflected: about old styling, fashions in design that had gone with some of the beautiful houses that existed. Much as she enjoyed seeing a simple room like the Wilsons' improving under her hands, she could find greater satisfaction in tackling something much more ambitious. That house up Cragg Vale had whetted her appetite, urging her to discover all she would need to know about the means she would have to employ to restore it to its original appearance.

I'll have to take on lots of ordinary work like this as well, though, she silently admitted. I'll have to build up the business in ways that I already understand before I can launch into lots of renovation of bigger places.

That evening when she went home her mother smiled as she greeted her from the kitchen doorway.

"There's another chap been seeking you to do a job, love. Charlie wrote it all down for you. I had flour all over my hands when the man came to the door."

Pamela thanked her cousin as he handed her the details. "If you go on like this, Charlie, I'll have to start paying you commission."

"Nay, lass, don't talk daft. I'm stuck here doing nowt, aren't I."

"Well, as from now, I'll put you in charge of taking messages for me."

There was a telephone number as well as the name and address. "I'll go out later on and ring them up," said Pam. But she had seen that the prospective client lived some distance away down Hanson Lane. "If I keep getting jobs that are a tidy walk from home, I shall have to find some way of carting all my stuff there."

"What you need is a little van," Charlie told her.

He was standing near the hearth, his back to the fire, and Pamela grinned up at him.

"A lot of use that would be even if I could afford one: I can't drive, can I?"

"If I still had my old van I'd offer to teach you, but it was in a bad way when the war started, it rusted away while I was abroad."

"Pity. I might have managed to buy it off you."

Today, though, looking at Charlie standing there, she could believe that he himself might soon be well enough to start up in business again.

While Pam was thinking this there was a knock on the door and Charles's mother came in.

"Hallo, Auntie Elsie, how are you today?"

"Not so bad, love. Tired out, mind you, allus am."

"Have you noticed your Charlie's getting back on to his feet, though? Been stood there a good few minutes now. That should cheer you up . . ."

Her aunt sniffed and gave Charles a look. "Haven't you sense enough to pick a better spot, lad? If you stop there

46

right up to t'fire like that it'll melt the marrow in your bones!"

Her son shook his head impatiently at her. "Nay, Mother, you're at it again, that's nobbut an old wives' tale."

"Happen so, but there's a lot of truth in these old sayings."

Mildred, who was listening from the kitchen doorway, greeted her sister, and at the same time winked at Pamela and Charles. She'd known their Elsie too long to expect her to relinquish belief in such dire warnings.

"Have you time for a cup of tea, Elsie?" she enquired, keeping her anticipatory smile in check while awaiting the usual response.

"Well, I wouldn't say no, love, if you're making one."

Before going out to ring her prospective client Pamela glanced towards her cousin. Charles looked to be sagging now as he stood in front of the hearth. He seemed exhausted after longer than normal on his feet; but she guessed he wouldn't move since his mother had commented on his position. Maybe Charlie possessed more of a stubborn streak than she had supposed. That could be a good thing when the doctors gave him the all clear, and he began struggling to work again.

Returning from the telephone with a date fixed for going to view the property in Hanson Lane, Pamela was thinking about the possibility of buying a van. It would have to be an old one, she wouldn't be able to afford anything postwar. Maybe she would have a word with Roger. Policemen always seemed to hear about bargains.

On the day that Pamela completed work on the Wilsons' house, she was beginning to feel pretty good. That morning's post had brought a note from Andre Malinowski accepting her figure for redecorating his bedroom. She had prepared an estimate for the Hanson Lane job and heard by return that they wished her to go ahead. They had appeared content with her stipulation that the work would be fitted in around the task awaiting her up Cragg Vale.

Roger had called in one evening when his beat took him near Parkinson Lane and she had sounded him out regarding finding a suitable van. He had promised to keep an eye open on her behalf and meanwhile had suggested his pal Leslie might be willing to deliver all her tackle, especially for jobs like the one at Stonemoor House where a quantity of materials were involved.

Dorothy had been there chatting with Pamela when Roger arrived, and interrupted when Pam's response to the offer was hesitant.

"You don't have to bother, Pam, there's my car, isn't there? I don't mind you having it during the day. I always walk to work; it's no distance, and it saves worrying about parking."

"Oh, I don't know," Pamela began, reluctant to be indebted, even to her best friend, especially while there was this petrol shortage. "And don't forget I still have to learn to drive."

"You can learn on that; it's so old you'll not do it any harm."

"I'll take you out a few times," said Roger, so swiftly that Pamela wondered if he had been waiting for an opportunity to see more of her. She was glad to take him up on the offer, but made a mental note that she mustn't ever do anything to mislead him. Roger was a nice bloke, and had always been a good friend, but she missed Jim so much that she couldn't believe she would ever really love anyone else.

Pamela had her first lesson the very next evening, and didn't think that she framed too badly when Roger finally let her take over the wheel. He had picked up the car

48

from Dorothy and after calling for Pam had driven as far as Savile Park.

Some of the roads around this open stretch of grassland were almost deserted, ideal for mastering the controls of the little car.

"When do you start out at Cragg Vale?" he asked as he slipped behind the wheel again at the end of tuition.

"On Monday. Why?"

"If Dorothy agrees, I could pick the car up from her again, and take you out there with all the stuff you'll need. I'll be on late turn, so that'd fit in just fine."

"Well, if you're sure. It'd be a great relief to get everything out to Andre's. I wouldn't mind then about going back and forth on the bus."

"How often do they run out that way?"

"I don't know yet, that's something I've got to find out."

Pamela also intended to learn more about the decor of the period when Andre's house had been built. She was pleased that finishing the Wilsons' room around midday gave her the opportunity to visit the library.

Almost all her life as far back as she could recall, Pamela had been a regular at Belle Vue mansion which had housed Halifax Public Library since 1889, the year her Aunt Elsie was born. It was her aunt who had introduced Pamela to the joys of reading, a fact which offset many of the small annoyances that Elsie's presence brought. But for her, Pam might never have learned to love books or to appreciate them as a source of knowledge. Her own mother had claimed for years that she had no time for sitting reading and, indeed, until comparatively recently had never used the library. Aunt Elsie, on the other hand, having a husband who'd survived until their only son was in his twenties, had been free to relax with the love stories that made her poor health seem more bearable.

49

Today, Pamela relished the feeling of anticipation with which she always approached Belle Vue. The mansion itself and adjoining conservatory set in a small park lent a sense of occasion. And only rarely was she ever disappointed with the books that she brought away with her. As a child, she had devoured every word so avidly that she often finished reading the three books allowed her within hours of returning home.

Although enjoying non-fiction and fiction equally, the desire to read up on the history of decorating was quite different. Normally, if she went for something factual it was biographical or perhaps an account of someone's travels. Exploring shelves that were fresh to her produced a sort of excitement. Pamela was glad there was plenty of time for investigating those which might be most useful.

Before too long she had discovered one which possessed several illustrations of early nineteenth-century interiors, and another that provided a history of wallpaper. She was thankful when she noticed one picture of a room which had windows and doors very similar to those in Andre's home. This seemed to confirm her own assumption about its period.

And when I've studied these thoroughly, she reflected, I may well be able to convince him that my ideas on restoring the whole of the interior have a solid foundation.

Pamela was surprised by her own eagerness to tackle that entire house. It felt extraordinary that even without a return visit she had developed this degree of longing.

I'd better be good! she thought, contemplating the work she must do on that first room there, and sensing already that she was on the threshold of something big.

On that first morning Pamela was grateful for Roger's company as well as for his arranging to convey all her equipment out to Cragg Vale. Knowing that a great deal could hang on the success or otherwise of this job at Stonemoor House, she had become more nervous than excited about the work ahead.

Soon after they had turned left at Mytholmroyd, Roger pulled in to the side of the road.

"Do you want to take over? It's quiet enough along here."

Pamela swallowed, shaking her head with a rueful grin. "Do you mind if I don't? I'm worried as it is, wondering what sort of hash I'm going to make of all this."

Roger smiled sympathetically. "Okay. I'll take you out for another lesson soon, anyway; happen at the weekend." He continued that he felt sure she need not feel overawed by the task ahead of her.

Andre's smile was welcoming when he opened the door to them, making Pam so relieved that she no longer felt too perturbed when Roger drove off after helping her unload the car.

"I'm on the lookout for a little van," she told Andre as she followed him up the elegant staircase. "In the meantime my pal Dorothy is letting me use her car. And Roger's learning me to drive."

Andre didn't comment immediately although he had glanced over his shoulder to catch what she was saying.

"You have some good friends, I think," he observed as they walked together along a landing.

"Yes, I'm very lucky that way. Things could be worse."

"That is so, indeed."

He sounded wistful, and Pam wished there was some way that she might help him to get to know people in the West Riding. It appeared he had not done so already.

"Didn't Roger say you're Polish? According to Mum, there's lots of Poles settling round Halifax. They have their own social clubs and all sorts, I'll find out about them for you if you like . . ."

51

"No," said Andre firmly. "Thank you, but I do not wish you to."

They had reached the room which he had decided should become his bedroom. As he opened the door and motioned her to precede him, Pamela sensed the momentary awkwardness between them slipping away. They both glanced about them.

"I think you'll be pleased you've chosen this one," she said. "Although it's plenty big enough it's not as enormous as some of the others. We get some bad winters up here, you know, and a house like this will take a lot of heating."

Andre's smile was amused. "I am accustomed to cold far worse than any you will experience here," he told her. "All the same, I think perhaps that I would agree. A room too large would not feel . . . what is your word – cosy?"

"That's right."

Pamela was setting down the items that she had carried upstairs. Taking out samples of wallpaper, she began unrolling them.

"I've brought a selection of papers for you to have a look at. They're all white as you requested, but some of them have quite nice designs in the texture. Of course, if there's nothing here that you fancy I'll have to search around . . ."

Andre was scrutinising the first sample, a frown narrowing his grey eyes. Pam couldn't be certain whether he disapproved or was simply giving his selection very careful consideration.

"These are all from among stock that I bought the other week," she continued when he said nothing. "They're prewar and I expect that means they're better quality than anything that we shall see around for a while yet."

Andre nodded and took the second sample from her. "If one can obtain any wallpaper at all, eh?"

"Quite. And I'll bet wanting white makes it more difficult. For years now paper for anything – books, magazines, or for writing on has been that awful drab stuff that's the result of salvaging. I can't think you'll get a very good white made out of that."

Pamela was thankful when Andre began smiling as he examined one piece of wallpaper.

"This could be the one, I like the effect. It reminds me of frost on window panes. Do you not think so?"

Pamela agreed. "I'm rather keen on the way the slightly shiny background gleams through the rest which you so rightly say resembles frosting." And, she added silently, there's nothing in this one to conflict with the period atmosphere of the room.

"Do you have sufficient to cover all the walls?" Andre enquired.

"Oh, yes. I only brought samples of those which I knew would do that."

"Then this is the one. And thank you. I shall look forward to seeing the room completed."

"So will I. I've never done anything all in white before. You are certain that's how you want the paintwork as well, aren't you?"

He had not changed his mind. It was no surprise, and Pamela stifled a groan as she thought of all the preparation that lay ahead of her, burning off the old brown paint as well as stripping the walls to bare plaster and making them good.

Setting to work, she was relieved that she had tackled Alice Wilson's place before coming to Stonemoor House. Painting her woodwork a lighter shade had involved almost as much preparation as would be necessary here. And the finished result had boosted her confidence.

Life in the WAAF had accustomed Pamela to long days and tiring physical work, enabling her to keep going even when the daily journeys back and forth to Cragg Vale increased her weariness.

Sitting in the bus and during the evenings at home, she was studying the books borrowed from the library. As well as preparing to try and influence Andre's thoughts on redecoration, she enjoyed discovering more about what she judged to be the period of Stonemoor House. One illustration in particular showed a large sash window which, with its narrow glazing bars, was a replica of those she had admired in Andre's house. Beside the window, wooden panelling echoed the dimension of its glass panes.

As she laboriously removed layers of paint from similar panels and doors at Stonemoor, Pamela began to admit that once they were repainted in white they could look quite effective. She remained thankful, nevertheless, that Andre's bedroom faced out towards the moors and, being on the second storey, wasn't conspicuous from outside. She still felt determined that the place ought to be renovated in a manner that resembled the original, and dreamed of an overall effect of old wood lovingly restored and walls decorated in the Regency style now becoming familiar to her from books.

On the Friday of her first week at Stonemoor, Pamela arrived to find Andre awaiting her with a smile of rare excitement.

"Have you thought about curtains at all?" he enquired almost before closing the door behind her.

"Curtains? Well, no, not really. You see, actually that's not quite my department."

"But surely it should be? You have such a good sense of the overall effect . . ."

Her grin was rueful. "Happen it's because I'm not much good at sewing. Although, come to think of it, my best

54

friend's an excellent needlewoman. Trouble is, these days, there's very little choice of materials. That's if you can lay your hands on anything at all . . ."

"Do you suppose this friend of yours might be willing to make curtains for my room, though?"

"Dorothy? Aye, I daresay she would. Maybe by now there is some cloth available. It's a bit since she was grumbling about there being very little in the shops."

Smiling, Andre shook his head. "You are misunderstanding. I explain very badly. I have some material here, I will show you."

Lightly, he ran up the staircase and hurried along to a room adjacent to the one where she was working. Pamela caught him up as he was turning from the bed to watch her expression.

"Gosh, but that's beautiful! Wherever did you get it?" she exclaimed.

At the head of the bed lay a bolt of satin from which yards and yards were spilling out in gleaming white folds.

"It came with the house," Andre told her. "Did I not say how I purchased the place from two elderly sisters? Both frail, they were glad to remove their few treasured possessions then accept a sum for everything else stored in the attics."

Pamela came further into the room and knelt on the rug by the bed to feel the texture of the cloth.

"This is beautiful stuff, really heavy. It would certainly hang very nicely. You are sure, aren't you, that you're free to do what you wish with it?"

"I am indeed. It was packed so very carefully, between layers of a special paper in one of the trunks, that I asked the younger Miss Norton if she knew that they had left it behind."

"And she did know?"

"More than that. Her behaviour became somewhat strange. 'If you can't use it, throw it out,' she snapped, and added that she never wanted to see it again."

Pamela was still examining the satin, draping it over one arm, when she turned to him once more. "This isn't really intended for curtains, you know, it's a different width. It's dress material. I wonder why there's such a lot . . ."

"Ah – I think I have a clue."

Andre walked briskly towards the dressing table and returned with an envelope which he handed across. "This was packed with it. The size of the envelope suggested it did not contain a letter; I could not resist the urge to take a look."

As soon as Pam did likewise she sighed. "Oh. Did you say neither of the old ladies was married?"

"So far as I am aware."

The exquisitely embossed card was dated 1902, a formal invitation to the marriage of Miss Sophie Norton with a Mr Sebastian Grey. From corner to corner it was deeply scored as though somebody had crossed through the lettering in considerable anger. Traces of pencil adhered to the indentations where they appeared smudged by an eraser.

"A wedding that never took place?" Pamela suggested, sighing again as she thought of Sophie Norton and how chastened she must have felt while she lived out the rest of her life in this old house.

"We must not sentimentalise," said Andre briskly. "Whatever the original purpose of this material, I do not intend it should be wasted."

Pam grinned at him. "And it will make super curtains."

After Andre had produced that lovely satin for her approval Pam developed even more enthusiasm for the job. As she worked on the final preparation of the

56

woodwork and began applying paint she was able to visualise the completed room. Even though the result might be rather monotone, the differing textures would add interest. And it was fun to be tackling something so innovative. Certainly a scheme that she would never have created; white was hardly the most appropriate shade here in the sooty West Riding.

Dorothy was happy to measure up and make curtains, and became ecstatic about the satin which truly was of far higher quality than anything she had seen, even before the war.

"When I have a minute I'm going to look up the previous owners," Pam told her on the way back to Halifax after Dorothy had been to Stonemoor House to take measurements. "Andre is beginning to show more interest in the history of his home. And I'm dying to discover all I can. If only so I can persuade him to accept my thoughts on making it look something like it would have originally."

"Do you think you can talk him round?" her friend asked seriously. "There is a lot of difference between that and his intention of having everywhere white."

"Don't remind me," Pamela exclaimed. "I'm trying not to dwell on the difficulties. All I can do is swot it all up, and pray I can think of some way of convincing him."

"And if you do – what then? Can you really manage to get that panelling to look as good as it would have all those years ago?"

"I'll have a damned good try! There'll be special techniques to learn, I know. But I'm prepared to read up on them, and Jim gave me a lot of basic knowledge which is coming back to me now. The first hurdle, though, is going to be getting Andre to agree."

To Pamela's surprise, this proved to be a less difficult task than she had expected. She had noticed as days

57

became weeks and she and Andre grew more easy with each other that he was interested in what she was doing. Whatever his own work might be, he appeared not to be practising it at present; he was always at home and seemed to have no occupation.

Once he had checked that doing so would not disturb her, he made a habit of wandering into the room to see how the job was progressing. As soon as Pamela began putting paper on the walls, a stage that she herself always loved, he became really enthusiastic.

That evening when she had finished for the day and was preparing to go home she found Andre downstairs in the hall, scrutinising the walls.

"You really believe, do you not, that this panelling should be restored to the way it must have looked when new?" he asked.

"As near as possible, yes. The wood is sound beneath that old paint, it seems a shame to cover it up again."

"And that is something which you could do?"

Pamela smiled. "I'd like to have a go. I would tackle a bit that wouldn't show initially – make certain that I'd not do any harm. In fact, if you'd let me experiment like that, I wouldn't charge you owt unless I found a way of getting a good result."

Andre smiled back. "What can I say? How resist such patent enthusiasm? But you must not think of giving your services free. I shall insist on paying for all the time you put in."

For days Pamela felt elated. And if she permitted herself to doubt that she was capable of putting all her ideas into practice, she hastily quelled such anxiety. So long as she tackled everything one stage at a time, she felt she would be capable of restoring that woodwork. She had learned a lot before the war, and another visit to the library had unearthed a volume on renovating old properties which had several chapters on how the woodwork should be treated.

That same book had a chapter on traditional wall coverings. When she showed Andre the illustrations he sat poring over the relevant chapter all afternoon.

"May I keep this overnight?" he asked. "I would like to study it more thoroughly."

He's really coming round to my way of thinking, Pam realised as she headed for home. She didn't doubt now that Andre would soon invite her to supply estimates for redecorating the whole house in the manner that she had suggested.

Roger took her out driving that evening and it seemed that in this also she was progressing. The hours spent on the roads around Savile Park had given her the opportunity to acquire clutch control and to familiarise herself with changing gear.

"It's time you ventured a bit further," Roger told her. "There won't be that much traffic about at this time, shall we try a run up to Norland?"

Pamela headed down Dryclough Lane and carefully negotiated the junction with Huddersfield Road. She was worried that the car might run away with her on Salterhebble Hill but Roger explained about changing down a gear and she felt the engine holding them back. The long straight stretch of Stainland Road presented no difficulties, and she was glad the way was clear while she was turning right in West Vale.

Approaching Norland, Pam felt she was indeed getting the hang of driving. Her hands were less tense on the wheel, and her legs no longer went into stress-induced cramps. Combined with the promise of success at Stonemoor House this produced a surge of satisfaction. I'll have to tell Jim as soon as I get home, she thought.

Roger took his gaze from the road ahead as he smiled

59

towards her. "Jim would have been right proud of you if he could only see you now," he said.

If . . . *If!* God, but she couldn't have forgotten . . . She couldn't have become so blinded by her own bits of success that she'd actually overlooked, even for a minute, this appalling weight of sadness.

Her eyes blurred, and she steered urgently towards the side of the road. "I'll have to stop," she muttered, and then the tears came. For the first time since the day that Jim died she let go and wept. Sobbing uncontrollably, tears washing down her face and dripping off her chin, she gave in to the grief that was ripping her apart.

Dimly she was aware of Roger reaching across to switch off the engine. And then he drew her towards him, holding her while the sobs shook her body.

"It's all right, love, you had to let go sometime," he murmured, his own voice husky. "Don't forget he was the nearest I had to a brother. I understand, Pam, I always will."

Thank goodness you do, she thought, thank goodness you're here.

# Chapter Four

For days after she had wept in the car Pamela felt disturbed, far more vulnerable than she liked. Breaking down so idiotically in front of Roger was bad enough, now she was afraid that it might happen again when she was with someone else. She would never convince people of her ability to cope with the job if she went to pieces while she was supposed to be working.

Fortunately, the work itself continued to absorb her, and prevented too much retrospection as well as becoming satisfying. On the day when she completed that first room for Andre and began to hang the satin curtains, Pam could scarcely contain her excitement.

Andre also was delighted. His grey eyes lit and his smile widened as he gazed all around, while in another white shirt and light grey slacks he looked as though the place was designed to feature him.

"You are very talented, I think," he exclaimed. "You have given to me exactly the room that I was imagining."

"Good." Pamela glanced over her shoulder towards him from where she was sliding the last few curtain hooks along the rail.

After a final adjustment to the curtains she descended the stepladder. Andre was at its foot, one hand extended to assist her.

"Thank you," she said, and felt her colour rising.

His hand still grasping hers, he looked into her eyes.

"But it is I who must be thanking you for transforming this part of my home."

When his fingers left her hand Pam experienced a strange chill, and was forced to check a shiver. However enigmatic he might seem, Andre was an attractive man and one whom she was beginning to like.

Pleased though she was to have completed this one room to Andre's satisfaction and her own, Pamela was quite sorry that her immediate task at Stonemoor House was finished. She had concentrated entirely on working here for the past few weeks, but had explained to Andre that until he was absolutely sure of what he had in mind for the rest of the house she must get on with jobs for other people.

Following her work at the place in Hanson Lane she had received requests for estimates from several homes in that area. These jobs would be short compared with the length of time that would be spent at Stonemoor if Andre should wish her to renovate the rest of the house. Pam wanted to get all such relatively easy jobs out of the way. If Andre needed her again, it would be for skills that she was still acquiring.

Whenever she could make the time to do so, Pamela visited the library to search out books that would explain more about renovation. From the start she had become engrossed in techniques that differed from the simple decoration that she and Jim had provided before the war intervened.

One aspect, at least, of her daily life had become easier since Roger's tuition had helped her to pass the test to drive a car. Roger also had gone along with her when she decided to offer for a second-hand van. Although nervous the first few times that she drove unaccompanied, Pam was beginning to enjoy having her own transport.

Roger's help had reminded her yet again that she

couldn't wish for a better friend. She thought sometimes of the old prewar days, and reflected that it seemed as though all the friendship that Roger had shared with Jim was now transferred to herself. Without it, she would never have survived. She liked to think that Roger would always be around, offering advice and practical help, plus this degree of stability.

Even though Pamela couldn't yet visualise ever marrying again, she was beginning to wonder if that might happen some day in the future. Losing Jim had left her feeling cheated out of having a family of her own. Maybe she could eventually settle with a partner like Roger who, if not someone with whom she would fall deeply in love, would always be totally dependable.

He seemed to have at heart the interests of everyone in her circle, including her young brothers and especially Ian. Not long after that first occasion when the lad had been caught selling demob shoes, he had been in trouble again, this time for dealing in clothing coupons.

Fortunately, Roger had heard Ian's name as soon as the incident came to the attention of the police force.

Pam would never forget the day when Roger arrived at their door. The concern in his brown eyes made her aware of his constant caring for them. And how much they needed someone on their side.

When he asked to see Ian, Pam noticed how swiftly their mother's worried frown reappeared.

"Don't tell me he's in bother again," Mildred exclaimed and turned to Pamela. "I was afraid this might happen. We were all too soft with him afore."

"*Is* Ian in now though?" Roger persisted. "I'm afraid this is quite serious. I've only just managed to persuade them at the station that if I have a quiet word it might be enough to stop this nonsense."

"He went upstairs a few minutes ago," Pamela confided. "I'll fetch him down."

Ian and Tom were in their attic room where Charlie was encouraging them as they constructed some intricate piece of machinery from the Meccano set which he had given them.

Pamela called Ian from the doorway but he took no notice. In three swift strides she was into the room.

"Ian," she repeated. "You can just stop playing with that. There's a policeman downstairs. He's come for you . . ."

Ian jumped and knocked over the model they were building.

"'Ere, steady on!" Tom rebuked him.

Ian pushed back his chair, regarding his sister with eyes wide with apprehension. He had flushed on hearing the word policeman, now his face paled equally rapidly. Hurrying from the room, he lurched against a heavy old-fashioned chest of drawers and stumbled.

The lad reached the living room ahead of Pamela who watched as very evident relief washed over him.

"Eh, it's only you!" he exclaimed to Roger before turning to face his sister. "You rotten thing – you did that on purpose, didn't you? Trying to make me think . . ."

"Trying to make you *think* is what we're all doing now," said Roger swiftly. "And, I might remind you, I may be an old pal but I am a real policeman. This isn't a bit of fun, Ian. I'm not leaving this house before I have the truth out of you."

He made Ian sit down at the table and took the chair across from him after setting down his helmet on Mildred Baker's red chenille tablecover.

"What were you doing trying to get folk to buy clothing coupons?"

"Clothing coupons? That weren't me," Ian blustered,

but his cheeks were scarlet while his gaze shifted from side to side then flicked towards the badge on Roger's helmet before finally resting on the red chenille as his head dropped forward.

"There's no point in lying, lad, you'll only make matters worse," Roger insisted. "You were seen and you were identified. You'll have to watch it from now on – the chap who spotted you was keeping an eye on you and your mate after that other time. You're getting a reputation already."

"But it wasn't me this time, honest."

"Where did you get the clothing coupons, Ian?"

"I don't know nowt about them," he protested, squirming uncomfortably.

· "Then you won't mind if I go up and take a look in your room, will you? Not if there aren't any more coupons for me to find."

Roger was rising but before he had moved away from the table Ian started to capitulate.

"It weren't doing nobody any harm. It wasn't as if we'd stolen them from somebody."

"Then how did you come by them, lad? You'd better explain . . ."

Beneath Roger's steady scrutiny Ian faltered. Looking on, Pam felt her annoyance with her brother turning to sympathy, and sensed from across the room that Mildred's emotions were undergoing a similar change. It was Mildred, however, who eventually spoke.

"Ian love, you'll have to tell Roger all about it. We're lucky he's come here today, you know. If it had been any of the others they wouldn't have thought twice before taking you to the police station."

Ian sighed, pondered for a minute and began speaking. "We weren't doing any harm, like I said. We haven't taken them coupons off anybody, no one's going short."

"Then where did you obtain them?" Roger demanded.

"Only from one of the stalls down the market. They were what the woman had taken off folk, when they were buying stuff, like."

Pamela saw Roger's smile which glinted in his eyes before being erased. When he spoke again it was quite sternly, but with a hint of understanding.

"That's still stealing, you know. Those coupons were not yours, were they?"

Ian shook his head, then took another breath. "No, but . . ."

"But you thought they weren't anyone else's? Is that it?" Roger shook his head pensively. "It's not that simple, I'm afraid, Ian."

As though sensing the explanation that would ensue, Pamela and her mother simultaneously went to armchairs and prepared to listen.

"It's like this," Roger continued. "Stealing coupons from someone in business, as you did, might seem to be less serious than taking them from a private individual, but it is still wrong."

"But . . ." Ian began, and was interrupted.

"I appreciate that you would believe you were not depriving somebody of their right to new things. But we've all got to consider what rationing is all about, what it's intended to do. Now, just supposing that we didn't have to have coupons for anything, but goods were still in short supply, what do you think would happen?"

"I don't know, do I?"

"Then I'll explain. Because there was still only the same amount of stock in the shops, there wouldn't be enough to go round. Like as not, prices would go up, and then those people who have plenty of money would be the only ones who could buy. Ordinary folk like us wouldn't get our share."

"That's making me think, and all," Mildred remarked. "Are you beginning to understand, Ian?"

The lad merely shrugged, and Roger went on again.

"And that's why what you were doing matters," he asserted. "By selling coupons as you were, you were giving those who could afford to buy them an unfair advantage. And by recycling the coupons – sending them round a second time – you were damaging the system. I know it's complicated, but when the government rations anything, the allocation they decide on relates to the goods available."

"How do you mean?" asked Ian, interested now.

"Well – if, for instance, you needed a new pair of trousers and your mother saved up the coupons and went to buy them for you, she might get to the shop only to find she was too late. Because some person who had more than their fair share of coupons was on their way home with the trousers you wanted."

Ian nodded. "Like if – like if, at school, somebody has more than one dinner and he doesn't hang on, then there isn't enough for everybody?"

"Is that another of your tricks, Ian?" asked Pamela severely. It seemed suddenly as though there might be no limit to his misdemeanours.

Her brother shook his head and grinned. "Not me, no. I don't like school dinners."

"Happen we should be glad you don't," his mother observed.

Pamela sensed the lightening of Mildred's mood, and recognised that her own spirits were rising slightly. Roger had evidently got through to her brother. Knowing the policeman as she did, she felt sure that he would not treat him too harshly.

"What's going to happen? Will you be locking me up?" asked Ian.

67

"Not yet. But I shan't guarantee that I won't do that if there's another time. This time, I'm just cautioning you to behave, but that is a serious warning. Any more schemes of this sort, my lad, and you'll be finished!"

Mildred Baker thanked Roger solemnly, and Pam echoed her thanks after she had walked with him to the door.

"You've been lovely with our Ian, and now you've explained, I'm sure he'll behave himself."

"Well, let's hope so. I don't want to have to take things any further. But you know how it is, there's too much black-marketeering and so on; we've got to stamp it out before youngsters like your Ian acquire a talent for it."

Waving him off, Pamela silently thanked their good fortune that everyone in the street had been used to seeing Roger arrive there in uniform. She couldn't have borne it if anyone suspected that either of her brothers was in serious trouble.

As Pamela had feared, their mother was greatly perturbed by Ian's second involvement in dealings that were shady. Mildred Baker, however difficult her life had been, had always been scrupulously straightforward with everyone.

"What our Ian needs is a steady job," she asserted to Pamela shortly afterwards. "He's outgrown school, and it isn't as if we could afford for him to go in for a lot of studying at the tech. The best thing would be for him to start earning as soon as possible. I've been thinking – it'd be ideal if you took him on. You've that many jobs coming in now, you must be wanting an assistant."

This was the last thing that Pamela wanted, but she quelled her own reaction, and tried to placate her mother without making any such commitment regarding Ian's future. She had been appalled by his getting on the wrong side of the law and was already praying that none of her potential clients should catch a whisper of it. Being asked to work in their homes depended upon her utter reliability. She had been determined to distance herself from her brother's petty crime. How could she ever contemplate taking him along with her?

Determined though she was that she would not take Ian on, Pamela could not shrug off her concern regarding his future. He and Tom were lovable lads, she didn't wish to even think about either of them turning out less than trustworthy.

Pamela suspected that the uneasiness of this long-awaited peacetime could be contributing to the refusal of Ian and others like him to conform. It often felt terribly unsettling, and she was sure her own bereavement wasn't the only cause of this deep-seated sense of disappointment. Certainly, there was the prolonged hardship of rationing, and beyond their own country little evidence of genuine peace. A few weeks ago in Jerusalem the King David Hotel had been bombed, destroying the headquarters of the British Palestine Army Command. Around the same time Calcutta was reported to be in turmoil following riots between Moslems and Hindus.

The only brighter news came from attempts being made to distract people from world crises. The Cannes Film Festival, scheduled originally for September 1939, was taking place seven years later, and a prize had gone to the British film *Brief Encounter*.

Pamela resolved to see it when she had the opportunity but, as always when feeling troubled, she was throwing herself into work as an antidote. Now that she had tackled several decorating jobs alone she was gaining confidence and thoroughly enjoying the challenge as well as the company which each task was bringing her.

She also was enjoying some of the rare leisure hours that she permitted herself. Ever since her return to Yorkshire she had relished outings with Dorothy and Charlie. Now that she herself could drive, she loved the sense of freedom bestowed by taking the van to the summit of one of the many local hills where the surrounding expanse of countryside invited them to explore.

For months now the three of them had taken days off to visit moorland hamlets or to leave the vehicle and stroll through ancient woods to clear their lungs of millsmoke. Charlie's health had improved at last and he was able to keep pace with the two friends, although none of them had a great deal of surplus energy. Pamela wasn't the only one who worked long hours: Dorothy spent a lot of time making curtains as well as continuing to assist in the baker's shop. Charlie himself was building up his plumbing business again, and also still helped both Dorothy and Pam to keep their books up to date.

Pam had been surprised that once he began recovering from his ordeal in the Japanese prison camp Charlie did not return to his mother's home. On one occasion she had mentioned this to him, but he had frowned and given an awkward shrug before replying.

"You know what my mother's like, Pam. She's never had enough about her. She'd soon be complaining that there was too much to do. And besides, it's lively at your place."

He had asked after a time if Pamela felt the house was overcrowded with him staying there. She hadn't had the heart to do other than assure him that the situation was perfectly all right. Charlie had improved in temperament, becoming affable, even talkative when he found a topic of interest. And he helped her mother – a fact that meant Pam would forgive him a great deal, especially while she herself spent so much time working outside their home.

There were occasions when she wasn't sorry to have someone of her own generation around. With brothers so much younger than herself and a mother who, however capable, could never be described as businesslike, Pamela sometimes needed someone like Charlie just to understand her problems.

Ensuring that she did not miss any requests for her to provide estimates for new jobs had proved difficult. While Charles had been convalescing at home, he had taken messages from people who arrived at the door when Pamela was out. As soon as he himself was working again, however, Mildred had protested that she hated writing down details of what her daughter's prospective clients required.

"I'm sure I'll get it wrong, then you'll be blaming me for losing business for you."

Despite reassurances, Mildred had remained uneasy and Pamela had decided to ease the situation by having a telephone installed.

From her mother's point of view, Pam couldn't have had a more perturbing idea. Persistently refusing to answer "that machine" she had let it ring on innumerable occasions when no one else was in the house.

"What can I do?" Pamela asked Charlie exasperatedly. "All I expect from her is to make a note of their name and number and to promise I'll ring them back."

"But she's not used to the telephone, is she, love?" he responded.

"And never will be, if she carries on like this!"

"You've got to look at it her way – nobody she knows has ever had a 'phone, she's never used one in her life."

"You're saying she never will do either, aren't you?" said Pamela ruefully.

"Aye, I suppose I am. But she's still a lovely woman."

That made Pamela laugh, and discussing the difficulty with Charlie persuaded her that anyone who wished to contact her would always ring again. They would not expect her to be at home during a working day.

"You're not short of work, anyway, are you?" he added.

That certainly was true, and especially so when Andre telephoned one evening to enquire if she was willing to do more redecoration for him at Stonemoor House.

"I have been thinking about everything you have told to me," he said. "And I believe perhaps that to have you work as you propose would be interesting. How soon would you be able to commence?"

Pamela told him how quickly she anticipated completing the jobs that she had in hand, and they arranged a date when she would return to Stonemoor. The preliminary visit which she suggested would be used for further discussion of his requirements and to enable her to outline the way in which she visualised restoration should be made.

Shaking with excitement when she hung up the receiver, Pamela drew in a long breath. She had won Andre's approval for her scheme, and now she could look forward to returning to Stonemoor House. To the most exhilarating challenge of her life.

Gazing out through the tall windows of Stonemoor House, Andre watched the early light glinting off the panes of a distant farm as the sun rose above the hill behind him. He had scarcely slept. All night long he had tossed in his bed within the room where she had created such exquisite perfection. He would see her at last. For the first time since those dreadful months when, pained by loss, he had merely existed, he felt alive once more.

Deciding to accept Pamela's ideas for his home had not been difficult. Listening to her, and reading up on the appearance of the house as it must have been all those years ago, he had seen the wisdom of what she advocated. The difficulty had arisen within himself, and during the first few days after she finished working here.

Never since that dreadful time when he had arrived in England – bereft of the wife who had died so tragically and yearning for the family left behind – had he missed anyone so greatly.

The days and weeks while Pamela had worked so hard to improve this one room of his home had integrated her into his life far more deeply than he would have wished or admitted. His most private condition of surviving in this strange land had been that he must rely on no one but himself. Only in that way, he had believed, might he avoid revelation of his true identity.

And now here he was, aching to see her again, listening and watching for her approach which, even this morning, appeared tantalisingly beyond his reach. The fact that her arrival was just a few hours away seemed to do little to improve his state of mind. He needed her now, and felt unable to believe that she really would be with him this morning, filling his home and his heart with all her positive enthusiasm.

Andre's inherent self-discipline took him from the window, to bathe and dress, and to make coffee in the ugly kitchen. Afterwards he began to tour the house, lingering in each room while he contemplated the changes she would make there.

He was in the smallest bedroom when he heard the van chuntering as it laboured up from the main road. By the time Pamela had hurried up the steps to his door, he was opening it wide.

"You saw me coming!" she exclaimed. "Or did you just hear my noisy old van?"

Andre could not reply. Seeing her again, tall and slender, her dark gold hair confined in a blue band that matched gleaming eyes, his breath was snatched from him.

He restrained the longing to take hold of her, gesturing instead that she should come through while he closed the outer door. And then they were together, at last, isolated in his home.

Pamela was removing her coat, gazing as she did so all around her at the panelled walls.

"Is it all right if we leave these and the staircase till last?" she enquired. "I've got a bit of a confession to make – I'm not quite sure yet how best to treat this wood."

Andre smiled, willed her anxiety to ease, and gave a tiny shrug. "This is a very big house, yes? You cannot do the whole of it at once, I think."

"So, you don't mind what I tackle next?"

Just be here, he thought, be here and eradicate that gnawing solitude. In the best possible way. He smiled. "I hoped perhaps that you would wish to decorate one of these rooms here . . ."

Beaming at him, Pamela nodded. "That's what I thought as well. That way, you'll have one room fit for entertaining friends."

*But you are my only friend.* He did not, could not say that. In its place he uttered trite little words about how pleased he would be to have the room restored. And inside his head, within his soul, he gave thanks that even the one room would keep her here for weeks.

Together, they decided the one for treatment was to be the room bedecked with hideous Victorian paper.

"This is going to require so much attention that I'll be glad when I have it off my mind," Pamela confided. "I've some good news for you, though – painting the woodwork white would be in keeping. I've come across a description of a Regency room like that."

"Regency?" Andre asked.

74

"Sorry – I still keep forgetting you're not English. The Regency period covered the first thirty or so years of last century. Which is when I think this house was built. That reminds me," she added. "I'd love to learn more about it. We could go and visit the ladies who sold it to you. Didn't you say they'd always lived here?"

Andre felt torn. A part of him yearned to be going anywhere with Pamela, yet he had to be so careful. Even after living here so long, he only left the house to buy in provisions and other necessities.

"If you don't want to see them again for some reason, I'll go on my own," she said swiftly, although she would be sorry if he didn't accompany her. "You've only to give me their address, I'll contact them. I could telephone them from home. I've had one put in."

Andre smiled. He loved her for being so ingenuous, despite her skill and the ability to run her own business, so unsophisticated that she was proud to own a telephone.

"You may make the arrangements if you wish," he began.

Pamela interrupted with a laugh. "You think I'm proper daft, don't you – I bet you've always had a telephone. My mum hates the thing, you know, refuses to answer it."

Andre continued to smile. "I was going to add that you should arrange for me to accompany you. I shall like to see the Misses Norton again. Do you suppose we should take a photograph of those curtains in order to show them how fine everything appears?"

"I don't know about that. Do you think they might wish they still lived here?"

Pamela went to collect dust covers and her tools from the van. On her way indoors again she suggested that Andre should make the call to the Nortons.

"Any time will suit me," she told him. "I haven't got anything arranged apart from coming here."

\*     \*     \*

75

Sophie and Hilda Norton now lived with a niece in a terraced house at Boulder Clough. Pamela enjoyed driving there with Andre seated beside her and exclaiming about the surrounding hills and valleys which he evidently had not seen previously.

"You've not been this way before then?" She had supposed that he might have visited Boulder Clough to see the Misses Norton.

Andre shook his head. "Whenever I have seen them it was either at Stonemoor House or in the office of their solicitor."

He exclaimed again when she drew up outside the terrace and he saw the elaborate exterior of the nearby Methodist Church.

"That does not resemble an English building, I am thinking."

"It doesn't, does it? Folk say it's French in style – Renaissance, if I'm not mistaken."

Andre nodded. "I would say so – just see those towers and the portico arches."

Hilda Norton and her niece were at the door of their home already, and despite the difference in their years looking remarkably alike. Both were of average height, plain faced, and as straight backed as anyone Pam had encountered during her service in the WAAF.

Only after introductions had been made and they were being led indoors did Pamela notice that Hilda Norton was far more fragile than her bearing suggested.

Entering the living room where tea awaited, Pam saw immediately that Hilda's sister was even more frail, a tiny body who glanced nervously in their direction. But then she smiled, and brown eyes behind gold-rimmed spectacles seemed to sparkle.

"Come in, come in,n and do be seated," she beckoned from behind a silver teapot. "Hilda mashed the tea the

76

minute she saw your van. It'll have brewed in a minute or two."

"You haven't given me a chance to take their coats," Hilda chided her. "Why must you always fuss so?"

"Because we want to hear all about the house, of course. About Stonemoor."

The final word left her tongue slowly, as though Sophie relished even the mention of her old home.

"And we want to hear all about its history," Pam asserted warmly. "As we explained, I need to learn all I can to help me make it look as good as I possibly can."

"Do you do all that on your own?" the Nortons' niece enquired, sounding incredulous.

"I've had to since the war, I'm afraid," Pamela confirmed.

The woman looked impressed. When she excused herself to attend to the ironing Pamela sensed that she was well suited to the domestic scene. And might perhaps have had little experience beyond it.

Sophie confirmed this as the door closed after her niece. "She's always busy like this, you know. Her husband works in a bank, and has to have a clean shirt every day."

"And likes his meals ready to the instant," Hilda added.

The room seemed overpowering, Pamela noticed as she went to sit on the sofa as directed. The furniture was early Victorian in style, and crammed in to an extent suggesting that it had been brought from the more spacious rooms at Stonemoor House.

"Do tell us how Stonemoor is looking then," Hilda prompted, after handing around slices of Madeira cake and cups of pale tea. "How much have you altered?"

"Only one room so far, the bedroom that faces towards the moors," Pam told her.

"That is my fault, I fear," Andre continued. "I was slow to become convinced regarding the best manner of renovating my home. But now all is well – Mrs Canning is to restore as much as possible in the style of the house itself."

"That's where you may help," Pam went on. "Andre could not recall the exact date when it was built. Can you tell us?"

"The house was completed for our great-grandfather," said Sophie Norton proudly. "The family took occupation in 1815 – just a few days after the battle at Waterloo. Robert Norton, our grandfather, was an infant at the time."

"You must have felt sad when you moved out," said Pam sympathetically.

"Naturally," Hilda agreed. "But we had anticipated for some time that we should be obliged to do so. Had Sophie married, of course, the outcome would have been happier."

"That was nothing I could help," Sophie asserted, giving her sister a reproachful look. "And you might not have had a home there as long as this, had Sebastian stood by his word."

"You're always saying that," Hilda said. "But you know as well as I do that father willed the house to us jointly."

Andre was looking uncomfortable, and Pamela tried to turn the conversation around by asking about the wooden panelling in the hall.

"There's so much paint on it that I haven't been able to tell yet what kind of wood it is."

"Oak," Hilda told her firmly. "That wood is oak. It never should have been painted, but oak wasn't fashionable at the time, or so we were told."

"That is probably true," said Pam, remembering what she had read. "And nor was panelling of any kind – that

78

had gone out somewhere around the turn of the century. But oak had been used much earlier than that."

"We always understood it was from our own trees," Sophie continued. "There had been tremendous gales when a lot of trees were lost. Our grandfather claimed he could remember the wind screeching round the place."

"After the oak was seasoned, our great-grandfather had it made into panelling," Hilda added.

"His wife, by all accounts, insisted it must be painted."

Listening intently, Andre had said little so far, but now he smiled. "And we intend that it shall be made to show its natural beauty once more, do we not, Mrs Canning?"

Pamela nodded. "But that won't be just yet – I'm going to work on some of the other rooms first."

"And the satin?" Sophie asked suddenly. "My bridal satin?"

"Has become exquisite curtains," Andre announced. "For my bedroom."

Nodding, Sophie smiled. "That pleases me," she said. "It is right that the material should remain at Stonemoor, that it should be put to good use after all these years. The wedding was called off, you know."

"Nobody wants to hear about that," her sister reproved her.

Sophie continued undaunted. "Sebastian and I were to have married in 1902, in the August – one week exactly after Edward VII was crowned."

"It's all history now, too long ago to be of interest," Hilda interrupted.

"I had waited so long for Sebastian – and I was over thirty before he even went away to South Africa. He finally came home when the war ended – the Boer War, of course."

"And then he threw her over, didn't he?" Hilda said quickly, sounding quite pleased about it.

"I'll never forgive him, nor forget, though he could have saved me from a loveless marriage. It was a cruel shock. Our family fortunes had taken rather a tumble while Sebastian was away."

"Father was incompetent where money was concerned."

"He was a visionary, Hilda, he wasn't meant to be mercenary." Sophie turned to Pamela and Andre. Her expression became dreamy. "Father was an inventor. He also had become profoundly deaf. He had worked for years to perfect an instrument to improve hearing."

"Sebastian had cultivated him all along, professing interest, and only so that he might be taken on to work with Father afterwards."

"It wasn't like that, Hilda."

"Wasn't it? Any road, some other inventor got there first."

"With his Akouphone, Mr Miller Reese Hutchinson brought out the most successful mechanical sound reproducer then developed."

"An aid to hearing, do you mean?" asked Andre.

Hilda nodded. "And when Sebastian got to know how Father had wasted years and most of his brass only to have that man beat him to it, that was it."

"Sebastian always was very ambitious," Sophie murmured.

"She's been better off without him," Hilda stated coldly. "I've looked after her, naturally."

The tale had saddened Pam, making her realise how lucky she had been to have had a loving husband in Jim. No one could take that from her. And she was young enough now to be able to look forward. She still had Roger's friendship, and his concern for her family. He had seen her through the worst period of her life.

Andre was asking more about Stonemoor House, and the sisters were explaining about the rooms that had been decorated in Victorian times, and those rarely used which had scarcely been touched in well over a hundred years.

"Our grandparents were typical Yorkshire folk," Hilda said. "They didn't spend where there was no need. And then Mother and Father lost so much on his schemes that they just about scraped by."

"We ourselves lived modestly," her sister added. "I hope you will forgive us now that the house needs so much attention."

Andre rose and crossed to give her shoulder a reassuring squeeze. It was the first time that Pam had seen him make such a gesture, she recognised that she had always thought him rather wary of others. Now, though, he was smiling as well.

"You must not feel perturbed, Miss Norton," he told her. "I am enjoying greatly the experience of having the house restored."

Pamela felt her own smile growing. She had needed to know that. All too frequently Andre appeared to exist in a brooding state where he contemplated the past which he seemed determined to keep secret. In the eye of her mind she pictured Stonemoor House quite plainly. I'm going to make you come alive again, she silently vowed to the place which became more dear to her with everything she learned.

# Chapter Five

Discovering so much of the history of Stonemoor House made Pamela so excited that she worked even more energetically, stripping bare the walls in that first downstairs room and preparing the woodwork.

Andre again made a habit of wandering in to watch, and was interested when she explained the various stages of her task. Fortunately, the walls only needed a few minor repairs to the plasterwork, the doors and other woodwork seemed in good condition.

As soon as Pam began painting, the room took on a brighter aspect, delighting Andre, and this in turn satisfied her. He had approved a striped wallpaper in shades of green, and she had made a mental note to thank Roger for insisting that she should buy up all that stock which otherwise would have been abandoned.

She would never have found anything suitable for this place. These months since the ending of the war had been grim, with restrictions continuing in the supply of all manner of household materials just as in food and clothing.

By the time the room at Stonemoor was almost completed, Pamela realised that Christmas would soon be upon them. And she hadn't seen Roger for weeks. She hadn't forgotten how good he had been to her, but she had become absorbed in her work. Realising what she had done, Pam was upset. Roger didn't deserve this. She must put things right, maybe invite him to join their family celebrations, if only to show that she hadn't intended to neglect him once she needed less help.

The previous Christmas seemed rather a blur when she looked back. Unable to come to terms with Jim's death, she had made no plans, choosing instead to fall in with her mother's arrangements centred on Tom and Ian. She could remember vaguely that her Aunt Elsie had spent a lot of time with them, and that it had seemed to be around that Christmas when Charlie had really begun to improve.

This year, Pamela was determined, would be better organised. She could afford to buy decent presents for the lads, Ian was to have that coveted saxophone and Tom to be invited to select a gift of similar value. She would ensure that Roger understood he was welcome to join them all whenever duty hours permitted.

Intent on issuing the invitation before anyone else mentioned Christmas to him, Pam telephoned Roger at home. She was relieved to have caught him in. Despite his long-standing friendship with Jim, she had never met either of Roger's parents. He so rarely mentioned his own family that she would have felt awkward if his mother or father had answered.

After she had explained why she was calling, though, Pam began feeling uneasy with Roger himself. He sounded different, somehow, almost as if he were reluctant to talk to her just then.

"Have I rung at a bad time?" she asked, about to promise to call him back.

"No, no – I was just – studying." Some male in the background laughed, there was a pause, and then Roger continued haltingly. "You – you say it's about Christmas?"

"Yes, love. Like I said, I didn't feel up to organising anything last year. And I'm that grateful for all you've done, for our Ian and all . . ."

84

"No need," Roger said dismissively.

"Anyway, I want you to come to us, whenever you can. I haven't seen you for ages. My fault, I'm afraid, being that busy . . ."

"No," Roger interrupted. "I've been busy, as well. I'm hoping to make sergeant in the not too distant future. That means work . . ."

She heard a man in the background murmur "work" and further laughter which, from the sound of it, Roger was trying to suppress. Most likely a fellow officer was there, helping him study. Roger promised to remember what she had said, but Pamela rang off feeling quite disturbed. If she hadn't found him always absolutely direct, she might have believed Roger was being evasive.

Her work at Stonemoor was slow, often laborious, but when a day's tasks were too mundane to occupy her fully Pamela let her thoughts focus on plans for Christmas. Her mother deserved a bit of a break: she herself could take on some of the preparations, Charlie would help with putting up decorations, and the lads might be persuaded to make paper chains out of the off-cuts she was saving from this wallpaper. Now that she had asked Roger to come in when he could over Christmas, she was determined that the house should be looking festive, and that they would have good food on the table.

In common with most households throughout Britain, the Baker family had been saving coupons and putting scarce groceries aside for the celebrations. One Saturday, Pamela and her mother had made a sort of cake and, although Mildred had bemoaned the absence of many ingredients, it did at least look like a Christmas cake.

On Christmas Eve Pamela told Andre not to expect her to work on December 27th which was a Friday. Many local people seemed to be extending the break to include the following weekend. Several mills, particularly in Lancashire and Yorkshire, had announced that they were taking more than the two days for Christmas, although this was mainly because of shortages of the coal that kept them running.

Pam was surprised when Andre frowned and sounded annoyed that she would be having the Friday off. She had finished the room begun after visiting the Norton sisters, and had started on another bedroom, but that still required so much work that its completion would not be in the foreseeable future.

"It needn't make any difference to you," she assured him. "You have one room that's ready for use, haven't you? And I'll leave everything tidy. Nobody who comes here will know that anyone's been working on the place."

But nobody will come here, thought Andre. Have you really not understood that there is no one in the entire West Riding whom I would invite? No one but you.

When he said nothing Pamela began to sense a part of what he was feeling.

"Haven't you been going out any more than when I first knew you?" she asked. "Haven't you made any friends? I told you about those local Polish clubs and so on. I could put you in touch with some of the folk that go there." Several of them lived near her own home.

"Polish?" Andre began, and stopped speaking. It was safer to let her believe what she would. "I have no wish to join anything."

Pamela had been applying undercoat to the window frame when she mentioned Christmas; now she returned to the painting but continued thinking about Andre.

"Tell you what –" she said after a few seconds during which she was conscious that he had remained standing near the fireplace and watching her. "Come to our house

86

for Christmas dinner. There'll be plenty going on, with my two young brothers. And Roger might be there – you know, the policeman that told me about this job. He's going to drop in when he's not on duty."

"Thank you, but no," Andre replied coldly. He would rather remain here alone than see her within her own family, and with that man.

On the following day Andre regretted his decision long before the solitary meal which he had been dreading even while buying its ingredients. Last year he had missed Anichka more intensely than at any time since she had been killed. He had also missed the family which he feared might always be separated from him.

So many things had gone wrong since he had decided that he could no longer stay in his homeland. Instead of making a new life for Anichka and himself, he had witnessed her death before they accomplished even one half of their journey to freedom. There had been no possibility of turning back, therefore he had been obliged to endure this protracted separation from his family.

Another year had passed and he was no nearer at all to improving this situation; he had not dared to put them at risk by making contact. And now he had been fool enough to grow attached to this woman who was surrounded by her own people – and her husband's friend who seemed about to slip into the dead man's place at her side!

She has so much, thought Andre, what right has she to patronise me with suggestions that I associate with people who are not even my own countrymen? Briefly, he paused, recognising such thoughts as unwarranted; he had led that policeman friend of hers to believe he was Polish. Just as he had created the same fallacy with every English person he encountered. He could not be too careful. Even so – it was all too easy for someone enveloped in home, family, friends and in the land where they were born to make unthinking suggestions about circumstances of which they understood nothing. If he were not so fond of Pamela Canning, he might begin to dislike her.

The day was long, and not improved by listening to the radio. His comprehension of English might be good, but that did not ensure his comprehension of their traditions! Andre felt starved. The substantial meal that he had cooked and eaten could not alleviate this massive emptiness. The broadcast by the British monarch left him aching for the culture in which he had been nurtured. Their Christmas hymns had him yearning for the faith of his fathers, a faith which for too long had been suppressed.

Towards evening, Andre wandered through the house, pausing in that newly refurbished room to absorb its beauty. Pamela had skill, she also possessed the admirable persistence which had led her to unearth details of how this room might have appeared when the house was new. Despite his mood, Andre smiled. Normally, he as much as anyone hated to have his ideas proved wrong. Here, he could only admit that Pamela knew what she was about.

When the walls and doors were completed and green curtains to match the wallpaper stripes hung at the windows, he had gazed entranced. The room was just as bright as if it had all been in white, but it also looked right with his furniture.

They had brought in the furniture together, positioning it after excited deliberation, and then had sat for a while before the fire which he had lit. Andre looked now at the embers glowing in the steel grate – an attractive grate that sat well within the carved marble chimneypiece. He willed away the days until Pamela would return.

Darkness moved in to enclose his home, shutting out the moors and distant farms, the lanes and black drystone walls. Andre went up to his bedroom. Closing the curtains, he glanced around at the walls with their illusion of frosting, at the paintwork gleaming in the pearly-shaded lamplight; and he thought of the millions of brushstrokes that had made the woodwork glossy. Her handiwork, her skill, produced for him.

The day slipped away while Andre stood pensively between fireplace and bed, and the plaintive sound of his violin soared unheeded by anyone save himself.

Christmas Day had gone rather well, Pamela thought. Her mother had consented to accept help with preparing dinner and had surrendered the washing-up entirely to Charlie and Aunt Elsie. Pamela had listened unashamedly to the pair, amused as ever by a mother and son who appeared unable to really communicate after thirty years' experience. Charles had become adept at washing-up in the Baker family's kitchen, but that didn't prevent his mother from advising him on just about every step of the process. Elsie also punctuated such advice with a selection from her inexhaustible supply of old wives' tales.

Charlie had enjoyed a glass of sherry before the meal and more than one bottle of stout afterwards. They had combined to unleash his tongue, and he was now treating Elsie to his opinion on the differences between her sister and herself.

"Aunt Mildred gets things done," he announced. "And she gets 'em done proper. You saw what a good spread she put on today."

"She had help, though, hadn't she?" Elsie interrupted.

"Aye, but only because there were such a lot of us. And me and Pam insisted. She'd have coped all right, she's that sort. You want to see her every day. Organisation, that's her byword. And that, Mother, is where you fall short."

"You don't know what you're talking about, Charlie.

It's all right for Mildred, she hasn't had my declining health to put up with. She's never been poorly like me."

"Only because she's been too busy to think about herself. Stopping here has been an eye-opener, I can tell you. Look how she had to take care of me when I first came home as a POW . . ."

"Are you trying to tell me something then, lad? Are you? If it's that wonderful here you'd better stay for good!"

Charlie, who'd had no intention of moving from the house if it could be avoided, evidently thought better of putting all his cards on the table.

"All I'm saying is – with a bit of organisation, you could look after yon place of yours a lot better."

"Nay, I'm not going to alter now. It suits me right enough. It's not dirty, you know."

"And nor is it tidy," Charlie muttered, but only Pamela heard him.

Pam was glad that her aunt had not heard that particular sentence. There was something sweet about Aunt Elsie, despite her unwillingness to do anything. And Elsie had always had a soft spot for Pamela herself. She had never forgotten her own embarrassment when Elsie was first introduced to Dorothy and had confided that Pam was "Our bit of Dresden".

Pam could only feel touched. However inappropriate the description of herself, she was glad that someone saw more than the fiercely practical side of her own nature. The side which recently she'd been compelled to encourage above all else. Whatever this work of hers was doing, it was providing a better life for her mother and brothers.

Far above them in the attic bedroom, Ian could be heard murdering some piece on his new saxophone, while out in the yard Tom was having a go with the dartboard that

Pamela had given him. Their mother had forbidden him to use the board indoors and, from the regular clinking of darts as they hit the wall instead or fell to the ground, Mildred had made a sound decision.

Roger had not arrived. Although disappointed, Pamela was not particularly upset. He could be on duty today; she supposed that all the married men in the force would be eager to spend Christmas Day with their loved ones. Roger Jenkins was just the sort who would change shifts to allow that. And there were several days yet when he might join them.

Feeling rested and eager to get back to work, Pamela drove out to Cragg Vale on the Monday after Christmas. Although she had enjoyed the days spent with her family, she had sensed that they were lacking in stimulation. The only change of company had been yesterday when Dorothy invited Charlie and herself for Sunday tea and the three of them with Mr and Mrs Stubbs had played cards afterwards.

"I've right enjoyed Christmas this year, you know," Charles had confided on the way home. "You can't believe how boring it used to be when I lived with my mother. I felt obliged to stay in a lot and keep her company. And that was afore the war – after being abroad, I'd have gone crackers suffocating there."

"I gathered the other day that you're not thinking of going back there," Pamela teased.

Charlie glanced sideways at her and grinned. "It'll do me fine where I am. Until I get a home of my own, that is."

Something in the way he spoke and the look in his eyes caused Pamela to wonder. Had Charlie got somebody in mind at long last? She'd noticed he was laughing a great deal while they were out. Was he becoming sweet on

91

Dorothy? He certainly had the air of a male showing off before someone he wished to impress. This wasn't at all like the old Charles, and seemed a substantial improvement.

The only cloud over the holiday had been Roger's non-appearance. Having heard nothing from him by the Saturday afternoon, Pam had telephoned to remind him of her open invitation.

Roger hadn't been on duty as she had thought he might be, but he had told her that he had got to go out later that day. She had been unsure whether or not that meant he was working, and was disturbed by her own reaction. She wasn't in love with Roger or anything like that, but they were friends and she didn't enjoy thinking that he had begun making excuses for not seeing her.

Today, heading towards Stonemoor House, Pamela was regaining a sense of proportion about Roger. He had sounded quite affable over the phone, saying he would see her before long. Learning to depend more upon her own resources was doing her no harm; perhaps when they did meet again their friendship would have entered a new phase. Having her rely so heavily upon him for emotional support couldn't have been much fun; they needed to enjoy their time together.

For the present, the work that she had in hand certainly was absorbing. She was looking forward to getting on with that second bedroom for Andre. Driving up the road from Mytholmroyd, with steep-sided hills to either side and the Stoodley Pike monument dominating one horizon, Pam felt the grandeur of the wintry countryside gripping her. In places the scenery was stark, especially like this when the woods stood dark and leafless, but it seemed an appropriate setting for Stonemoor, the house that she was learning to love.

Dressed all in white, as he had been at their first

meeting, Andre was smiling his welcome before she had unloaded the van. There were shadows under his grey eyes, but he still looked striking. Pam had to collect her wits, remember where she was, and what she was doing.

They talked for a short while as Pamela set out all her tools and inspected the paintbrushes which she had left clean and ready for use. Andre had said no word about Christmas and, sensing that he might have spent the whole time alone here, Pam didn't ask if he had enjoyed the festival. He appeared happy enough today, she had no intention of inviting further reproof for becoming too interested in his affairs.

While she worked, however, Pam began considering Andre quite seriously. The man was so fiercely reticent about his past, about his homeland and about the events bringing him to Yorkshire. Despite the weeks spent working like this with no one else to intrude, she knew little more about him than she had learned from Roger.

Why did Andre so rarely emerge from Stonemoor House? He had so evidently relished the outing to visit the Norton sisters, had even exclaimed about the scenery during the journey until he made her long to take him all over Yorkshire. Yet still he appeared to go out only the short distance to shop for food and other essentials. What could he be concealing?

And there was his accent. Having been away from Andre for those few days, Pam was again acutely aware of the way he spoke. Ever since he'd refused to meet Polish people, she had wondered from time to time if he came from somewhere other than Poland. His determination to avoid others was almost paranoid. Was there a sinister reason for hiding his identity? Could Andre even be German?

Pamela could well understand that he would need to conceal that fact – even guessing that it might be so was disturbing her. She had no wish to work for someone whose nation had been responsible for such carnage, and whose airforce had caused Jim's near-fatal 'plane crash.

Applying paint and then beginning to plan the papering of that room, Pam found her thoughts straying repeatedly to the enigma concerning its owner. But no matter how frequently she reflected that he could be German, she was unable to ignore her instincts about him.

She liked Andre Malinowski. Even without revealing personal details of his past, he had become an engaging companion. He often spoke now of the Misses Norton, and enough about the period when Stonemoor House was constructed to show that he was studying English history. He laughed when Pamela teased that he was trying to prove he knew more than she herself about the early nineteenth century.

"That is not true, you know," he told her firmly. "I wish only to learn, and perhaps to feel less disadvantaged when you put me right on how my home should be renovated!"

He laughed again at her surprise and held her gaze with those intense grey eyes which today appeared provocative. Pamela felt the breath catch in her throat, and a sudden inner pulsing, the passion which for too long had been neglected.

Much later, as she was preparing to go home, Andre said something which seemed to confirm that his attitude towards her was altering.

"I am thankful that you work here once more. You make my home come alive. And I think also that you have a similar effect upon myself. Please remember always that I am telling you how you are doing far more than making my house beautiful."

His words shook Pamela, creating such inner disturbance that she felt quite relieved that it was time for getting away for a few hours. Andre had attracted her from the start, but she had attached no more importance to the fact than she might to finding any stranger attractive. The old adage "Handsome is as handsome does" had been well rehearsed by Mildred Baker throughout the years when Pam was growing up. The good sense instilled had endured and, even while falling in love with Jim, Pam had looked for more than the excitement generated by the proximity of a personable man.

Marriage had taught her to value a stable relationship, and during her service in the WAAF she had learned to contain her own feelings. She had seen enough of affairs that occurred when the attraction between people who were thrust together wasn't resisted. Having spent these recent months as a single woman, she had believed she possessed enough acquired wisdom to remain level-headed about the man currently employing her. Only now she realised how much she liked Andre . . .

Thoughts of Andre were driven from her head as soon as Pam parked the van outside her mother's house. Roger was standing at the gate, looking blessedly ordinary, and smiling as she got out of the vehicle.

"I've been waiting for you, your mother said you shouldn't be long," he told her. "I was wondering if you'd like to come out for a meal. I feel bad about not taking up your invite to call at Christmas. And there's something I want to ask you."

Something to ask her? Pamela's heart began racing. Had Roger realised at last that they ought to be spending more time together – perhaps even that they might do worse than commit themselves to spending the rest of their lives that way? This was more like the stability that she needed – not just ephemeral attraction, but a relationship that already had some real substance.

Pam beamed at him. "I'd love to come out with you, only I'll have to have a wash and get changed."

"That's all right." Roger followed her indoors.

In the living room Mildred was reading the evening paper while Tom was engrossed in a library book. Both were trying to concentrate despite Ian's determination to master a tune on his saxophone.

"It's Glenn Miller," Roger told Pam after Tom and her mother had said hallo. "*Moonlight Serenade*, he's been telling me."

"I'm glad you said," Pamela whispered with a grin. "I'd never have known."

Ian failed to hear beyond the sounds his instrument was producing, but Tom gave them a wink.

Their mother set aside her newspaper. "How's your first day back at work gone, love?" she enquired, and nodded approvingly when Pam confirmed that all was well. "I'm glad you're going out, any road," Mildred added. "You've not had that much of a change of company during Christmas."

When Pam reappeared she was pleased to see that Roger had an arm across Ian's shoulders while he explained some refinement of the saxophone to him. Roger always seemed to fit in so well with her family.

He suggested that they might go to the Picture House café in the centre of Halifax, and Pam was happy to agree. Just seeing him again felt so reassuring that she'd be content anywhere.

During their meal Roger asked how the job at Stonemoor House was progressing.

Pamela smiled. "Slowly, but it's lovely work. Not easy – I don't mean that, it's quite a challenge – but it's so interesting. Did I tell you I persuaded Andre to go for my ideas on renovation? It's all going to be in a style compatible with the period of the house. In some rooms, we're hoping I can preserve original wall coverings. Then there's the hall and stairs – the walls there are panelled. We found out before Christmas that it's oak under the layers of old paint."

"I'm glad you're doing so well, Pam. Jim would have been proud of you."

"I hope so. He'd also have been asking if I'm not taking on more than I can handle! Jim always made sure I kept at least one foot firmly on the ground, bless him." Pamela grew silent for a moment, thinking. "I'm glad I've seen you again, at last. I've been meaning for ages to thank you for urging me to start the business up again. And you couldn't have known what a good turn you were doing me, getting me to buy all those materials."

"I'm pleased they're coming in useful."

"There's so little available even now, I'd have got nowhere without that stock. And if you hadn't taught me how to drive, I'd never have coped with travelling back and forth to Cragg Vale. If there's ever any way I can do owt for you, you've only to say."

"Well, actually, there is . . ." Roger stopped speaking, causing Pam to wonder if he was about to broach something important, something very important to both of them. And the time felt right. With a person who was so familiar to her she could be ready to begin planning the future.

When Roger eventually continued speaking it was of a matter so mundane that Pam had to look away, silently cursing herself for being fanciful.

"You know that friend of mine – Leslie Rivers? Well, he's moving into a nice little flat. It needs decorating, and I thought you should be given first refusal of the job."

"That's nice, thanks." Pamela struggled to appear businesslike, and to accept the reaction setting in after the excitement that had arisen over nothing. "I'll certainly

97

take a look at it. I suppose Andre will understand if I want to give a day or two each week to working somewhere else. That job at Stonemoor is going to take forever, he can't really expect me to lose custom in the meantime."

Although originally disappointed that Roger hadn't been about to make some more personal suggestion, Pamela didn't feel unhappy by the time they were saying goodnight. They had discussed her work, and Roger had then gone into some detail about all that he must accomplish if he was to be promoted to police sergeant.

This reminder that he was engaged in advancing his career had made Pam feel better about their friendship, and about her own ambitions. Roger was busy and so was she. He wasn't going to be perturbed if, for the time being, they didn't see much of each other. It was a relief that whilst hoping to marry again and have a family, she could happily continue with this work that she found so engrossing.

Content though she might be with her own work, Pamela could not ignore the troubled start to that January of 1947. Everybody felt dissatisfied with the state the country seemed to be in. The National Coal Board that had come into force on New Year's Day headed an industry fraught with difficulties. Despite the potential for replenishing sorely depleted supplies, substantial absenteeism was reported from the mines. The situation became so bad that one week later, steelworks were closing because of lack of coal.

Ian, who had left school at Christmas to begin work as an apprentice at a foundry in Elland, was delighted when prevented from going to the job which he already hated. But even he ceased to smile when the strike by hauliers stopped fresh food reaching the shops.

"What's happened, Mum?" he asked when Mildred

served up a meatless stew consisting mainly of potatoes and dumplings.

His mother gave him a wry look. "I'll tell you what's happened, my lad. More folk like you that aren't overfond of work are coming up with a lot of reasons for hanging about on the streets instead." A hard worker herself, Mildred had never had time for men who went on strike. "If they'd seen as much short-time as I have over the years, they'd just be thankful that they have jobs to go to."

"Don't worry, Mum, I'll see what I can do about getting us some decent food," said Ian, an offer that sounded thoughtful, until his mother remembered some of his past attempts at raising money.

"We'll manage, thank you very much," she told him firmly. "And I mean that. I don't want you embarking on another of your schemes."

"Are they opening up any civic restaurants round here?" Tom enquired, looking up from his homework. "They were telling us in Current Affairs at school that they're doing that to feed folk in London."

"I don't know, I'm sure," said Mildred. "London's London, isn't it? – they're different down there."

Pamela had arrived home just as her mother was stating this, and was given a resumé of the discussion by Tom who had developed an interest in social affairs.

Pam heard him out, feeling glad that her youngest brother had this serious side to his nature, and then she reassured him.

"We'll soon be all right again, any road. We had the wireless on today, and it's just been announced that servicemen are being used to distribute supplies of food."

But by the time that the benefit of this was being felt, the threat of further stringencies appeared in the newspapers.

"I thought your country won the war," Andre remarked

99

ruefully, when it was announced that the meat ration was reduced to one shilling from one shilling and twopence weekly. The Government also was predicting a cut in bread rationing, and no improvement in supplies of bacon, eggs or fish.

"But there is to be a slight increase in butter and sugar rations," Pamela pointed out.

Andre laughed. "That is what I like about you – you always seek the good news."

"You might as well, mightn't you? No good crying into your beer."

"Especially when beer production is threatened with being cut!"

"Is it? I hadn't heard that."

Andre smiled. "You evidently do not drink much beer. I believe the cuts are due to shortages of wheat."

The deprivations seemed to hit all the harder as the weather grew extremely cold. Freezing temperatures overtook the whole of Britain by the end of January, and even fell to -16 fahrenheit.

The journey to and from Cragg Vale grew hazardous on icy roads, and Pam wondered how much longer she would be able to reach Stonemoor House. This might have been the opportunity to do the work required by Leslie Rivers, had his new flat been in a more urban situation.

She had been surprised when Roger gave her the address and she found that his friend intended living near the reservoir at Causeway Foot. Visiting Leslie there, Pam decided the place was rather nice, if remote. With a view over the reservoir, it was the upper storey of a cottage and was to be given its own entrance gained by an external flight of stone steps.

The interior was in a good state of preservation and would need only a few coats of paint on the woodwork and the pale green distemper which Leslie had chosen for

100

the walls. Having only one bedroom, a living room cum kitchen and a tiny bathroom, the place was so small that redecorating completely should not take up too much of her time.

Leslie seemed pleased when Pamela told him this as she went around measuring up and calculating quantities of materials.

"Now I've got the flat," he said, "I want to move out of my mother's house. There's no sense in paying rent and not living here."

Coming on her own to meet him at the flat, Pam had felt uneasy. She hardly knew Leslie and, apart from the brass band, didn't know what his interests were.

It was about the band, however, that Leslie began speaking, making her forget any awkwardness while she listened to accounts of concerts that sounded very familiar after attending so many before the war, when Jim was playing. It struck her then that Roger never talked about the band; she had even wondered if he had lost interest in performing.

Pam realised now that Roger had most likely been careful not to mention brass bands in case that resurrected too many memories and made her loss more painful.

I must have a word with Roger, she resolved. It's time he understood the way I feel about Jim. There mustn't be anything that we can't discuss. Suddenly it seemed obvious that Roger had avoided becoming involved with her because of the past. She'd have to make him see that even though she had loved Jim so deeply, she could think about the old days and remember the good times. And still could look forward to a new life. Jim wouldn't want anybody to be doomed to be lonely. The things that Roger and Jim and she herself had shared would always remain as a bridge. A link that could make the future not only acceptable but more comfortable, really happy.

# Chapter Six

It had snowed for days, turning the steep-sided hills enclosing Cragg Vale into an enchanted place, mystical, with fields and trees unfamiliar in their white dressing. Even the dark drystone walls had vanished under the snow so that only houses and farm buildings stood out against the pale landscape.

Beneath the wheels of her van the roads were treacherous. The protracted frost and heavy snowfalls meant that even on days when the wan sun appeared, nothing thawed. Feeling secretly foolish, Pamela had begun carrying additional clothing with her, a spade in case she might need to dig her way out of one of the many snowdrifts, plus a supply of biscuits. She had told no one of this, but was determined that if the weather worsened she would not be unprepared for its attempt to maroon her.

Mildred Baker would have been relieved to know of her daughter's forethought. With the quality possessed by most mothers of refusing to believe her own offspring entirely responsible, she had chided Pamela for even venturing beyond the end of the street.

Each time that she reached Stonemoor House safely, however, Pam experienced the thrill of accomplishing another challenge. And while Andre continued to compliment her on the efforts to arrive there, she felt well rewarded.

She had finished that second bedroom for him now,

103

and was beginning on the laborious preparation work in another downstairs room. She had noticed that Andre seemed to relish the heavy snowfalls, and teased him when he remarked on how the snow had been banked up to a height of four feet or more against the door that morning.

"I cleared it away, naturally," he told her. "I felt sure you would be here shortly after your usual time."

"Don't count on that tomorrow, though, or the next day!" Pamela exclaimed. "There's no guarantee that I shall make it this far."

"I know, I know." Suddenly, he sounded grave. "And I do not wish that you should endanger yourself on my behalf. Why do you not remain here while the weather seems determined to resemble the Arctic?"

"Stay with you? I never thought of that."

"But why not? I have two lovely bedrooms now, have I not? And only one of me."

Pamela laughed as she began tackling the tasks that she had planned. But when the snow started falling yet again and continued throughout the day, Andre reminded her of his suggestion.

"I could ring my mum and let her know," Pamela said.

"And she surely would be thankful to hear you are not about to attempt that journey to Halifax alone."

This wasn't the only reaction when Tom, who answered, handed over to Mildred! "Of course, I don't want you risking your neck. But you be careful, think on. You will be on your own there with that chap."

Believing her mother's reservations unfounded, Pamela settled to enjoy staying in this house which interested her so completely. It would be really good to feel, however briefly, that she belonged here. A feeling which she suspected had been developing for months.

She was surprised to discover that Andre was an accomplished cook who provided a warming casserole, spiced with enough unfamiliar ingredients for it to seem deliciously foreign. He appeared pleased that she approved the dish, but when Pamela expected their conversation might hover around various foods and their origins she again was surprised.

"I have been learning more about the countryside here," Andre announced, after offering biscuits and a cheese that seemed to bear no relation to the pungent soapy substances to which Pam was accustomed. "I read of Daniel Defoe's visit to Blackstone Edge which is, I understand, only a mile or two up the road here."

"That's right. You've never been there then?"

Andre shook his head. "I am thinking that we should explore. We may take the opportunity while you are staying here perhaps?"

"In all this snow?" Pamela was incredulous. But she also felt intensely excited by the prospect. In fact this entire experience was becoming enhanced by intensity. Now that she wasn't working, the sheer charisma of this man was too powerful to ignore.

"I am not foolish," Andre assured her. "I would take good care of you."

Pamela laughed, and with exhilaration rather than disbelief. At that moment Andre was riveting her with his grey gaze. He might have been willing her to agree to everything he would suggest, and she suspected that he would need to exert no more than a fraction of his will in order to win her co-operation.

"We might have a go tomorrow," she heard herself saying. "See how far we can walk up that way."

Her blue eyes were sparkling, revealing her delight generated by the prospect of taking time off work. *To be with me*, thought Andre, and smiled as he continued speaking.

"Daniel Defoe, I fear, found the area hostile, but he was not a strong Yorkshire lady. I feel sure you will not be daunted!"

Laughing again, Pam shook her head at his flattery. "They do breed 'em tough in the West Riding. Although I'm not sure we're all that ladylike."

"But I *am* sure of that, Mrs Canning," Andre remarked quietly.

"You'd better make that Pamela, I think, don't you?" she continued. "We've known each other long enough, and I am stopping here and all."

They talked on about the locality, and yet again Andre surprised her, this time with an account of events at nearby Hollingworth Lake. "I was interested to learn that Captain Webb trained himself there for swimming the English Channel."

"You've learned a lot more than ever I have!" Pam exclaimed. "You make me feel as if I'm ignorant."

Andre shook his head. Did she not know that he was entranced by her many and varied skills, and by the self-assurance enabling her to create rooms as elegant as the one in which they were sitting?

He smiled across at her. "I would say rather that you always have been too busy working to laze around and study the journeys of others, or their reflections."

Pamela slept well that night in the lovely high-ceilinged room where she could feel well content with her own work. With time now to study what she had achieved, she noticed that both woodwork and walls revealed that her craftsmanship had increased. Words she had read years ago in Thoreau's *Walden* came back to her: "Drive a nail home and clinch it so faithfully that you can wake up in the night and think of your work with satisfaction." We're becoming very literary all of a sudden, she thought with a wry smile, but she was glad that relaxing with Andre had somehow resurrected this long-neglected part of her.

When they awakened next to morning to discover fresh snow, but also blue skies beyond the surrounding hills, Andre insisted that they should make the most of the respite and take the walk which they had promised themselves.

"I shall not complain if you fall behind schedule," he said.

Pamela had guaranteed that her work would finish to time. "I don't want concessions. And you don't have to bribe me to go out with you!"

There was more truth in that than she would have him read from her light tone of voice. Wearing a thick sweater that echoed the grey of his eyes, Andre was looking well, all wariness removed and a new vitality evident in every line of his body. Pam wanted to learn what had effected these changes, and hoped her improvements to his home might have contributed.

Even thickly clothed and wearing Wellington boots, they found all too quickly that trudging through the snow was far more difficult than they had supposed. Once they reached the road that sliced through the valley, they discovered a track of sorts made by some early-morning vehicle. Here, though, just as elsewhere, a dense snow-covering obscured the ground, beneath which yesterday's wheels had rutted the ice. To either side the wind that still battered their ears and stung their faces had whipped up drifts that stood shoulder-high.

"Are you used to snows like this?" Pamela asked.

Andre grinned. "You could say that I am."

But still he told her little else about his homeland. The longing to know more about him grew into an ache deep inside her.

After an hour of struggling uphill, he enquired if she was all right, and ought they to turn back?

"I'm not defeated yet," Pam answered. "Even though I will admit that this quantity of snow has rather exceeded what we generally expect in Yorkshire!"

"Are we far from Blackstone Edge now?"

"It's difficult to be sure – there's so much drifting that some contours of the land have altered. And I've only been up here two or three times, it's not all that familiar to me."

Now on much higher ground, they were able to see beyond the immediate hilltop to the distant horizon, and here clouds were forming. Over to the west, further clouds were surging in, bustling along with the wind behind them.

"We ought to return home," Andre announced. "I will not risk having you caught in the blizzard that's threatening."

"Is this only on my behalf?" Pamela asked, stamping snow off her boots as they turned in their tracks. "Aren't you a tiny bit concerned for your own wellbeing?"

Andre gave her strange look from beneath long eyelashes. "I think perhaps that now I *am* concerned to preserve this life."

Pam's shiver was unconnected with the climate. Briefly, she felt perturbed for this man who clearly had at one time felt such disregard for his own safety. And I can understand that, she thought, recalling the massive abyss created by Jim's death.

But that was long ago, and now Andre reached for her hand, to assist as they sought a less hazardous route back to his home.

A weird light in the sky behind them made them glance over their shoulders before travelling further downhill. Beyond iron-grey clouds the remaining sky was washed with an angry yellow, an unearthly colour that presaged abnormal weather. Beneath the smouldering clouds the rim of the moor appeared black while snow, whipped by the keening wind, soared and fell, soared and fell, too restless to settle.

Stonemoor House looked welcoming and blessedly solid as they approached. Hastening where they could, they had remained ahead of the blizzard, and now reached the front entrance as the initial scattering of flakes began falling.

Andre stoked the fire in the kitchen range and they ate soup, sitting close to the blaze until numbed fingers and toes tingled.

"We must go that way again," Andre insisted. He told Pam of reading, in a journal written by Celia Fiennes, of the precipice at Blackstone Edge and of a "causey". "Tell me, Pamela, please – what is a causey?"

"Sounds like an ancient word for causeway to me. Was this journal old?"

Andre smiled wryly. "If you call 1698 old."

"There you go again, teaching me something fresh about the West Riding and its past! And there is a paved road up yonder that's reputed to be Roman. I reckon that'll be what she saw."

"Then we must see it also."

Pamela liked the prospect of exploring further with Andre. He would benefit from going out, even if they only shared their walk with the elements. And it would do her no harm either.

However harsh the weather outdoors, she felt that it had refreshed her today. Working throughout the afternoon, she discovered that even monotonous tasks were accomplished more swiftly. When not obliged to concentrate completely on the job in hand, she let her mind stray ahead to the parts of the house still requiring renovation. The kitchen should be tackled before very long. Sitting there a short while ago, she had recognised again how uncomfortably it contrasted with the feel of the whole of Stonemoor.

Snow had fallen consistently and heavily from the moment that they had come back into the house. To Pam's astonishment, she found when ceasing work in time for dinner that it had drifted up to all but cover the tall ground-floor windows.

Wireless bulletins told of entire towns isolated by snow, trains cut off amid drifts, and doctors compelled to resort to horseback for visiting patients.

"I'd better ring my mother, if you don't mind," said Pamela. "Tell her that we're all right, and check that they are."

The intention remained no more than that: the telephone was completely dead.

"I am not surprised," said Andre. "No wires would withstand the weight of all that snow."

"And the wind won't have helped," Pam added. It was wailing all about Stonemoor now, whistling in the chimneys and rattling at the sash windows.

She slept less well than previously, despite choosing an early night because the trudge through all that snow had produced aches in many muscles. Beyond her room the ceaseless flakes fluttered against frosted panes, barely audible yet sufficient to scratch at weary nerves. The wind had dropped slightly, but now and then arose to send ice-encased branches crackling in the trees.

"Just be still," Pam murmured. "Please."

On the edge of sleep, she hovered, sensing that it needed only a few moments of quiet to tip her into unconsciousness. But the disquiet was within herself now, a once-familiar craving, the deepest need to belong. And this was not permissible. She might fantasise about her love of Stonemoor House, but nothing more than that.

Andre employed her; at most, was only a friend. She must not even think of his ever becoming the answer to this intense yearning.

Albeit uneasily, Pamela slept, but not for long. Reflected light from the white world outside revealed the hands of the ormolu clock set at one-thirty. The relentless wind and the snow it carried were no longer the only sounds to disturb her.

Somewhere in this house a violin was playing. Exquisite though the strains were, at that hour of the night they were a painful intrusion. The music was a piece from somewhere in her distant past, a melody that once had pleased her. Tonight, it did not please: it sounded quite eerie against the wailing of the wind. Anywhere but here, she would have hurried to locate its source and ask that it should cease.

Pamela felt trapped, locked by the snow in a home with this curious man, foreign and still half-stranger. Andre. Considerate by day and now, in the night, disregarding her needs. Fleetingly, foolishly, the thought occurred that *his* needs could be the cause of his wakefulness. Needs that would never be assuaged by the playing of a violin.

I'm not obsessed with sex, Pam asserted to herself, I never have been. I can't be thinking like this, feeling this desire. Even with Jim that had been one aspect of their life, but only one. And she was here purely on account of work. It was her business that mattered, the job now providing more success than she might ever have imagined.

The violinist halted, went back and played several bars again, confirming the performance as live, rather than a recording. But then Pam had *known* this was no mere record. The name of the piece tormented still, tantalisingly out of reach. For so many years she had listened to little beyond brass band music. Rousing tunes to set your feet tapping, they were easier to understand. And the men

111

who played them, were they more readily understood? – Was Jim? And what of Roger?

Pamela smiled to herself. What could be more matter of fact than a policeman's life? Who more direct than Roger? She liked to know where she was with people, did not mind the absence of surprise; her life already had delivered one surprise too many.

The violin persisted, and began to irritate. She wished again that Andre were someone more familiar. Someone ordinary like Roger who would accept her reproach for disturbing her sleep.

The sounds that had annoyed must at some time have begun to soothe. While the last thing she felt like was sleeping, Pam's eyelids closed and she knew nothing more until the morning.

Andre was in the kitchen behind windows where daylight was now obliterated by the snow piled against them. He turned and smiled when Pamela walked in chafing her hands to warm them. In each of the rooms that they used, fires blazed continually, but elsewhere about the house the cold was appalling.

"I shall clear the snow away out there after breakfast," he said when he'd greeted her. "Get it back from the windows, at least."

He was beside one of the tall store-cupboards, sorting groceries.

"D'you want any help?" Pamela asked. She couldn't picture any other man she had known addressing a domestic task so cheerfully.

Andre shook his head and grinned. "I have relied upon my own resources for quite some time now. You would be amazed by my abilities."

Pam smiled. "Well, perhaps by your willingness."

He shrugged as he turned to face her completely. "As

112

you will have observed, I am no longer pursuing my career. And so the tasks I take on now are of no consequence."

His career? she thought, and began to wonder, then wondering became feeling certain.

"What was that piece you were playing in the night?" she asked. She had decided not to criticise, but she was determined he should be aware that he had disturbed her.

"Piece? I do not understand." Andre was staring towards her, his eyes as cold as the ice frosting the nearby window.

"Violin piece – I'm not much good at the classics, but it was something I'd heard before." When he said nothing, Pamela persisted. "You were playing, weren't you?"

"You are mistaken, I think. I was not playing any instrument." His tone was polite, infinitely dismissive.

"It went on and on, keeping me awake. I was not mistaken."

"I might have switched on the radio, perhaps."

At one-thirty in the morning? And to hear an instrumentalist pause and play that section over again? Did he believe she was stupid? Pam could have hauled these arguments before him, but chose not to. Andre was trying her patience, but she would not risk an argument. For a while at least, she was living here. And afterwards nothing would induce her to give up the work begun on Stonemoor House. She had loved each step in its redecoration, no one was going to deprive her of the satisfaction of continuing. Some of the most interesting work still lay ahead, there were walls to restore to something like their original, and there was all that panelling to be tackled.

"I think that perhaps you heard music from one of the other houses out there."

Pamela forbade herself to show any hint of a reaction

113

to his words now. Andre could be infuriatingly enigmatic; he must learn that others need not be quite so responsive as usual.

"There is no violin here," he stated firmly, as though that left no room for disagreement on the matter.

Again, Pam refused to acknowledge the statement but it remained there, in the air between them, marring the relationship which almost had seemed to promise something ideal.

Pamela worked long days, and refused to leave the house, even when Andre set out on foot to replenish their stocks of food. He had lied to her and she could not forget that, even while laughing together or discussing the job in hand, even while talking of other matters. And they did talk a great deal, sometimes as she worked, always in the evenings. Now, though, Pam could never be sure of the truth in the words he was speaking.

When vehicles began passing along the road below the house, and the slow thaw daily revealed more of their surroundings, Pamela dug out her van and spent several long, cold minutes swinging the starting handle. Andre had not offered to help; she sensed his reluctance to have her leave, and was saddened because of the one episode which now prevented her from experiencing similar emotions so wholeheartedly.

On the evening when Pam finally arrived home the welcome warmed her heart. Tom and Ian both looked up with a grin as she came indoors and their mother came bustling out of the kitchen to kiss her.

"You have been all right, love, haven't you?" Mildred asked.

"Of course, Mum," said Pam, giving her shoulders a squeeze.

And then Charlie came pounding downstairs. "I saw the

114

van draw up," he said. "I was just getting changed after my work. I couldn't do my shirt up fast enough!"

"That's nice, Charlie, thanks," Pam responded, and was enveloped in an enthusiastic hug.

"It's been right quiet without you," he told her as he let her go.

"What – with these two brothers of mine around – and Ian with his sax? How's the playing going, Ian?"

"Not so bad now. Roger's been coming round a lot coaching me."

"That's good of him." She liked to think of Roger making himself at home here, especially when that involved doing what he could for Ian. Following her stay at Stonemoor House she felt bewildered. She had expected to love living there, but not to have Andre make her want him. If *want* was the right word. She wished she had been spared that particular torment, especially while the man responsible continued to conceal so much. She felt quite relieved to be home, and reassured by having a friend like Roger who was so open and straightforward.

Pamela did not have to wait long before seeing him. They had finished their meal and she and Charlie were clearing away the dishes when Roger arrived.

Both Ian and Tom made a beeline for him, but it was Pam whom he was seeking.

"I saw your van going past the end of the road when I was heading to the station to sign off my shift. I've been trying to ring you while you were out at Malinowski's place."

"The lines have been down, haven't they? Sorry you couldn't get in touch, though. Was it something important?"

"We –" Roger checked himself, hesitated, and began again. "Leslie was wondering how soon you could do that job for him. He wants to move in afore so long,

115

and it'll be easier all round if you're able to complete the decorating first."

"I dare say I could start next week. I'll have a word with Andre – that's assuming the phones are working again. I don't see how he can complain, I've been there long enough. And he does know that I've got this other job lined up."

"I'll tell Leslie what you've said. I'm seeing him tonight."

"Oh. All right." Pamela had been hoping that Roger intended spending some time with her. But she made herself smile. Until a short while ago he might have supposed she was still up Cragg Vale. She could not blame him for making other arrangements. "If it is okay for me to start on the flat, what do I do about picking up the key?"

"I – I've got one here, I'll leave it with you," said Roger removing a key from his keyring and handing it across.

Pamela grinned. "You came prepared! You both thought I'd be willing to get cracking next week then?"

She rang Andre that evening, she didn't want him to complain that she was giving him no warning that it would be a week or two before she continued with the work at Stonemoor.

He sounded cold and distant with her, not at all the man with whom she had talked and laughed, and struggled through snowdrifts. Pam marvelled that they had ever got on so well together, and then she recalled his lie about the violin music. Andre was like two people, and only one of them could she understand. She felt more thankful than ever to be about to work for Leslie Rivers. Roger had seemed delighted that she was decorating this flat for his friend.

The empty rooms felt larger than ever now that they were silent, yet too many reminders lingered for Andre

116

to dismiss her. There were pots of paint, of course, wallpaper in rolls and brushes that she had cleaned and left to dry. All these had their scents, but it was her scent which obtruded the most – in the bedroom that he now considered hers, in the bathroom next to it.

He was being a fool, he knew, her absence was to be but a few days, but having relished her presence for so long this parting came all the harder.

Andre made himself a meal, and ate listlessly without really tasting the food. The night stretched ahead, limitless time which he could alleviate with nothing.

He went to the cupboard and took out his violin case, opened it, and gazed at the instrument, but left it where it was. He had no heart for playing when it resurrected such memories.

Why, why, why had he told Pamela that untruth? Did he really trust her so little? How could he have grown so attached to her, and still feel unable to unlock at least one secret from his own history?

How could he even hope that they might at some future time mean a great deal to each other, while he felt like this – afraid to confide? They could have shared so much more, his music, the story behind the life that had shaped him, tales of the culture in which he had been reared. Instead of that he had shut her out. The hurt in her eyes had spoken of the injury to their relationship.

Would she ever believe him now? When these long days ended and Pamela came home to Stonemoor House, would she even listen?

On the day that she drove out to begin on Leslie's flat, snow started fluttering down again. Combining with the quantity remaining from the heaviest snowfall in decades, it made the approach roads dangerous. From the windows of the flat, however, Pam was happy to see how the fresh fall had whitened the drifts previously dusted with soot from the mill smoke. And this time the snow was light, by mid-morning she was looking out on to blue skies and the sun glinting back from ripples on the surface of the reservoir. Compared with Stonemoor House, the preparation work here was easy, the entire job would be simple. And might be accomplished swiftly. Not that Pamela wished to rush the work.

She was enjoying evenings spent at home. Tom had taken up painting – not her kind, the sort that involved watercolours and delicate brushes, and sitting at the living room table. Pam hadn't known her youngest brother had any artistic inclination and was fascinated. She had spent one entire evening, just watching. While he painted, Tom talked as he never had in the past to her. He was copying a photograph taken the previous summer, of moors and the sky, a farm in the foreground and a bridge over a brook.

Pam hadn't understood how much Tom loved the countryside. She wished he was with her today. The snow out here had blue shadows and mauve where the line of the hill folded, then there was the water and the way it stirred, the dappling of sunlight. Tomorrow, she might bring a camera, capture the scene for her brother to interpret.

She would see Roger tonight, he had promised Ian another saxophone lesson, and she had heard Mildred inviting him to stay for supper. We need to talk, Pam thought, Roger and I – and away from my family. For ages now they had had no time on their own, no time for their friendship which felt as if it had been suspended. She hadn't intended to neglect so much through being occupied with her work. Only this morning, her mother had mentioned that Roger had got his promotion and was now

Sergeant Jenkins. Pam felt awful about not congratulating him, but she had not known. And somehow not knowing made her feel all the worse. She'd been afraid before that Roger might believe that since she'd ceased to need his help she had lost interest. But these days she suspected that before very long Roger would need *her*.

No one had said, but she had assumed from the start that Leslie had taken on this flat because he was getting married. She could imagine that when that happened Roger would miss him a great deal. He and Leslie had known each other for almost as long as he had known Jim. Pam had sensed that Roger had turned to Leslie increasingly since Jim's death. They were the two friends who still played in the band, weren't they? Would Leslie even have time for band practice once he had a wife? She knew from her own experience that adjusting to married life was time-consuming, and became all-important.

Roger could have been waiting for this promotion before settling down. He was well turned thirty, and showed an almost fatherly interest in her brothers; he must want a family. She believed he was as ready as she herself for having a real home. And she liked the idea of looking after him. It could work very well. Her business could be organised to accommodate his career in the force, she would schedule her jobs to be at home when he came off shift. And nobody but Roger understood how she had felt about losing Jim.

Pamela smiled. Although it was all a dream, as yet, it did have some foundation, and not the silly head-in-the-air stuff that so frequently went wrong. Marriages needed friendship between the partners, it was when that was missing that there was no lasting bond.

Later the same day, sitting in the living room while Roger was giving Ian tuition, Pam considered all that she had thought that morning. She watched Roger and saw how, out of uniform, he still had that upright stance which made him appear distinguished. Even absorbed as he was with coaching her brother, the air remained – a man of some standing. A man to admire.

That was it, she thought, she admired Roger. She respected him for the job he did, and certainly for his treatment of her family. This might not be being in love, but it was real, a feeling to be valued.

As so often, there was too little time to talk, and none to speak alone. Tom was painting again while Charles, also at the table, was updating his books. For today, Pamela would have to be content that she'd had the chance to congratulate Roger on his promotion.

She did, however, see him to the door when he was leaving. He asked how her day had gone at the flat, and smiled when she told of her progress. His lips when he smiled always softened, removing the sometimes austere look that he had when on duty. Pamela began wondering how it would feel to kiss him.

Towards the middle of the second week of working on the flat, Pamela started when she heard a key turn in the lock. She was applying a final coat of paint to the bedroom door, one of her last tasks here. Rushing to the head of the stairs, she saw the door in the hall below opening, and Leslie stamping snow off his boots.

"You didn't half make me jump!" Pam exclaimed after they had greeted each other.

"Sorry," Leslie said. "Didn't Roger say I intended coming out here?"

Pamela shook her head as he came up the stairs to her side. "I haven't seen him for a day or two. Although, as a matter of fact, I've been thinking that might alter – that he and I might shortly be seeing more of each other. He's been good to me since Jim died,

120

that's brought us together, and – well, with you getting married . . ."

Leslie was staring strangely at her: she might have been speaking in a foreign tongue.

"Well, you are, aren't you – getting wed? That's why you've got your own place, isn't it?" Pam prompted him.

Leslie shook his head. He was beginning to smile. Feeling rather idiotic, Pam went back to painting the door. While she had turned away the paint had begun to dry slightly, she needed to concentrate now as she began brushing in so that there was no ugly line.

Leslie was watching her; she sensed his amusement, and wondered what its cause might be.

"I thought you knew, Pamela. I thought you'd understood and agreed to keep it to yourself. That – that Roger had explained."

"Explained? Explained what?" She couldn't leave what she was doing, and suddenly she did not want to. She had a dreadful feeling that she was going to hate what she was about to hear.

A little behind and to her right, Leslie shifted his position slightly, as though to stand more firmly. When he began to speak, the assertiveness in his voice willed her to accept what he was saying.

"We've never liked making a secret of it, but we're not daft – we can't risk being sent to prison. Still, you'll not let on to anybody, I'm sure. It's quite simple, Pamela – this flat is where Roger and I shall be living. It's off the beaten track, and far enough from his local station to prevent his colleagues from dropping in."

For a few moments Pamela failed to comprehend any reason why Roger's fellow officers, or anyone else, should be concerned about his sharing a friend's flat. But then, perhaps realising that she had not grasped its full

121

implications, Leslie went on to reveal further facts about the relationship.

"Roger and I have been more than friends for a very long time; we decided to give our love a chance by making a home together where we no longer have to pretend. No matter what the law says, we've got to have somewhere where we can be true to ourselves, to each other . . ."

There was more, but Pamela was too sickened to grasp what he was saying. *Love?* Between Leslie Rivers and Roger? *Roger?* So shattered that she literally was afraid she might vomit, Pam inhaled slowly and deeply several times. The smell of the paint, which normally she scarcely noticed, hit the back of her throat and made her eyes sting. She coughed slightly, and continued painting. She hardly knew Leslie Rivers, did she, she couldn't let him see how upset she was!

Despite her distress, Pam could feel his gaze boring into her back, willing her to make some response. She drew in another breath, and summoned enough composure to reply.

"No, I didn't know. But now that I do I certainly hope you'll both be happy." Was that the right thing to say? she wondered. It was the kind of phrase she would have used to any heterosexual couple.

"Thanks," Leslie said. "And I know we can rely on your discretion. You've been a friend of Roger's for a long time, you wouldn't cause him any trouble."

Pamela said nothing further while, like an automaton, she finished painting the rest of the door.

Leslie had returned downstairs, and she couldn't have been more relieved. She would have to get out of here. She needed to go right away and consider these facts when she was quite alone.

Pam replaced the lid on the can of paint and set it to one side with her brushes. She was too upset to hang around cleaning them while that man was in the flat.

"Will you be here tomorrow?" she asked, thrusting on her coat.

When Leslie told her that he would not, Pamela resolved that she would if necessary spend every minute of the next day here, in order to complete the job, and get right away from the place for ever.

Instead of going home, Pam drove the van a short distance to park beside the reservoir. She needed to think, and couldn't imagine ever being able to think about Roger again while she was anywhere near her family. They knew him, for heaven's sake, how could she ever bear this burden without a murmur?

Skirting the side of Ogden Reservoir, Pamela began to walk. The wind seemed keener than ever here, coming off the water after sweeping across the snow-covered moors. This was some of the wildest, and most invigorating country in the area, with the distant ruins of Top Withins reminding her that she was nearing moorland beloved by the Brontë sisters. Thinking of them and of the strangeness depicted in some of their tales, Pamela began to feel her agitation quietening. The Brontës knew that some things in life were beyond explanation. They might not have encountered anything of this sort, but she somehow felt quite sure that they would have tried to understand.

And can I? she wondered. Can I ever comprehend the nature of what is binding Roger and that Rivers man together? At present it felt as if she never would, or could. She could only give it time. And if the devastating loss of her husband had, with time, become bearable to this degree – enabling her to work, and to enjoy that work, then she might perhaps adjust to anything.

I just wish I hadn't been so blind, she thought, so blind and such a fool that I'd even hoped that Roger and I could have some kind of a future together. Already, she wondered how the supposition had grown.

Her only consolation, as she trudged out her distress over the snow-covered tussocks of the moor, was that no one in the world need ever know what she had dreamed.

# Chapter Seven

Pamela was driving quite slowly as she set out for Stonemoor House. The weather had improved and a slight thaw had despatched some of the ice which had made the roads so dangerous, but it wasn't on account of physical conditions that she was taking her time. She was savouring her relief that this day had come.

Ever since the truth about Roger had shattered her, Pam had looked on returning to Andre's home as the escape that might keep her sane. Throughout the final day at Leslie's flat she had worked unremittingly, constantly hauling back her thoughts when they meandered towards the relationship that appeared so unnatural, and thinking ahead instead to tasks awaiting her at Stonemoor House.

Life at home had felt no easier as she struggled to seem her usual self while memory resurrected all the occasions when Roger had been a part of their lives there. Ian mentioned that Roger would be calling in two days' time to give further music tuition, and Pam was appalled, recalling now the way in which she'd actually been glad to see Roger's arm placed affectionately across her young brother's shoulders. Could she even let the saxophone lessons continue without giving Ian some warning? But how could she do that when she had promised to keep the secret that had disrupted her life so cruelly? She must rely instead on the fact that Roger never saw Ian alone.

Pamela hadn't yet permitted herself the luxury of

examining the news in the light of her own feelings about Roger. After her immediate reaction, she had chosen to concentrate on less painful issues. And to remain deeply thankful that no one had known of her own ideas about the future she might have had with Roger Jenkins.

When she had turned left out of Mytholmroyd, Pam began looking forward to the rest of the day. The road was blessedly familiar, and the surrounding hills in their covering of snow brought memories of that blissful walk with Andre.

The house, as she approached, was bathed in sunlight which warmed gold-toned stonework and gleamed from its windows. Pamela felt as though she was going home, and wished with all her heart that she was.

Andre had the door open by the time she had unloaded and locked the van. Mounting the front steps she realised he seemed like an old friend, and longed to rush to him and recount all her troubles.

"Pamela, how pleased I am that you are here!" He extended a hand to help with the equipment she was carrying.

Pam surrendered a pile of dustcovers to him. "I'm not sure you should have to help! You're paying me to get this job done, remember?"

Andre laughed and went through into the room that she was decorating. "I am so delighted to see you that I could reward you simply for coming to Stonemoor House."

She gave him a rueful grin before beginning to set out her tools. "And *I* feel as if I should be the one paying you. You'll never know how thankful I was to get away from that place."

"I certainly shall not if you do not confide in me. What has happened, Pamela?"

"Nothing," she said, and nothing was what she revealed during the next few hours.

Andre spent most of the time watching her, and seemed intrigued when Pam began experimenting as she tried to clean the wallpaper which, in this room, was original and over 130 years old.

She was using a homely method learned before the war, and she found herself smiling as soon as Andre exclaimed.

"That looks like bread, Pamela. Tell me that it is not bread!"

"Ah, but it *is* stale bread," she told him. "It can bring off surface grime, and without damaging the paper. It's all I dare try on something so precious."

The work was slow and laborious, however, and not quite so effective as Pamela had hoped. Before the day ended she had discussed the difficulty with Andre and sugggested that only the paper within the decorative panel should be preserved. The remainder of the walls could be distempered in a toning shade, one that would have been used in the early nineteenth century.

"The rest is too dirty," Andre agreed. "And, as you say, a more severe treatment would risk ruining the paper's surface. I think your idea of applying a colour wash will be ideal."

Pamela was pleased by how readily Andre now accepted her thoughts on how his home should be renovated. He was showing a substantial understanding of all that she hoped to achieve, and had acquired enough knowledge of Regency styling to be able to confirm that her notions were acceptable, not only to him personally, but as a means of restoring the original ambience of the house.

Following the occasion when she had stayed at Stonemoor, Andre now expected Pamela to eat with him at lunchtime, and he made no secret of enjoying her company. Feeling shaken and raw as a result of learning the truth about Roger, Pam was glad to relax with someone who seemed content to make the most of their amiable encounters. In contrast with that shattering piece of news, the disturbance caused by Andre's denial of playing the violin now appeared so trivial that she dismissed it.

Despite being happy to be working at Stonemoor again, by early afternoon Pamela felt exhausted. She also felt torn. Her own home had become a place where she could no longer discuss the matter that was troubling her. Terrified of inadvertently revealing what she had learned, she couldn't just let go there. Ordinarily, she would have explained how tired she was and would gladly have headed back to Halifax. Now, because she felt so awkward about the situation, she struggled on, growing increasingly miserable.

Andre brought in a tray of tea at four o'clock, and insisted that she should set aside her work and join him on one of the sofas which had been moved to the end of the room and covered with a dust sheet.

"You are troubled today, Pamela," he remarked, handing a cup and saucer across. "Can you not tell me the reason?"

His voice was more gentle and concerned than ever in the past, and as warm as she had heard it. The ache of disillusionment turned into a massive yearning to explain what she was feeling. But how could she when she had vowed to keep the truth to herself?

"Have you had bad news within your family perhaps?" he persisted. "You know I too have suffered, I should like to try to understand."

"You'd never understand this. No one ever could understand it."

"Well, I shall not if you do not speak of it to me, that is for sure," he remarked stiffly. "And you will never know then if this matter is quite so terrible as you fear. My experience has been wide, my dear – I have not always

128

lived in this seclusion. You might be surprised by the extent of my understanding . . ."

His quaint un-English phrasing made Pam smile when she felt least like smiling; more importantly, it made her realise that because Andre was so unlike anyone she knew, he could be the one person to whom she might talk.

"I've been so shattered that I hardly know what I'm doing," she confessed. "So confused by what I've been told that I scarcely know who I am any longer."

"You should tell me everything," Andre prompted. "Trust me."

"It's this old friend – an old friend of my husband's, actually. He's been good to me since Jim died, and I was even beginning to wonder if he and I, eventually, well – you know . . ." Pam paused, swallowed. "I've been such a fool, Andre, but never in a million years would I have begun to suspect. He – oh, God – even talking about it is so awful!" She faltered again, wondering which words to use. "He – he isn't interested in women, not in that way, do you understand what I'm saying? He's setting up house with another man."

Pam felt hot all over, much too embarrassed to even look at Andre. She had needed so desperately to talk about this, but now that she had she felt no better. What could Andre say? After all, Roger was breaking the law. She tried to find comfort in something ordinary like drinking tea, but her hands shook so abominably that she was forced to replace the chattering cup and saucer without one sip.

"You have never before encountered a similar relationship, I think," Andre began. "Naturally, you are perturbed." He sounded almost amused; maybe the facts were not as dreadful as she supposed.

"That's right," she admitted. "But it is illegal, isn't it?"

"How old are you, Pamela?"

"I shall be twenty-nine this year. I suppose that makes me seem young for my age, incredibly stupid."

"While I am ten years older, and yet I should hate to believe that I have lost the capacity to be surprised. Agreeably, or otherwise. And you have come across nothing like this, not even during the war, in the forces?"

"There were rumours, but not about anyone in our squadron. Or not anybody that I knew. Just – gossip about folk being sent away. I can't believe this is happening, that Roger could be locked up."

Andre turned her to face him. His grey eyes regarded her steadily, assessing the damage the news had done her. After a moment he smiled.

"In your circumstances, anyone would be perturbed, although I am sure your friend will be too circumspect to be arrested. But you should not let this turn you against him. He, I am sure, is still that same person who has been kind."

"No, he isn't, he can't be. I don't want to even think about him with another man."

"Then do not think of it. One month ago, one week even, you considered this friend to be exactly like everyone else. But, you know, he has not changed at all from what he was then – only your perception of him has changed. Can you not see that?"

Sighing, Pamela shook her head. "Oh, I know what you say makes sense, but it makes no difference to what I feel. He's not the same. It's just all so horribly unnatural."

"To you, yes. Also to myself, because we are endowed with feelings whose essence has been indoctrinated in us. But not to those who, like your friend, have other compulsions. Their nature is such that, for them, a different conduct would seem abnormal."

"I wish I could think like you, Andre. You sound so wise, so logical. You must believe I'm terribly naïve!"

Smiling at her, he shook his head. "Not at all. Innocent perhaps, but that is not a failing." He kissed her cheek then, affectionately.

Pam felt reassured, comforted. And her shakiness appeared to be coming under control. She began to drink her tea. When she finally set her cup aside, she gave Andre a long look before speaking.

"You've known a lot of people, haven't you, Andre? And many of them very different from the folk I've moved among, even in the WAAF."

He nodded. "Our cultures are not very alike, I think. Many of my friends were of the sort which you English people would call eccentric. Artists, some of them were, and performers of various kinds. A few were academics. And among them all several had denied the heterosexual love which we accept as the norm. In the main, I would say, they were no worse for that."

"What sort of life did you have in – in your own country? What did you do?"

"One day, I will tell that to you. For the present, I cannot."

"Well, it's certainly given you a broader outlook."

Andre grinned. "I am pleased it seems that way. I like to believe that I have acquired the ability to judge things for myself, but without being judgemental."

Judgemental, thought Pam. Yes, she was afraid that was what she was. And being aware that she should not be that way made things seem all the harder. Especially the prospect of meeting Roger again.

"I wish I knew how to tackle this. I can keep it to myself, I'd not put him in any danger. But I'm going to hate seeing him again."

131

"Do you have to see him – at least before you have adjusted to what you have learned?"

"Tomorrow night. He's coming to my mother's. He's a regular visitor there, that's what makes it so much worse."

"You do not have to be there, do you? You could go out for the evening. You might stay here for the night. Tell everyone you are so busy that you cannot return to your home."

"Isn't that just putting off the awful moment, being a coward?"

"Or being kinder to the person involved – if otherwise he were to read in your eyes the distaste that you are feeling."

Since it was not until the following night that she would remain at Stonemoor House, Pam was able to explain the arrangement to her mother. Mildred seemed perturbed, but prepared to accept the idea.

"I suppose if you were going to do owt wrong you've plenty of opportunity without staying the night. I've brought you up right, happen everyone'll understand it's only to save a bit of time."

"Aye. Petrol an' all while it's still in short supply."

Pam couldn't have known how relieved she would feel to be avoiding an encounter with Roger. All day long while she worked she felt the weight slipping away from her shoulders and when evening came she was in just the mood for enjoying Andre's company.

Once again, he proved how adept he was at cooking and smiled when she exclaimed delightedly that he had managed to produce an interesting meal from their rations. This time, she had insisted in advance that he must accept some of her coupons. When she had stayed with him previously she had only been able to recompense him afterwards for what he had used.

132

The dish today was basically lamb, but in such an exotic sauce that Pamela could scarcely recognise it from the lamb she had eaten at home.

Andre laughed when she complimented him, and teased her with the thought that he was influencing her to become more cosmopolitan.

Pam laughed with him. "I've never considered myself as that before!"

"Not while you were in the forces?"

Pamela grinned. "I never got any further than air bases in this country. The only thing was I met a lot more new people than ever I would if I'd stopped in Halifax."

She asked what he had done during the war, but Andre's reply was evasive. Sensing that his wartime experiences were painful to discuss, Pam did not press him to reply. He did speak later of his peacetime way of life, which did indeed seem to involve meeting a great many artistic people, although again he did not confirm in which branch of the arts he had worked.

Curiously, Pam noticed that she was unperturbed when Andre failed to explain his past completely. They were good friends, of that she was certain now, and she felt that was all she needed to know about him.

During the night, however, Pam did wonder for a time if their friendship was being strained unduly. She awakened, as she had on that other occasion, to music from a violin. This time, she reminded herself that she approved everything that Andre believed about refusing to judge the behaviour of others. Even though he had disturbed her into lying awake, she could accept that he must have good reason for denying these sounds which now drifted eerily through the darkened house. Only the atmosphere of his home seemed altered, not Andre himself. His wish to conceal the existence of the instrument need not cause her to question how good a friend he was.

133

Pamela had been warmed by his concern and had sensed a new tenderness in his manner towards her. And although her emotions felt so raw that she was afraid she would never contemplate more than friendship with anyone, knowing that Andre cared meant a very great deal to her.

Working at Stonemoor House was increasing Pamela's interest in antiques. She was delighted when Andre suggested one day that she might go with him to an auction to be conducted by one of the London houses in a local mansion.

"I need to replace beds," he told her. "And to purchase more furniture for these downstairs rooms as well as the bedrooms."

Pam was delighted that he wished her to attend with him, and felt flattered that he regarded her knowledge so highly. I have studied, I know, she reflected, but this seemed a splendid reward for reading up on an interesting period of history.

For once Andre seemed to have dismissed all his misgivings about going out, and to be more at ease than Pamela herself in the huge room where the auction was held. He had warned her against making any movement that might be misconstrued as a bid, and consequently she felt afraid of moving so much as a muscle.

Once bidding began, however, Pam became fascinated. The auctioneer might have been an actor or the conductor of an orchestra, so skilfully did he encourage bids and with such rapidity.

Her excitement increased each time that Andre became interested in something. She was also amazed by the high prices commanded. After he had succeeded in taking only three items, she suspected that their total cost would have furnished the whole of her mother's home. He acquired a pair of carved and painted armchairs, exquisitely gilded and made in 1815, and a sofa table of mahogany inlaid with ebony.

He was less successful regarding the other furniture he required. "The beds listed here are of the wrong period," he complained.

Andre seemed to console himself quite adequately, nevertheless, with a rosewood sideboard that had two pedestal cupboards, one fitted as a cellarette, the other a platewarmer. To further enhance his dining room, he took a set of chairs which had a brass inlay to match the sideboard's.

"When they are delivered, you shall help me decide where these may best be placed," he promised.

On the way back to Stonemoor House from the auction they passed quite close to Boulder Clough. Andre decided to call on the Misses Norton.

"It'll be nice to see them again," Pam agreed, "and to check that they have survived all that snow all right."

Sophie Norton was the one who welcomed them at the door on this occasion, fussing like a sparrow with a young brood while Hilda urged from within the room that they should come right in at once.

The tea ritual was enacted as before, but with a little more disturbance for their niece was out for the afternoon. Sophie tried to insist that she must prepare the tray, but Hilda took over and made quite a production of bringing tea into the room.

The sisters soon assured them that the snow had troubled them not at all. Moving in with their niece had been a godsend. They had been cosseted near the fire, while every item of shopping was purchased on their behalf.

"But tell us how it was at Stonemoor House," Sophie begged. "I used to love the place in winter."

Together, Pamela and Andre described the walk they had taken, and the way they had relished the wildness of the scenery.

"And the old house withstood all the elements, I'll warrant," Hilda exclaimed. "It was built for folk who understood how bleak it could be out there, you know."

"It protected us well," Pam assured them.

"Just as you are protecting it internally," added Andre, giving Pam an appreciative smile before he turned to the sisters. "You would not believe the concern Pamela is showing your old home; her patience is boundless."

"And Stonemoor will reward you," said Sophie. "It's a home that knows when it is loved."

The sisters listened intently while Andre explained which rooms had been renovated now, and what still needed to be done.

"You haven't tackled that panelling yet then?" Hilda asked quite sharply.

Pam confessed that she hadn't had the courage to begin on restoring it. "I need to know a bit more about treating woodwork. And besides, if I leave that till last I shall be able to concentrate more fully."

"Pamela has engaged so many skills already," Andre said. "I can well understand the need to devote more thought to a technique which will be so different."

"And are you setting aside other work, in order to give all your time to Stonemoor?" asked Sophie.

"I hope you're not turning jobs down," her sister added.

"I've done the occasional one elsewhere." But Pam did not mean to dwell on that flat she had decorated. "I can always advertise again when I'm free to take on more work." She was so enjoying the challenge of Stonemoor House that she hardly ever worried about obtaining further jobs.

"Your reputation will become your advertisement," Andre asserted. "You will soon have no need to publicise what you are doing."

Pamela hoped that might be so although, since Andre avoided other company, she wondered how news of what she accomplished there would reach others.

Both she and Andre became enchanted when the sisters began describing Christmases at Stonemoor in their grandfather's day when large family gatherings had filled the house with laughter.

"There was music as well, and plenty of it," Sophie exclaimed.

There is music now, thought Pam, and gave Andre a look. He seemed quite ordinary today, and benign. He hardly appeared the kind of man who would not only take to playing the violin during the night, but also have cause for denying that he had done so.

"Then there were walks in summer," Hilda remarked suddenly. "Quite long walks, over past Stoodley Pike and on towards Todmorden. Do you remember, Sophie, that day when the peat was smouldering?"

Sophie nodded, seeming excited by the memory. "Sebastian was with us that day. He saw us over the danger."

"I don't recall him being there," her sister said waspishly.

"No, well – you wouldn't, would you? But he was there all right."

"Smouldering?" Pam enquired. "You say the peat was smouldering?"

"Indeed yes," Hilda affirmed. "On fire below the ground we were crossing. Every so often a hole appeared in the dark earth. You could see it glowing red underneath."

"And smoking," her sister added. "It was hot through

the soles of my boots. Without Sebastian's help, we'd never have reached home again."

"So you say," sniffed Hilda. "You don't mention the other things about your Sebastian, the times when he angered Father."

Sophie smiled to herself. "It was only a little misfortune. And only because he – well, he was home for such a short time, we had so few days together . . ."

"Father was most particular," Hilda continued. "Only for her own good, of course. Sophie was always to be home by nine-thirty. And if she wasn't home by then, he let them both know all right! Father was a church warden, you see. And if Sophie wasn't in the house, he went across to the church and set the bell ringing."

"Such a noise it was," Sophie exclaimed, covering her ears now as though the sound reverberated there. "Him being deaf, he didn't realise how loud it really was. Sebastian was quite startled the first time that it happened."

So she was late more than once then, thought Pam, and caught Andre's glance. He was just as amused as she herself was.

Approaching Stonemoor House, Pamela sensed how her love for the place was developing. Picturing the Norton sisters growing up here was almost as good as having her own family inhabit the house. She would feel their presence belonging in the very walls, and even in the silence might imagine she heard the songs of past Christmases.

This love she felt for his home was somehow increasing her affinity with Andre. Their friendship had made her all but dismiss the disturbance created by everything that she had learned about Roger. As days passed and winter turned to spring Pam discovered she

138

was losing the rigidity caused by her unease about her old friend.

She and Andre laughed together and talked, and became familiar with each other's likes and dislikes. And Pam found him more and more attractive. Even while she worked, she frequently became aware of their being alone together. Andre came into a room, and her entire being awakened to his approach.

Pamela was particularly thankful that working for Andre seemed to fill her life. Away from Stonemoor House, she was beset by difficulties and managed precious little relaxation. Both Charles and Dorothy were too busy working to indulge very often in the outings which the three of them had enjoyed. And although Pam had resolutely refused to treat Roger any differently, their encounters had become more rare with his moving to the flat out in the country. When he visited now it was only briefly to coach Ian with his saxophone.

She could not begrudge Ian that one interest and someone with whom to share it, especially when that person could exert a powerful influence regarding keeping within the law.

The lad was in their mother's bad books, this time for walking out of his job. Asserting that she would stand no such nonsense, Mildred had marched him straight back to the foundry. After a long talk with the manager there, she had persuaded him that Ian should continue his apprenticeship. That was when Ian himself had ruined everything by refusing to do any such thing. And the manager had seemed thankful to seize that as a good reason for washing his hands of him.

"You'll do something, Ian," Mildred had assured him as soon as they arrived home. "You needn't think you're going to get away with doing nowt towards your keep."

The boy had grinned reassuringly. "I know that, Mum,

139

I'm not daft. Don't worry, I'll soon be bringing some brass in."

However lacking in application he might be, Ian was not short of enterprise and at the end of the week he had brought home a larger sum than he would have been paid in the foundry. Unfortunately, the fresh source of his earnings had been discovered during the next few days. A neighbour had spotted the lad scrambling about in the coal yard. Curious, he had followed him to the rows of scruffy houses where Ian was selling the coal that he had gathered.

"You'd better talk to him, Pamela," their mother had insisted, driven almost to tears. "He's that heedless with me, it's a waste of my breath saying owt."

Moved by the contrite expression in Ian's eyes, and the half-smile that still reminded her of their father's, Pam had tried to explain how wrong it was to make a profit out of something as scarce as coal.

"You know how short fuel supplies have been this winter, and that they're likely to continue this way with the miners being promised a five-day week. Nationalisation's caused terrible unsettlement throughout mining. Then there were hold-ups not all that long ago, with everything brought to a halt by the snow."

Ian had grinned. "I know all about that. But it's only stuff that there's a shortage of that you can sell easy, isn't it?"

"But you *mustn't*, love, not when it's against the law."

"All right then, you tell me what work I can do . . ."

Mildred had heard Ian's final retort, and when he had gone to bed she reminded Pamela of her original suggestion. "You could set him on to work with you. He's the size of a grown man now, I'm sure you could make use of him."

Once again, Pam explained that if she was to take

somebody on, it must be a trained man. But she hadn't entirely dismissed the idea from her mind. She was fond of both of her brothers, and felt sure that Ian was foolish rather than downright bad. He might respond well to being made to work with someone who kept an eye on him. So long as none of her clients ever discovered what schemes he'd been trying.

On one thing Pamela remained determined, though; Ian would never be asked to work with her at Stonemoor House. She needed her time there to be quite separate from her life elsewhere. A time when she could feel at home with Andre.

His sudden announcement that he was going away from Stonemoor for a short while therefore seemed all the more alarming, dropped as it was into their conversation over dinner one evening. Pamela had remained at the house for the past week. She had long since ceased to create reasons, even for herself, when she needed to stay there. And now here Andre was, telling her he would be away, but not where he was going, nor really for how long.

Despite their recent closeness, Pam sensed his old reluctance to confide, and thought better of pressing for details of his destination. She did ask where she might contact him, but received only a solemn shake of his head.

"That will not be possible, I fear. But there will be no need, I am sure. You know the place as well as I do. The area surrounding Stonemoor House appears to be less of a mystery to you than it still is to me."

He went on to say with a smile that now the weather had improved there was no risk of her being stranded at the house. "Although I should be pleased if you were willing to stay here during my absence. That need not be alone, if you are more comfortable with company. You have brothers, have you not? Perhaps one of them could be persuaded to sleep here?"

141

Pamela could feel the colour slipping away from her face. If Andre had been aware of the suggestion that her mother had made regarding Ian, he couldn't have inserted a more pointed reminder! But Andre did not know, and he must not learn how worried she was about Ian, least of all of his inventive methods of raising money.

"Or if not one of your brothers, perhaps that friend of yours who made the curtains . . ."

"Dorothy, you mean? Oh, I don't know. In any case, I don't mind stopping here on my own."

Andre smiled. "You must do as you wish. But I shall like to think of you in my home."

Pamela felt a warm glow running through her as Andre finished speaking. He seemed to be confirming that she had not been entirely wrong to feel at home here with him. She knew at once that she would work especially hard during his absence. There was nothing she would like more than to delight him by how much she had achieved while he was away. Or, she admitted silently to herself, nothing that she was likely to get! She had been attracted to Andre from the start, a force which had combined with this growing affinity until she now felt that she was really alive only when she was with him. But such emotions were very private, and must remain so; she was enough of a realist to be sure that someone who had so much experience of the world – to say nothing of owning a house the size of this – would not contemplate committing himself to anyone at all ordinary.

Despite these efforts to remain level-headed, Pam found she was savouring the next few days, her awareness more acute as though she might be impressing on her memory the way it felt to have Andre near. She was going to miss him so intensely, and knew already that not knowing how long he might be absent would become a form of torture.

Andre also appeared subdued on the morning that he left Stonemoor House. They had talked hardly at all during breakfast. She had caught him looking around him in the rooms that she had completed, and had sensed his need to carry an impression of his home wherever he was travelling.

Startling her slightly, he drew Pamela into his arms at the foot of the staircase when he was about to leave. He hugged her to him until she felt the urgent hammering of his heart, and every button of his coat where it pressed into her.

"Take care of my home, but I know that you will," he said quite lightly. "And take care of yourself," he added, his arms tightening around her.

"And you take care, Andre." Pamela was overwhelmingly aware that, wherever he was going, he could face danger. "Come home safely."

"To you," he murmured emphatically. "Of course I shall."

Andre kissed her then, full on the lips, a kiss that lingered and deepened, charged with desire, but more than that – with all the emotions which had developed between them.

He made as if to turn away, but then she was in his arms again, crushed against him while he stirred with a passion that she had only half suspected he felt, and hungry kisses sent the blood rushing to her mouth.

They heard the cab approaching up the lane. Pamela felt him easing away from her and raised her eyelids to find his grey eyes, intense with longing, searching her face.

"I have to go." His voice sounded husky.

She could not watch him being taken from her, but listened to his taxi driving away and, already chilled and quite bereft, found she was crossing her arms over her

143

breast, clutching at her own sleeves as though she might lock in all the affection of his embrace.

But she must be practical. "Decision time now," she murmured aloud, with a glance all about her to the deserted hallway and staircase. Could she ignore the hint that was more timely than Andre could have guessed when he uttered it? Could she continue to dismiss the urge to do something to help young Ian?

# Chapter Eight

"I shan't stand any nonsense, you know. There'll be no messing around. And if one word gets out about the scrapes you've been in, that'll be the finish. Even before you get started."

They were in the van driving out to Stonemoor House. Beside her, Ian was grinning as if he had been handed the world on a gold salver. He gave her a long, loving look, and Pamela was reminded yet again of the father they had lost.

"Do you remember Dad?" she asked, before Ian went on with the assurances that he was grateful and knew how to behave, which had been repeated frequently since she arrived home earlier that evening.

"'Course I do." He stopped, shrugged the shoulders that, these days, reached higher than her own. "A bit. He was kind, wasn't he, sort of gentle . . .?"

"Aye, he was, love. He might have had a manual job, but he was a true gentleman. And Mum's like that, even though she has to be tough with us at times. That's why I want her to be proud of you."

"But I'm not clever, not like you."

"You haven't found what you're good at yet, have you? You could be clever with your hands – that's what we're hoping. And trying you out like this, while there's no one there but us, we'll learn the truth without any embarrassment."

145

It was for her own sake that Pam had decided to take Ian to Stonemoor House now. If he were to make a mess of things there, she couldn't have borne that if Andre were present to see. No matter how capable she might seem, her brother's ability would reflect on her.

Their mother had been ecstatic when Pam came home a few hours ago with the announcement that Ian could accompany her to Stonemoor. Even the list of misgivings that Pam had rattled off had failed to cool Mildred's delight.

I'm glad I'm giving him a try, if only for her sake, Pamela had thought. And Ian's absence might also help his younger brother. Tom tended to seem rather over-shadowed.

"I'd no idea it was anything like as big as this!" Ian exclaimed now while Pam was driving up the track towards Stonemoor House. "And are you really going to decorate the whole of it?"

"Decorate, or renovate where necessary, yes. On the inside, that is. We haven't decided yet about the outside paintwork." The exterior was well preserved, and Pam wasn't desperate to do more than what she was tackling indoors. Although repainting the window frames and doors would be simple enough.

"What will you do with this then?" Ian enquired a few moments later, setting down his case and looking around at the hall panelling.

Pamela smiled. "Good question!"

"You'll have to do a fresh coat of paint all over, won't you?"

"Not if I can help it. I've started reading up on treating this sort of wood – it's oak, by the way – only I'm going to get the rest of the house finished first. Andre's agreed to that."

"Andre," Ian repeated. "That's foreign, isn't it? Is

he French?" He had learned French at school, up to a point.

"He is foreign, yes. Not French though, I thought he were Polish, only . . ." Pam let her voice trail off. She didn't like being reminded of the apparent secrecy surrounding Andre's nationality.

". . . Only what?" her brother prompted.

"Just – I've never been told where he comes from. It doesn't matter."

"Perhaps he's a Jerry, that's why he won't say," Ian suggested over his shoulder, as he began opening doors leading off from the hall and looking into rooms.

"Come here, you," Pamela snapped, and recognised that her annoyance with Ian had more to do with his reminder that Andre could be German than the eagerness to explore.

"I've got to find my way about here, haven't I?"

"Yes, of course. But I won't have you poking your nose into everything. This is Andre's home, and we have to respect that. Do you understand?"

Ian nodded. "Yes, in a way. But you've stayed the night with him, it's not as if . . ."

"Not as if what?" If she was to have any peace of mind at all, she needed to know what was going on in this young man's head.

"Well – not as if you only worked for him."

"But I do. Andre is paying me, and paying me well. The fact that we've become friends is just – well, something that makes working here all the pleasanter."

"Only 'friends'?" Ian asked. "Come off it, Pam – I'm sixteen now, remember. I know what goes on."

"Well, nothing has been 'going on' here, I can assure you!" said his sister fiercely.

"But he's not married, is he? You've never said owt about him having a missus."

"Andre's wife is dead, that's as much as I know."

"And is he missing her like you missed Jim at first?"

Pamela did not answer, but the question was making her think. For a short period Andre had, at times, seemed desolate. But for months he had appeared more adjusted, happy even . . . She would like to believe that he was. Would like to make up for what life had done to him.

"Hasn't he even kissed you?" Ian persisted.

Again, Pam did not reply.

By the time she had shown her brother around the parts of the house he would have access to, and allocated him a bedroom, it was eleven o'clock. Ian seemed genuinely surprised by the quality of the work she had carried out so far, and said he was eager to learn some of the craftsmanship involved.

"That's the spirit," Pam approved. "Learn as much as you can, and remember what I keep telling you. There's to be no messing about here. And no prying into cupboards and drawers. I know you. And I'm not going to have anything happening that'll make folk stop trusting me in their homes."

Although Ian groaned after receiving another lecture, Pam sensed that was only because he felt such a reaction was expected from him. Her intuition was insisting that she could be right to feel that showing some faith in the lad might bring out the best in him.

Taking Ian from room to room, she had gazed around as if it was all strange to her, and was thrilled by the nineteenth-century ambience she had recreated. Her colour schemes brightened the house, and made her wish it was her own. Pam smiled ruefully and silently reproached herself for becoming pretentious. Something closely akin to sinfulness in someone who'd grown up in a row of back-to-back houses!

During the first few days that Andre was away, Ian

148

worked well under her instruction. Pam had decided this was the best time for tackling the kitchen. They themselves could have makeshift meals whenever cooking something more complex proved difficult. And any mishaps in here, where the floor was tiled and the work surfaces were marble-topped, should be less catastrophic than in any other room.

Even while being certain that she must give her brother this chance, Pam had been visualising all the potential hazards. The days that had elapsed without major problems hadn't yet convinced her that she should dismiss all her fears. She was keeping a close watch on Ian, and explaining very fully each time that she set him a new task.

She had first shown him how to remove the old wallpaper which someone had varnished over in an effort to keep it clean. The varnish meant that stripping the walls became prolonged, but Ian kept at the job without complaint. And with surprising regard for the surface of the walls, as well as for everything within range of him.

"If you always work this carefully, you and me might get on," Pam had told him after a couple of days.

"You'll have to be setting folk on permanent to work for you, won't you?" Ian remarked. "Now that you're being so successful."

"Happen so, but I shall need people experienced in the trade, don't forget. Don't let this experiment start going to your head!"

Pam was removing stains from one of the marble worktops. Treating it with a swift wipe over of lemon juice, she immediately rinsed with water before the acid could penetrate the marble surface. As soon as it had dried she rubbed in a little oil and polished with soft cloth.

"That looks better, doesn't it?" she exclaimed.

"Can I have a go at that?" Ian asked eagerly.

149

"I'm not so sure, love. You've got to get the lemon juice off quickly before it can eat into the marble. What you can do, is start washing down those walls. We've got to have them perfectly clean. Andre wants them painting white."

"White? Won't that be boring?"

"Boring or not, it's what I've promised him."

Pamela discovered that Ian had difficulty accepting how readily she accommodated all Andre's ideas. Remembering the early discrepancies between Andre's notions and her eagerness to retain the correct period style, she found her own difficulty now was in recalling that such conflict had ever really existed.

Stonemoor House felt strange without its owner. All too frequently, Pam caught herself wondering where he was. And if he was safe. Andre's refusal to disclose his destination had left her feeling that he was in some kind of danger. She wished that she knew when she might expect him to return.

Andre had confided in no one else. For some months (ever since there had been more than one or two rooms restored and furnished) he had been employing a woman who came in twice-weekly to clean. Pamela had contained a rueful smile when first introduced to Mrs Singer, for the woman had been deaf from birth and was unable to speak. She might have been chosen for her inability to gossip about her employer.

With time Pam had grown accustomed to communicating with Mrs Singer, as Andre did, by writing everything down. And she had learned from her that he had left no note regarding either his whereabouts or the date of his return.

Pamela became glad of Ian's company as well as his willingness to learn. Living and working in Andre's home, she could not avoid reminders that he was absent. Not that she needed any such reminders; with Andre so far away she was discovering the strength of the role that he had assumed in her life. Pam had anticipated that she would miss his friendship, but she also yearned for him with a passion that had as yet been permitted no expression. Or none beyond that kiss. Busy though she was, she often recalled the feel of his mouth on hers and his arms about her, and was obliged to still a gasp of alarm when longing surged right through her.

Two weeks after Andre's departure she and Ian stood back to admire the kitchen as it gleamed white from every cupboard that they had painted, and from the walls. During one time when Pam was not at the house Andre had had a modern cooker installed which now looked more at home in its brighter surroundings.

Ian had asked what they were to tackle next and Pamela took him into the downstairs room where she had been working recently. The distemper there had turned quite patchy as it dried out and she intended applying another coat. But this was something that she could not entrust to a beginner like Ian. And she dared not leave him to work unsupervised elsewhere.

"I think you'd better watch me for a bit while I do this distempering. I'll try and explain how I'm applying it, so you won't get bored."

Her brother did grow bored, however, and decided instead to go up to his bedroom. "I think I'll write to them at home," he announced, astonishing Pam.

"That's a grand idea," she approved. "Mum will be delighted."

Pamela hadn't finished repainting one wall when she heard a slight thud from the room above her head.

Ian came clattering down the stairs and ran into the room. His face was ashen and his eyes staring in horror.

151

"Come quick, Pam. I've knocked the bottle of ink over."

"Where's it gone?" she demanded, aghast, and went hurrying after him up the staircase. "On the carpet?"

"No, but it's all over the floorboards and seems to be soaking in."

"Never mind, it was an accident," she said. Ian had been very careful until now, she mustn't let her own alarm emerge in too severe a reprimand.

As he had said, the ink was soaking into the floorboards and spreading. But he had had the sense to right the bottle, and had left it on the floor which at least confined the stain to one area.

"I'm going to try washing it off first," she told him. "I doubt if that'll get it all out, but we might get rid of the worst. I'm only thankful that ink didn't land on the carpet." If necessary, she could restain a section of the floor.

She warned Ian to stay where he was while she went in search of cloths for mopping up and a bucket. She had no suitable clean stuff left among the materials she had brought with her. After locating the bucket, Pam began searching for something old that she might utilise. She recalled seeing an ancient torn curtain in one of the hall cupboards and went to look for it.

The cupboard seemed to have acquired a mass of additional items since the only other occasion when she had seen inside it. Pam could only think that Mrs Singer had tidied things away here. The torn curtain was nowhere to be seen but, growing agitated while she thought of the ink that would be drying, she continued searching.

A stack of newspapers and magazines had been pushed back towards one far corner where it was so dark that Pam could not make out what stood beyond them. Leaning into the cupboard and reaching across the newspapers, she touched some kind of material that felt soft to her fingers. Maybe this was something which she could use.

The cloth seemed to be caught around an object wedged in behind the stack of papers. Pamela was obliged to tug quite vigorously in order to pull it towards her. And then as the material came away, the object concealed by its folds slid sideways with a thump.

What now? thought Pam, praying that she hadn't damaged anything. Hardly daring to look, she thrust herself across the newspapers, and stretched down into the gap between the heap and the wall.

The case she recovered was very old, a music case. She wasn't in the least surprised to find it contained a violin. So, she had been right about the music she had heard! But why was the instrument hidden at the back of a cupboard like this, and why had Andre denied its existence?

The wretched ink stain which had driven her to search could not be ignored; Pam was obliged to replace the violin in its case and the case in its hiding place. She pushed the material around and in front of it again. This wasn't the cloth she had seen before, anyway, and nor was it suitable for cleaning up.

Pam eventually trudged back upstairs, bearing a square of cloth torn off one of her dustsheets. She had been reluctant to resort to that – with every kind of material still rationed, the supply of old sheets and so on for use as dustcovers had diminished.

Removing the stain from the floorboards took a great deal of time and an equal quantity of patience. Washing did remove a little of the ink, but where each board joined the next it had penetrated more deeply. Pam eventually resorted to applications of permanganate of potash solution followed by hydrogen peroxide to take out the surplus colour from the potash.

"I'll give the area another coat of stain when this has

dried out, and no one'll be any the wiser," she told Ian who had watched, apologising profusely throughout the process.

Although she could not say so to him, Pamela was far more perturbed about the violin that she had found. Even to her inexperienced eye, it looked very old and she suspected it could be extremely valuable. Finding it concealed at the back of a cupboard as she had, she'd sensed immediately that Andre had some good reason for keeping its presence secret. Why otherwise would he only play when he believed her to be asleep, why did he never use the instrument at other times? He certainly had sounded a magnificent violinist, too good to keep his expertise a secret.

After Ian had gone to bed that night, Pam returned to the cupboard and carefully took out the case. Examining the violin for some mark or signature, she finally noticed when peering through an ornamented hole that the inside of the instrument's base bore an inscription.

Carrying it to the nearest electric lamp, she looked more closely, studying the writing which was so old that it was all but indecipherable. Could that really be Stradivari? An expert would recognise other qualities, the varnish used and, of course, the tone of the instrument. But she was no expert, she could only make assumptions about its origin – and worry!

Pamela certainly was worried now. The violin and its concealment seemed to shriek to her that they had no place in this home in the heart of Yorkshire. The longer she considered the few facts she knew, the more afraid she became that Andre hadn't obtained this violin honestly. Was it a trophy of his war? Was he capable of theft? She remembered the conjecture that he might be German. The German armies hadn't hesitated to loot treasures all over Europe.

\*　　\*　　\*

154

Still disturbed by the way that discovering the violin increased the enigma of Andre Malinowski, Pam was thankful that he appeared quite ordinary when he returned to Stonemoor House. He arrived one Thursday afternoon, looking cheerful, if tired by travelling. And he seemed delighted to meet young Ian.

"You must show me which part of this is your handiwork," Andre said to the lad as soon as he had approved the redecorated kitchen.

"This bit of wall here, and over there." Ian pointed them out while a flush of pleasure stained his cheeks.

"And are you going to follow the same career as your sister?"

Ian shrugged rather awkwardly and darted a glance in Pamela's direction. "I'd like to, but I don't know if our Pam thinks I'll ever be good enough."

"We shall have to see," she responded. "I think we'll have to try you out on places that are rather more modest than this. You first need to learn basic techniques really."

"But what am I going to do until you're working on a more modern house?" Ian asked.

Pamela had no immediate answer, a fact which was perturbing her when she drove Ian home that evening. The whole family gave them both an enthusiastic welcome, and listened while Ian chatted on about the work he had done, and Pam described the newly decorated kitchen at Stonemoor House.

"It does look smashing, Mum. But I'm not sure you'd be keen on all that white paint round here. I suppose it's not so bad out at Cragg Vale, there aren't so many mills pouring out soot."

"And are you taking Ian on permanent?" Mildred asked.

"Not straight away, I'm afraid," Pam admitted, and

cringed when she saw the frown that she'd anticipated on her mother's face. "I'm sorry but I just can't do it. He needs a good grounding in routine jobs, and he'll not get that so long as I'm working for Andre."

"But surely Ian needs to learn all sorts of stuff – the same as you had to?"

"Not straight away, though, Mother. That's all I'm saying. And Stonemoor House isn't the place for a beginner to be practising."

Mildred was still not satisfied. "You can't keep picking the lad up, then dropping him again. That's not good for him. Our Ian needs keeping busy."

"I could use somebody to do a bit of labouring," Charlie suddenly announced. "I've got a big job on, plumbing an old house that's being converted into flats."

Pam was thankful when both Ian himself and their mother seemed pleased by that idea. If she was to employ her brother in the future she needed time to work out what kind of training he must have. For the present, she wanted to be free to concentrate on Stonemoor House. And much as she had appreciated having Ian around while its owner was absent, she couldn't really picture the lad remaining there now that Andre had come home.

Andre had seemed disappointed when Pam had driven away with Ian as soon as they finished work for the day.

She returned to Stonemoor House, of course, on the Friday, but did not arrange to stay there over the weekend. While at home she had telephoned Dorothy to discuss some curtains that she had agreed to make for Andre. When Dorothy remarked that she had not seen Pam for ages, they arranged to go out somewhere on the Saturday evening.

It was early summer now and the two friends decided to drive as far as Hollingworth Lake. When Charles heard their plans he invited himself along and as they set out it began to feel like the old days, immediately postwar, when they had relished such outings.

They strolled beside the lake, enjoying the fresh air and the sense of escaping from the industrial landscape. Charlie was in high spirits, teasing both young women and reminding Pam how much better he was than after returning from the war, less than two years previously.

Leaving Hollingworth Lake, they took the road over towards Ripponden, and stopped for a drink and a snack at a moorland inn before continuing on to Halifax.

Once or twice while they were out Pamela wondered if she herself had changed. She noticed the light-hearted banter continuing between the other two, but felt somehow distanced from their frivolity. And when they were travelling close to Blackstone Edge where the road from Cragg Vale emerged to join with the highway they were on, she experienced an intense longing to be with Andre.

When Monday came and she arrived for work to be greeted with his hope that she intended to stay at Stonemoor, Pam smiled inwardly as she agreed. Perhaps his period away from the house had made him miss her. Certainly, *she* seemed to be discovering that no other company entirely compensated when she wasn't with Andre.

He appeared to be more interested than ever in all that she was doing, and in Pamela herself. During their meal on that first evening he began asking about her past. There seemed no limit to his questions about her schooling, about her life in the forces, and about her late husband.

Pamela was surprised that she was able to speak quite freely of Jim, expressing how shaken she had been by his death, without feeling that she might give way to tears. For virtually two years now she had lived as a single woman and, especially through the work she had taken on, the experience had imbued its own strength.

"I shouldn't like to live on my own, or not for ever," she told him. "But I'm not frightened of my own company any longer. And I can believe that there might be better days ahead now."

"And for me also," said Andre, his grey gaze locking with hers across the table. "Your restoration of my home has somehow served to represent the reconstruction of my life."

"I'm glad, Andre."

Warmed by his words, and reassured simply by having him near once more, Pam began to hope that she and Andre might one day be more than friends. If only he were more forthcoming about his own history, she thought, I really would believe I was beginning to mean a lot to him.

During the second night of this stay at Stonemoor House, Pamela awakened suddenly, conscious that some sound had jolted her out of sleep. Had that been the big outer door closing? She lay for a few minutes, listening intently for a noise but at first hearing nothing. And then all at once there were hushed voices below in the hallway, a stair creaked and then another. A short while later she noticed voices again, together with somone moving about in the attics above her head.

What a strange time for somebody to arrive! Pam thought, but there could be a quite ordinary explanation, she supposed, especially if that person had travelled a long distance.

There was no sign the following morning of anyone except Mrs Singer and Andre himself who was glancing at the Daily Telegraph while he waited for Pam to join him for breakfast.

158

"You have a visitor, I believe," Pamela began when she could no longer contain her curiosity after they finished eating.

"A visitor? No – you are mistaken," Andre contradicted her smoothly. "Why should anyone come here?"

Unable to doubt the evidence of all that she had heard, Pamela was baffled. Short of accusing Andre of lying, she could do nothing. But her agitation grew with each hour that she remained in his home while he maintained his pretence that nobody had joined them there.

Totally perturbed by this development and unable to question him further, Pamela continued to work, and to work quite feverishly because he had destroyed the ease she felt here. How could she have imagined only less than a week ago that she and Andre might have some kind of a future together? She had been misled by her emotions again, just as she had over Roger. She could never live with somebody who was less than straightforward about so many areas of his life. I must complete my work on this house quickly, she thought, I could never bring myself to desert Stonemoor until the whole place is restored.

Pamela couldn't for the life of her think why Andre should wish her to stay overnight in his home while he seemed intent on concealing as much as possible from her. *She* certainly couldn't endure there being no relief from the tension generated by the enigma surrounding him, and by the attraction which continued to shake her. Without explaining her reasons, Pam drove back to Halifax that evening. If Andre remarked on her decision to travel back and forth, she would give the excuse that she needed to spend time looking for future work.

That couldn't have been more true – it was ages since she had taken on even a small job away from Stonemoor House, and her work there would not last for ever. She had one more room to finish and then the task of renovating the woodwork of the hall and staircase. After that was done she would have no immediate prospect of further work.

"You could apply to decorate these flats where I'm putting in fresh plumbing," her cousin Charles suggested as soon as Pamela mentioned the situation to him.

She felt relief flooding through her. "Thanks, Charlie – that's a splendid idea. How soon will they want that doing?"

"Well, the plasterers are still in there. They've had everywhere rewired. In fact, part of the house only had gas lighting."

Charlie gave her the developer's name and Pamela telephoned his home number that evening.

The man sounded keen to employ her, but added that he was going to invite tenders for the work.

"That's all right, I understand," said Pam and arranged to visit the site in order to measure up and begin calculating estimates.

"It'd be a good job to get, would yon," Charlie observed. "Being divided into flats like that, there'll be plenty of folk getting to know what you're capable of. Better by far than working for only one chap like you've been doing for long enough."

That made sense, Pamela knew, but coming away from Andre had affected her so that, despite her misgivings, she couldn't bear to think about the time when she would no longer be going to Stonemoor.

Pam was reflecting how attached she had become to Andre as well as to his home while she drove out there the following morning. Even though he had never repeated the kiss that had transformed the day when he had left her in his home, the passion with which she longed for him remained alarmingly potent. She also believed that she still read affection in his lovely grey eyes.

160

She was discovering that she was unable to disregard all this even when he made her unhappy with his secrecy. I only want him to trust me, she thought, and realised that events in his past were responsible for his current behaviour. Perhaps, given time and her understanding, Andre would learn that he could depend on her.

Parking the van in front of Stonemoor House as usual, Pam glanced upwards and noticed that paint had begun peeling from the outside of one of the window frames. Although they had not intended that she should redecorate the exterior of the building, she was concerned to discover that it needed attention.

Instead of going up to the door, Pam walked around the outside of the house, skirting the shrubs that in some places grew beside the walls. Most of the windows of the ground floor appeared to have sound paintwork, it was only when Pam was returning along the third side that she noticed another spot where the paint had begun flaking. Here, there were no shrubs and she was able to walk on the grass growing close against the foot of the wall.

Pamela was testing the edge of the flaking paint with a fingernail when a sudden movement within the room made her look inside. She saw Andre then and the girl with long fair hair whose dash across the room had attracted her attention. Andre had caught the girl to him in a fierce embrace and now was covering her head with kisses while he pressed her close against him. The moment seemed so tender and intimate that Pamela immediately drew back, aware that she was intruding. Turning, she started hurrying back towards the front entrance. She felt appalled by the scene she had inadvertently witnessed, and not only because it proved that she herself could never be the person whom Andre loved. *That girl had only looked about fifteen. And Andre was years older than Pamela herself was!*

161

No wonder he had so readily rationalised the relationship between Roger and Leslie Rivers! Andre himself was capable of something that seemed only slightly less abnormal. Sickened by picturing Andre making love to that child, Pam ran to sit in her van. She struggled to steady her emotions and realised how utterly shattered they were.

Eventually Pam calmed sufficiently to leave the vehicle and retrace her steps to the house. She must ensure that her expression remained impassive while Andre introduced her to the girl. Whatever else, she must give no sign of surprise even, much less censure.

There was no evidence of anyone but Andre anywhere in sight. Even though Pam was relieved to be avoiding an embarrassing introduction, she found her agitation increasing. Andre evidently had sent the girl away to hide – presumably in the attics. And following what she had seen, Pam could understand why he had needed to conceal the girl's presence from everyone who would condemn such a strange liaison!

Before the end of the summer Pamela heard that she had won the contract to decorate the flats. She was extremely thankful. Although she still had work to complete at Stonemoor House, she was glad to alternate that with jobs that took her away from Andre's home. He appeared happy to accept that she needed to look elsewhere for work that would secure her future. Indeed, Andre seemed very happy now – a fact which Pam found less than pleasing whenever she contemplated the existence of the girl who was living secretly with him.

For herself, Pam could only feel saddened that, at this stage in her work when she should have been thrilled by how splendid the house was looking, everything about her time there was spoiled.

162

She was now keeping away from Stonemoor as much as she could, and sensing whenever she worked there that Andre seemed somehow different. No doubt because she was keeping him from his child-lover.

Dorothy and Charlie both appeared glad that Pam now had most weekends free for going out, although Pam was beginning to notice that her friend seemed to be quite keen on Charlie. After intercepting several longing looks sent by Dorothy in his direction, Pam eventually asked Dot if she wished to be left alone with Charles more often.

Her friend's laugh was rueful. "Nay, love, things are all right as they are, so far. I don't think that cousin of yours sees me as more than another pal! There's been times when you've not been around and we've gone somewhere on our own, but it's never led to anything further."

"But you wish that it would?"

"Aye, I suppose I do, Pam. It's not a grand passion or owt. But he's a decent bloke is Charlie, and since he got his business going again he's lost all that dejection that used to get on my nerves."

"That was only the result of being a POW, I think."

"Yes, I dare say you're right. But now he's over that, he's so comfortable at your Mum's that I'm afraid he's never going to shift himself."

"I wish there was something I could do," said Pam. Dorothy was a lovely woman who would make any man a good wife.

"Happen it's too late," Dorothy said. "I often think I must be getting too old for marriage. I'm not the only one, am I? There's many a hundred left on the shelf because the men they might have wed got killed during the war."

There must be some way I could help, thought Pamela. If Dorothy is keen on our Charles it's time somebody brought him to his senses and made him realise what a grand life he and Dot might have.

The prospect of bringing the pair together gave Pam something different to consider, and occupied her mind while she was so perturbed about the situation at Stonemoor House.

# Chapter Nine

Since she no longer slept the night at Stonemoor House Pamela had no means of knowing whether the girl she had seen in Andre's arms was staying there. And she did not wish to know. She would not have believed how shattered she would remain as a result of witnessing that embrace. Until that day she had supposed that she had recently become toughened by life, less vulnerable to its surprises. Discovering how entirely Andre could damage her composure was a shock.

Despite all her misgivings about Andre, Pam was enjoying the final stages of her task there. Removing the old paint from the panelling had been laborious. It was inadvisable to either burn it off from the original wood or to use sandpaper, but she had tried sharkskin, a traditional means of obtaining a smooth surface on wood.

She was now relishing the actual restoration. Using her own blend of beeswax and turpentine she was gradually endowing the wood with a patina that would last. Slow though the process it was, each day increased the beauty of a small section of those panelled walls. And she could not deny her delight when Andre complimented her on the successful results.

Although immensely satisfied by all the work which she had completed on Stonemoor House, Pam often felt torn when she reflected on how soon she would have no further reason for coming here. The house had become a part of her life. All the additional skills which she had needed to learn had given purpose, ensuring her survival after Jim's death had wrecked everything. No matter what her future brought, the time which she had spent here would always be linked with her recovery from that trauma.

All but one wall had been renovated by the day when Pamela used up her turpentine and went out in the van to buy more. She had expected to have to drive some distance to obtain another supply, but on impulse stopped at a tiny shop just short of Mytholmroyd. She was pleasantly surprised that the owner could supply what she needed.

Arriving back at Stonemoor, she hurried straight into the hall, and there they were, Andre and the girl. Although not embracing quite so closely as Pamela recalled from the other occasion, he had his arm about the girl, and was smiling as he kissed her.

"Don't mind me," Pam said quite briskly, as they both started and turned towards her. "I'll keep out of your way."

"There is no need," said Andre. "And now that you have seen Tania, I am happy to introduce you. The pretence has continued for long enough. And if anyone had followed her to my home, that would have emerged long ago. There should now be no need for concealment."

Feeling bewildered, Pamela could only try to gather her wits and appear gracious, and she walked towards them with her right hand extended while Andre began introducing the girl.

"This is Tania," he was saying, "my daughter whom we finally succeeded in bringing to England."

*His daughter!* Pamela hoped she was containing her gasp, but she felt so shaken that she was aware of very little beyond Andre's voice announcing her own name and the cool grasp of the girl's hand on hers.

"As you can imagine," Andre continued, "having my

166

daughter join me here makes me very happy. Since her mother's sad death we each were alone for too long."

For a short while the three of them talked; Pam mustered enough composure to say that she hoped that Tania would be happy in Yorkshire. And the girl began asking questions about the work which Pamela was doing for her father, and pleased her by admiring her flair for decor.

Meeting Tania affected Pamela profoundly. The weight of believing that Andre might have taken such a young lover fell away and, almost overnight, Pam felt all the old attraction that she had been repressing. Instead of contemplating keeping away from the house, she again wondered how she would ever survive away from there.

They had already decided that any exterior paintwork in need of attention should merely receive another coat – a conclusion that had seemed welcome while Pam had so many misgivings about the girl. She could hardly make excuses now for extending her work at Stonemoor, but the prospect of never seeing Andre again began to eat into her.

At home in her mother's house, her brother Tom remarked on how subdued Pamela had become, and assumed that she was worried about future means of ensuring that more work began coming her way.

Pam was pleased by the lad's concern. Tom was always so quiet that she often wondered what he was thinking. Learning that he cared enough to remark on how she appeared was heartening.

Charlie grinned across at them both as soon as he heard what Tom was supposing. "Then she needn't be worrying at all," he exclaimed. "Pam knows there's the work on them flats coming up. And I'll certainly put in a good word whenever I hear of owt else that wants decorating."

"There's another house I heard of only t'other day,"

Ian announced. "Not as big as Stonemoor, but it could be just as old. Out at Northowram, it is. The chap who's having one of the flats where Charlie and me are working has a brother who's bought the place. Newark House, it's called."

Pam smiled at Ian. "Thanks for thinking of me. I'll have to consider setting you on to advertise my work, shan't I?"

"No. Just set me on again to work with you, that's all."

"I think Ian prefers the jobs you give him to labouring for me," Charlie exclaimed.

"Only because I never got round to landing him with any real work!"

Pamela was wondering already if she would feel obliged to employ Ian once she moved on from Stonemoor House. Certainly, she would need to think of employing someone before very long, but she'd always visualised the person being an experienced decorator, hadn't she?

"I can't be doing with plumbing for so much longer," Ian said.

"Oh, and what's wrong with it?" his mother enquired sharply. She had enjoyed the freedom from anxiety while the lad was employed.

"It's all that dust, isn't it? It'll ruin my wind. I can't do with that now I'm regularly playing the sax."

"You're performing with the brass band now, are you, Ian love?" Pam said, and wondered why she hadn't been told. "I hadn't realised your playing had come on that far. Jim would have been suited."

"Not the brass band," Ian contradicted. "It's a dance band we're forming, to play Glenn Miller's music and so on. We're practising already."

Pamela was pleased when Andre asked her to accompany him on another visit to the Norton sisters. He wanted to invite them to inspect Stonemoor House as soon as Pam's work there was completed.

"I am so thrilled with the place that I must ensure that they see how delightful it looks."

Driving out to Stonemoor wearing a mid-blue New Look costume instead of all the old clothes normally worn there, Pam was experiencing a worrying mixture of emotions. Happy though she was to be going somewhere with Andre, the strangeness of this smart copy of a Dior outfit with its long skirt and sloping shoulderline seemed to symbolise the changes overshadowing her life. She had calculated that in just one more week she would have finished all that she had set out to do in Andre's home. His evident satisfaction was in no way going to compensate for the prospect of losing regular contact with him.

Aware that before long she would be surrendering this key which had made her feel that she belonged at Stonemoor House, Pamela unlocked the door and went through into the hall. From the room off to her right she could hear Andre's raised voice and Tania's, which sounded as if it were complaining.

Sure enough, when the girl spoke again she appeared as agitated as her father had seemed. "You make me believe you are ashamed of me, do you realise that? You bring me all this way, yet you will not permit me to leave the house."

"For your own wellbeing, Tania, as I have told to you. One day you shall go wherever you wish, but not yet, not yet. We must not risk your being discovered."

Pamela noticed their accents had grown stronger with emotion. Hating the sensation that she was eavesdropping upon, she opened the door and took a few paces, saying "Good morning" as she approached them.

Father and daughter faced her simultaneously, but their reactions couldn't have differed more sharply. Andre's grey eyes were beaming approval as, with hands out-stretched, he walked towards her. Tania, meanwhile, gave a toss of that golden mane of hair and treated Pamela to a prolonged hostile stare.

"You look quite splendid, Pamela," Andre exclaimed, catching both of her hands in his, then raising her left one to his lips. "I have never seen you as glamorous as this."

While Pam was thanking him, Tania came stomping towards them and made as though to push past. At Pamela's side, however, she seemed to think of something and glared at her father.

"I know now why I am not wanted today. You do not wish me to be there, spoiling things, while you are taking *her* out."

Andre released one of Pamela's hands and surprised her by taking the girl quite roughly by her upper arm. "That is not the case, and well you know. I have explained until I am wearied by explaining. You are not to leave this house before I can be certain of your safety. You are all I have left, Tania, too precious to risk losing."

"But they wouldn't find us here, you told me that when Uncle Ilyia brought me to you. You must be quite paranoid to believe anybody from Russia would take the trouble to trace us to this godforsaken place!"

The word Russia sent Pamela's mind racing. Was that where Andre and his daughter originated? But the Russians had been our allies, surely, she thought; why should these friends of hers be in any danger here in England?

"Yes, we are Russian – *White* Russian," Andre told her while his daughter's feet were heard clattering up the wooden staircase. "I think it is time that I should tell you a little about me."

Going with him out to her van, Pamela felt relief pouring through her. Andre was about to tell her the truth at

170

last. And so many of her doubts might be laid to rest. She hadn't realised it until today, but she had never entirely dismissed the fear that he could be German. Starting the engine and heading towards the main road, Pamela was smiling. From the sound of it, Andre was simply a man who had escaped to freedom in her country and eventually had succeeded in bringing his daughter here as well.

Settling into the seat at her side, he began speaking at once. "I shall tell you all now that I have begun. But I think perhaps I should ask you to drive a little way first and then stop the van. I would hate for my story to distract you from driving."

She drew off the road high on the moor where the green hills stretched, line upon awesome line, into the mauve-tinged distance.

"I have thought your country quite small," Andre began with a smile. "Compared with the vastness of my own, England is tiny. Today, however, your landscape appears to reach towards infinite space. Perhaps it also contains the infinite freedom that I never remember in my homeland."

Andre paused briefly then took hold of her hand. Pamela felt his fingers begin stirring over hers while deep within her longing surged, as powerful as the wind which, even on a summer's day like this, careened across the moors.

"My family home was in Minsk, and in 1918 my father joined a White volunteer army which was led by Czarist generals. They allied themselves to the Cossacks. My father died in the conflict with the Red Army, and my mother decided then that in order to survive she must feign allegiance with Trotsky and Lenin. I was ten years old, my sister four or five."

Andre stopped speaking, his fingers working furiously over hers as he struggled to subdue emotion.

171

"Years afterwards I found it hard to forgive my mother the lip-service that she paid for the rest of her days to the Communist regime. But now I believe I understand. I almost would do likewise if that were to keep Tania alive. But I digress – we lived out this lie and, because my mother was a talented singer, we lived quite well. Even the revolutionaries could never bring themselves to destroy all forms of art. My mother began again to perform as soon as Russia had settled to a kind of peace."

Andre went on to explain that even as a ten year old he had begun to feel an affinity with the British. That was after their force landed at Archangel in 1918 to aid the White Russians. It was too late by then to help the Romanovs who had been executed, but hope was established within the young boy – hope that survived and led eventually to his escape following the end of the second world conflict.

"I would not pretend that everything in my own country was bad," he admitted. "My family ensured for me a musical training. Fortunately, I inherited Mother's ear if not her voice. I played professionally in many of our great concert halls."

"Played the violin?" asked Pamela softly.

"The violin, yes. Perhaps I was foolish to conceal my playing from you. But I hope you may understand. I was quite recently come to your country when first we met, and still so afraid that I was being watched. I was too well known, you see, for defecting easily without detection. And after my wife was shot while attempting to get away with me, I became too angry to remain entirely discreet."

"How did you escape?" Pamela asked. From what she had heard, the Communists were reluctant to permit anyone to leave the USSR.

Andre sighed. "I had friends, sympathisers who assisted.

Our original plan was aborted as soon as my wife was killed. That is the reason why Tania has joined me only now. We had left her behind with old friends from my university days, until I was able to contact them and arrange for Ilyia to bring her to me."

"You went back to Russia then, just the other week? Wasn't that terribly dangerous?"

Smilingly slightly, Andre shook his head. "Not quite all the way. To go any further would have meant taking too great a risk. But I met up with Tania again in the middle of the Baltic, aboard a tiny boat. I had used a similar route when I made my escape."

"But how? – I don't really understand."

"It was very complex. When Anichka was shot my sleeve was grazed by a bullet but that was all. Because I dropped to the ground beside Anichka they were convinced I was dead. The men drove off, and I tried to carry her, but she was dying and knew it. She begged me to leave her – to stay alive for Tania. Leaving her was the hardest thing I have done. I turned back, but Anichka pleaded with me again, before lapsing into coma. We were in the Ukraine, heading towards the Black Sea. I ran and ran through the forest that night, then set out in the opposite direction to foil the guards. I travelled overland, always by night, avoiding all border areas. The journey took weeks, but I no longer cared for haste – I had left Tania where she was safe, all I needed was to reach the West eventually."

"And how did you complete the rest of the journey to England?"

"By boat as far as the Swedish coast. Afterwards by stowing away aboard a merchant ship that was crossing the North Sea."

"The whole journey must have been a dreadful ordeal!"

"I only knew that it was something that I must do, and I

was concerned for my own safety only in order to provide a home for Tania."

Learning his story was unleashing all kinds of emotion in her. Pam felt quite in awe of his determination and courage, but most of all deeply thankful that he had survived.

"I'm very glad that you finally ended up in the West Riding," she told him, and felt his fingers tighten over her own.

"And so am I," said Andre, turning to smile into her eyes. "You have made such a difference to my life. I hope that we always shall remain friends."

"And so do I," said Pam fervently. If she had doubted in the past that she needed more than friendship from Andre, today's revelations had confirmed that; but being friends mattered a great deal to her, and did at least maintain some contact between them. Knowing how much Andre had endured, she understood now that she might wait for ever if she expected commitment from him. But she herself still had a lot to achieve, she was prepared to invest time in this relationship.

Sitting with the Misses Norton, and watching Andre as he appeared totally relaxed while he talked about Stonemoor House, Pamela found remembering the ordeal of his escape incredibly difficult. He might have been any cultured person who had suffered nothing worse than the rationing and the air raids in her own country.

She mentioned this to him during the journey back to Stonemoor.

Andre smiled. "But relaxing is so simple over here. You should not forget that in Russia there had been no kind of freedom since I was a small boy. When one exists in any tyrannical state there is a perpetual condition of tension. After removing yourself from that, the difference is blessedly restorative. Of course, the

174

process is helped by repeated contact with someone like yourself."

He kissed her cheek and Pam gave him a sideways look.

"Why now, Andre – when I have to concentrate on driving?"

He laughed. "As a promise perhaps, for when we find a more suitable occasion."

Pamela could hardly wait for them to arrive back at Stonemoor. She felt sure now that Andre was just as attracted as she was to him, and that he no longer intended to conceal his feelings. She was disappointed to find Tania watching from one of the front windows and then rushing to greet her father as soon as he came through the door.

The girl's greeting was in Russian, and she did not comply when Andre told her to speak in English. Pamela could not mistake Tania's determination to obstruct any attachment between Andre and herself. But she was prepared to take into account the separation father and daughter had endured, and to let them have the time alone together which they evidently needed.

Leaving them behind, Pamela recognised once more how deeply she had been affected by Andre's story. She felt quite overwhelmed by the warmth of having him confide in her. Considered alongside all the uncertainties that he had faced, it seemed to indicate that the trust growing between them was infinite. Pamela remembered an earlier sentiment that she had experienced; and now she knew for sure that she longed with all her heart to make up for everything that life had done to him.

When hardly any renovation remained to be completed at Stonemoor, Pamela had tried in earnest to secure future work. After seeing the extent of the task of redecorating those flats, she had reached a big decision and employed

175

an experienced man to assist her. Ted Burrows was apprentice-trained, but after leaving the army in 1946 had failed to find regular work within the trade. Supplies of decorating materials were still difficult to purchase. Pamela was glad that the stocks which she had taken over had not only kept her business running, but were now about to help provide work for someone else. She was also thankful that Ted was willing to turn his hand to anything and seemed to think that working on the flats was marvellous.

She herself had discovered that Stonemoor House had spoilt her for tackling more mundane jobs. The careful thought that went into renovating somewhere old suited her, and she longed to establish herself sufficiently well to be able to specialise.

Pamela had been delighted when the house mentioned by Ian turned out to be just what she needed.

The purchasers were middle-aged and appeared to have plenty of money to spend on redecoration. Newark House itself was about half the size of Stonemoor and had been built in 1875. None of the original decor remained, but the new owners seemed as eager as Pamela herself to recreate the ambience of its period.

I am going to enjoy this, she thought, on the day that they accepted her provisional estimates. With a whole new period to research, and the challenge of sorting out suitable materials, she would feel her skills were being extended.

The first thing that she noticed, that the place possessed no wooden panelling, came as a relief. Although she had no wish to rush this job, she needed to complete it more quickly than the work at Stonemoor House. Well rewarded though she had been there, Andre's reluctance to advertise his presence had prevented her from publicising all that she had achieved in his home. She must ensure that all future jobs brought her name before potential clients.

Pam was feeling quite insecure when she finished the last few tasks at Stonemoor House, and not only because the work which had sustained her for many a month had ended. Despite all that he had said regarding their friendship, Andre made no arrangements for seeing her again, and when Pam said goodbye she felt her heart plummet.

She suspected that she knew his reasons for simply letting her go. During those final few visits to the house, she had been dogged by Tania's efforts to make her feel uncomfortable. Realising at an early stage that the girl resented her, Pam had resolved to put up with that, and to do nothing to cause trouble between Tania and her father.

In an attempt to crowd out the desperation with which she was missing Andre, Pam began cramming her leisure hours. She arranged visits to the cinema and to the local repertory theatre with Dorothy and with Charlie, and insisted that they must make the most of the last few weeks of summer by getting out into the Dales or taking a run to the coast.

Dorothy was still very busy: her curtain making wasn't sufficiently well established to support her, consequently she still served in the baker's shop. On occasions this prevented her from joining her friends, and Pam hadn't the heart to refuse Charlie's suggestion that they should go somewhere on their own.

Her cousin was amusing company now that he had fully recovered from his wartime imprisonment, and was free with his dry sense of humour. Pam found she was laughing a lot during the day that he drove her to Scarborough. The weather was disappointing with a sea fret refusing to budge from the shore, obscuring the castle from view and dampening her hair until it clung about her head. Somehow, the awful climate only heightened their sense of the ridiculous, and their homeward journey was accompanied by a light-hearted rendering of several of the old wartime songs.

When Charlie drew up and parked a few streets from home Pamela frowned suddenly.

"You're surely not thinking of getting fish and chips, I hope!" she exclaimed. They had eaten a substantial lunch and later had taken tea in one of the big hotels.

Charles shook his head. "I just didn't want to go in yet awhile."

Pam felt embarrassment creeping right through her as soon as he rather awkwardly drew her to him.

"Oh, Charles," she began, and then hesitated, wondering how on earth to protest without sounding unkind.

Charlie smiled. "I know," he murmured against her ear. Evidently he had misinterpreted her exclamation. "It's been a long time, Pam. Too long, and I've been a fool to make you wait."

He kissed her then, full on her mouth with lips that began to stir. Appalled, Pamela tried to push him away, but she didn't want to be too brusque, and Charles seemed oblivious to anything but his own desire.

The kiss went on and on, and Pam realised that she would have to be quite firm and put him right about his assumption that she reciprocated his feelings. When she finally broke away, she was breathing deeply with embarrassment and could feel heightened colour stealing from her neck up over her entire head.

Still smiling, Charlie nodded. "I can see you're just as inflamed as I am myself. It's a bit of a shaker really, isn't it, discovering what's been simmering away below t'surface all this time."

"But it hasn't, Charles, don't you see . . .?"

178

His smile only deepened, and he tried to pull her close again. "Okay – so it's come as a bit of a shock to you. But you needn't look so perturbed, Pam love. We've no reason on earth to fight this. Or not for more than a week or two. We'll get married. There's nowt to stop us. And soon, very soon."

"No, Charles. Oh, God – this is awful. I'm not the one for you. It's not me you should be asking."

"But we've always been right good pals, ever since we were little. And you've been champion to me – putting work my way with this new contract you're getting." He had been pleased with her suggestion that he try for the plumbing work in Newark House.

"That's only because you're family, and a damned good plumber."

"You wanted us to work together, you don't know how much that means to me. And that's how it's going to be from now on – only we'll be working for our future. A future in our own home."

"No, Charles. I'm sorry but I just don't think of you in that way, not at all. You're my cousin and I've always been fond of you. I'm glad we still get on but – well, that is all."

His expression darkened and he abruptly pulled away from her. "I'm not good enough for you! That's the top and bottom of it, isn't it? You've got bigger ideas. I should have seen it, I suppose, with all your working in grand houses, and that. Well, I didn't see. I just thought – all these months, I thought we were becoming well suited."

Charles fumbled as he switched on the ignition, and they roared off and around the corner. Neither of them spoke a word as they got out of his van and went into the house.

Mildred was sitting beside the hearth, knitting away at a cardigan for her sister. There was no sign of either Ian or Tom, and Pam was thankful. The fewer people

179

who witnessed their entrance, the better she would be pleased.

"Hello, you two," Mildred greeted them. "Have you had a nice time? What was the weather like?"

Charlie did not give her so much as a glance never mind a response. Pamela could have thrashed him when he strode across the room and began stomping up the stairs. She had intended behaving as though nothing untoward had happened. He had not only generated an atmosphere but left her to explain.

"What's up with him?" her mother demanded. "Has summat upset him?"

Pam made a rapid decision that, since the truth had to be told, she might as well tell it tonight.

"*I* have actually," she admitted. "But it wasn't intentional. I couldn't be expected to know what was going on in that mind of his, not when he's never so much as breathed a word until today. If he'd even given a bit of a hint, I'd have found some way to let him down lightly."

"What about? What have you been saying?"

"That I won't marry him."

"Won't? I know you're cousins, but that doesn't necessarily mean you shouldn't get wed, love."

"Happen not. But not being in love with him seems a good enough reason to me."

Mildred was looking concerned. "Eh, Pam love, you shouldn't be hasty like this. Charlie's a decent chap."

"I know, I know."

"You can't expect to feel like you did before about Jim. He were t'first man you fell for. It'll be different this time."

"I dare say it will. And it *won't* be with Charlie. I've told you – I don't love him, not in that way."

"Well – if you want my opinion, I think you're proper silly. You could look a lot further and fare a lot worse."

180

"I won't dispute that. But I'm not just looking for somebody I can rub along with. If I marry again, it'll be because the life we'd have together would be pretty wonderful."

Her mother sniffed. "Aye – well, I've heard sentiments like that afore! And I can't say as I've noticed them marriages turning out any different for it."

Pamela had nothing further to say, but her silence seemed only to provoke Mildred. "I'm surprised at you, you know. I thought you were old enough by now to have more sense."

Being reproached for not accepting Charlie's proposal made Pam feel grossly misunderstood. How could her mother even think that she should marry Charles when she didn't love him? I shall be unpopular now, she thought, I shall have to keep out of the way until this is forgotten.

Pamela was greatly relieved that Charles had finished his job at the flats so that whenever she went there to discuss the work with Ted Burrows there was no risk of bumping into her cousin. At home, of course, there was no way of avoiding him, and she felt terrible about the strained atmosphere there. Even reminding herself that she had done nothing to invite Charlie's proposal made her feel little better.

Pam was exceedingly thankful that she had this new job ahead of her which would need some researching as well as the actual hard work. As soon as the library reopened after that dreadful weekend she began reading up on Victorian design.

She had been planning for some time the order in which she should tackle the rooms when an awful thought struck her. Some time ago she had suggested Charlie for the task of renewing all necessary plumbing. They would be working in the same house, and she could not believe that would be at all comfortable for either of them.

*　　*　　*

Living under the same roof as they were, Pam was frequently able to learn when Charles intended working on Newark House. Occasionally, she arranged to go there on days when he was called to attend jobs elsewhere. This system couldn't last, but it did ease the situation a little. Pam knew that they couldn't continue forever virtually ignoring each other, as they now were, but each time that she had tried to put things right between them Charles had snubbed her.

Her interest in the job compensated to some degree for the awkwardness. She was putting her whole heart into bestowing a suitable air to the high Victorian rooms.

One concession had been agreed – that the window frames and doors should be painted white rather than the dark brown favoured during the period. In the drawing room this lighter paintwork was needed to offset the wall-paper which, although closely resembling mid-Victorian styling, tended to be quite dark. It was heavily patterned flock, predominantly gold and red with touches of green, one of the many that she had acquired in that first purchase of stock from the old widow.

Pam was secretly amused to recall that she had wondered at the time if anyone would contemplate having something so old-fashioned. And now she was just very glad that the people at Newark House thought that it looked ideal. I wonder if I'm old-fashioned really as well, she wondered. I do so love restoring places with a bit of history to them. And I seem to have romantic notions concerning marriage!

Her mother had tackled her again about turning down Charlie's offer. The renewed criticism hadn't exactly been unexpected, but it had distressed Pamela.

"I'm surprised at you, you know," had been Mildred's all-too-familiar opening words. "From what our Charles

182

says, you've been leading him on ever since he got home from the Far East. He thinks you have a cheek chucking him over when you've been behaving like that. And I can't help but say I agree wi' him!"

"But I've never led him on. It was only because I felt sorry for him that Dorothy and I got Charlie to start going out with us. As a matter of fact, I had begun to think that he and Dot would make a go of it . . ."

Even while she was saying the words Pam realised that she had been too perturbed by Charlie's proposal to wonder how Dorothy might react. But now her mother was preventing her from considering that for she emphatically continued her criticism.

"You know, Pamela, I'm disappointed in you. It looks as if you think it's clever to be in a position to turn Charlie down. Because he's only a workman. You've found a way of making a good living, but you're letting that go to your head. You're meeting rich folk wi' plenty of brass, and you look down on a man who does a decent day's work. I only hope that them as you think of as quality come up to all your grand expectations, lady!"

Every word stung, and all the more sharply because Pamela felt that they were unjustified. Her mother was calling her a snob – something which she most certainly was not.

Pam had never felt more hurt. She still could hardly believe that Mildred, of all people, wanted her to marry a man whom she could not love. She wished with all her heart that she could explain how she really felt, that she could bring Andre here and let everyone see what manner of man he was. And how deep her love for him was becoming. At present, though, that prospect seemed as remote as flying to the moon! She had heard nothing

183

from Andre since she had finished the work at Stonemoor House. And if Tania's attitude towards her was any guide, it would be many a long month before she was granted the opportunity to see him.

# Chapter Ten

Although the work she had begun on Newark House was interesting it didn't quite succeed in making Pamela feel better about her life. She had been persuaded to take Ian on permanently as her apprentice. His presence beside her while she worked was preventing her from rationalising all the distress that she had felt since Charlie's proposal. Had she been working alone, she might have used the time for analysing where she had gone wrong. As things were, she was beginning to believe that she was singularly lacking in perception. How otherwise could she have failed to see how seriously her cousin was misinterpreting her behaviour towards him?

As soon as Ian started working with her it seemed as if getting away from home had given him the freedom to voice his opinion. He quickly made it plain that Charles had got in with his version of events, and Ian for one thought Pamela was a prize idiot.

"You could have built up a smashing business between you – with him doing the plumbing and you decorating places afterwards."

"But marriage isn't only about working together, is it, Ian?"

"No, but – he's not old or anything, is he? And he's not bad looking. I'd like Charlie for my brother-in-law, he's always been good to me."

"Soft, you mean," said Pam, smiling at her brother.

185

"I'll bet he's never crossed you since the day he was demobbed."

"So – somebody's got to be on my side."

"My, aren't you hard done by! I had no idea how you've suffered . . ."

"And he's been kind to our Mum, helping in the house an' that. Not so much since he's been working a lot again, but he helped before."

"So he did. And I daresay he'll make somebody a really good husband. It's just that that person isn't me – all right?"

It was not all right with Ian. He'd calculated that if she and Charles had married and combined their businesses they would always have had plenty of work for a certain young brother.

Pam shook her head at him and laughed. "And you'd have been able to pick and choose which jobs you'd condescend to do, I suppose?"

"Naturally. Seriously, though, Pam – can't you tell him yes now? He'd never move away from home then and . . ."

"Hang on a minute," Pamela interrupted. "Where do you think I'll be living if I ever do marry again? I shan't be stopping with you lot! Don't you think I deserve a bit of peace after all these years?"

"You lived there before, with Jim."

"Aye, so I did. But only because we were saving up."

She insisted then that Ian must cut the chatter and concentrate on work. But she knew in her heart that this was partly to avoid his reminders of an embarrassing and uncomfortable situation. She wished that she could somehow eradicate that wretched proposal and all its repercussions.

On the other hand, Pam realised suddenly, she could reconsider her refusal: marrying Charles would please a lot of people, and it could do one thing for her. Niggling away at the back of her consciousness since the day that Jim died had been the unacceptable prospect of never having children of her own. Charlie was good with kids, she pictured him having patience with them as he had with her brothers.

Persisting with instructions regarding the tasks in hand, Pam kept Ian off the subject of her private life and, to some extent prevented herself from dwelling on it. Her brother had matured quite a lot since he had spent that short time with her working at Stonemoor House. She supposed she could thank Charles for that, and wished that the old ease still existed between them so that she could have walked into the house one evening and given him credit for the improvement in her brother.

Certainly, Ian was bright and, in the main, did not need twice telling. Having explained in the past how to strip off wallpaper, she could leave him now to prepare a wall, and without gouging out too much plaster. He soon learned to use filler on any cracks and seemed to have more patience than Pamela herself when sanding down woodwork.

Their mother was delighted that reports of his work were good, and Mildred's relief to have Ian in a steady job was compensating Pam for the family disapproval of her decision regarding Charles.

Away from work, as soon as Pam had read up on the redecoration planned for Newark House, she found that she had more than enough time for considering her life. And she was plagued by this feeling that she was particularly adept at misunderstanding the significance of relationships. The trouble between herself and Charles had reminded her of another time, not all that long ago, when she had formed entirely the wrong idea about Roger's attitude towards her.

187

Whatever's the matter with me? she wondered, and couldn't imagine ever really recovering from these doubts about her own judgement. In the old days, she would have turned to Dorothy, but she admitted privately to being worried about seeing her. She had no means of knowing how Dot would react to all that had happened since they last had met.

Pam was still trying to avoid her when Dorothy arrived one day at Newark House, ostensibly to begin measuring up to make curtains.

As soon as they encountered each other Pamela realised that her friend knew. All the old ease had vanished and instead Dorothy tossed that head of gleaming black hair and stared at her, hazel eyes hardening until she no longer looked beautiful.

"I'm still going to make these curtains, you know, no matter how awkward we find working in the same house. But you might as well know that Charlie's told me."

"Oh," was all that Pam could say immediately, but Dorothy made up for her lack of words.

"How could you do it, Pamela? You've got a nerve, I must say – leading the poor chap on like that, then giving him the elbow. If you ask me, Charlie's too good for you, far too good."

"But it wasn't like that," Pamela protested earnestly, close to weeping after all the criticism she'd received, and now her old friend was here and hurting her by completely failing to understand.

"Come off it! Charlie's too shy to ask a girl to marry him if he hadn't had some encouragement. You must have been making up to him."

"I wasn't, never for one moment."

"You had plenty of opportunity, living under the same roof for long enough. How could you, Pam? How could you, after all I'd said?"

"I didn't do anything, you've got to believe I didn't. If I had done, I'd have accepted him, wouldn't I? Wouldn't I?"

"I don't know. I'm not sure about anything any longer. I thought you understood the way I felt about him. You might have had the decency to be equally straightforward with me. I can't fathom what sort of a game you're playing! There we were, talking about a fellow like we've allus done, you and me. Then the next thing I hear is Charlie saying how fed up he is because you've turned him down. And made him feel a right fool into the bargain."

"Nay, I'll not take the blame for that. He took me completely by surprise. If he felt a fool afterwards, that was his own doing."

Dorothy turned on her, her eyes blazing. "You would say that, of course. Nothing's ever your fault, is it? Is it? You've allus got to lay the blame on somebody else. Pamela Canning can't ever be wrong, can she? That wouldn't do – not when she's intent on thrusting herself up the social ladder."

Sighing, Pam shook her head. "If you only knew . . .! I'm not a bit like that."

"Aren't you? From where I'm standing, you are exactly like that. Look at you now – working in another grand house. Because you think you're a cut above folk who do decorating for ordinary people. Any road, I've had enough. If you and me happen to work in the same place in the future that's going to be all. You won't be seeing me again anywhere else."

Sighing, and clattering her stepladder, Dorothy went about the house measuring every window, without speaking another word. After the outer door had closed behind her and a car engine started up, Pam let out a long sigh of despair. She could only be thankful that the owners of the house hadn't yet moved in. She would have been horribly embarrassed if they had witnessed that little scene.

Her own brother had heard it all, naturally. He came through from the next room as soon as Dorothy had departed.

"Does she really fancy Charlie?" he enquired eagerly. Now that he had adjusted to learning that Charles and Pam might never marry, he was showing a lad's natural curiosity about adult pairings.

"You evidently heard what Dorothy said," his sister told him quite sharply. She hadn't enjoyed being reminded what Dot's feelings were.

"So, all we've got to do is bring them together," said Ian seriously. "Then they'll both be all right."

"I think there's enough damage been done already. Just you leave this alone, Ian." But all the time that she was telling him this, Pam was wondering if it might be possible to thrust Charlie and Dot into each other's arms. Marrying him herself just because this might be her last chance of having children didn't seem very honest. She suspected that only by seeing Charles settled might she forgive herself for becoming caught up in this wretched business.

For weeks Pamela thought of nothing but her job. Ian was becoming very useful, working uncomplainingly and fetching and carrying while she was paper-hanging or doing intricate paintwork. He also had mastered the least taxing painting tasks, although his tendency to scatter drops about meant protecting everywhere in his vicinity.

With decoration of the flats completed Ted Burrows came to join them at Newark House and the work there seemed to surge ahead. The new owners visited from time to time inspecting progress, and declared that

190

they were well pleased with the appearance of their future home.

Pam was thrilled when the offer of further work came from acquaintances of theirs who had inherited a house of similar size and period. If only her personal life had a little hope on the horizon she would have been completely satisfied.

As things stood, the unease induced by the misunderstanding between herself and Charlie made her uncomfortable in her own home. Outside it there was nothing but work, and the everlasting yearning to see Andre once more. She hadn't heard one word from him.

Looking back to the months when she had worked on Stonemoor House resurrected all the attraction that she had felt towards him along with the rapport that had developed between them. Separated from Andre, Pamela now felt more alone than she had since the early days following Jim's death. And this time she seemed to lack even one friend who might care about her feelings.

Receiving a telephone call from Andre just when she seemed enveloped in despair felt like the answer to a prayer. Pam was so exultant that she could have sung.

After asking how she was, Andre explained that he had wished all along to include her when he arranged for the Misses Norton to visit Stonemoor House.

"Unfortunately, Hilda Norton fractured her ankle and healing has taken a very long time. Now, however, they are planning to come to see the place. On a Saturday afternoon."

"At this time of year?" Pamela asked, rather surprised. For they were into December and the first snow of the winter lay on the hills surrounding Halifax.

Andre laughed. "They insist that they can wait no longer. I am sending a hired car for them. But I wish that you should come here first, I need your reassurance that the house is looking its best. The Nortons are invited for the Saturday before Christmas – could you possibly spare me some of your time on the previous Saturday?"

"It depends what time of day that would be. Our Ian always goes to a band practice on Saturday mornings and I pick him up afterwards."

"You could bring Ian also – the two of you are invited for lunch. And then during the afternoon you and I may inspect every room here at leisure."

The prospect of being with Andre again sounded wonderful. Pamela felt infinitely better for having that to look forward to. And if she might have preferred going there alone, the possibility that Ian might keep Tania occupied seemed to compensate.

Ian was pleased to have been included in the invitation and promised not to keep his sister waiting when she picked him up at the school where his band practised in a hired room.

Pamela had bought herself a new dress. Of a soft woollen material, it was in a dusky pink shade, with unpressed pleats falling from its narrow waistline to the new length which swirled only a few inches above her ankles. As with her other good outfit, in contrast with her working clothes it felt totally impractical, but it gave her the sensation that she might be more feminine than she often suspected.

Her brother seemed almost as excited as Pam herself when he got into the van after placing his saxophone in the back. All the way out to Cragg Vale he talked, firstly about his rehearsal but then of his longing to see Stonemoor House.

"I was beginning to think I'd never get to see it finished. And now I've learnt how to do decorating I shall be more interested."

Pamela laughed. "You say that as if you'd mastered

all the skills you'll ever need! Is that what you really think?"

"Well – no, not quite, I suppose. Not enough to do all that you can. But I've not done so bad, have I? And I really am finding it interesting."

"I know, love, I know. And I'm very glad."

"It's a pity our Tom doesn't want to learn. That way, we could have really made sure we kept the business in the family." Tom had announced his intention of studying commercial art.

"It might not be a bad thing for him to be in a different line," Pamela observed. "If there's ever another slump – which heaven forbid – we might be glad one member of the family's working. There'll always be the need to see Mum's all right, she's not getting any younger, you know."

But the day was not for serious contemplation. And in any case Pamela's mind was racing with excitement to the extent where sensible conversation was growing difficult. I'd better try and calm down, she thought, or I'll not get out one coherent word when I see Andre!

After she had parked the van outside Stonemoor House, Pam noticed Ian leaning into the back to pick up his saxophone.

"You're not thinking of inflicting that on anyone, I hope?" she said. Ian needed to learn that not everyone shared his enthusiasm for the instrument.

Her brother was shaking his head. "I'm just taking it inside so's it'll be safe – all right? You can't be too careful."

Andre had the door open before they had mounted the steps leading up to it. He was wearing the white shirt and slacks which had appeared so striking when Pamela first met him. Today, his smile was so warm and welcoming that she felt that she might be coming home. He grasped

193

her hand as the three of them exchanged greetings, his grey gaze linking with hers to send tremors coursing through her. She hadn't forgotten how attractive he was, but recognising this afresh produced a pleasurable shock.

"Where's Tania?" Pamela enquired, and then as they all stopped speaking she heard her. From one of the upstairs rooms an exquisite soprano voice drifted down towards them. "Is that her . . .?"

Smiling, his eyes suddenly brimming, Andre nodded. "She inherits my mother's voice. I hope very shortly to arrange for her to receive training. In Russia she was having classes, over here – well, I do not know of a conservatoire."

"She's very good," said Pam. "You must be extremely proud."

She noticed her brother then, gazing upwards, his cheeks glowing beneath their faint down. Turning to follow his gaze, Pamela saw the girl as she approached the bannister rail, the song dying on her lips while she paused to look towards them.

"Come along, Tania," Andre called. "Pamela, you know, of course. And now I should like that you meet her brother, Ian."

Tania had grown while Pam had been absent, she appeared quite fragile with her slight figure and long pale tresses. The gown she wore was also pale, a soft green that somehow emphasised her youth despite its lines of the utter simplicity that gave away its cost.

Ian emitted a long, low whistle. While Pam was itching to nudge him into remembering where he was, Tania came running down the stairs to smile up at him.

"I'm Tania," she announced, sounding far bolder than she looked. She said a brief hello to Pamela and turned back to Ian. "Is it a trumpet you've got there?" she asked, indicating his instrument case.

194

"A sax, actually – saxophone," he added, remembering that she was foreign. He wanted Tania to understand all about his interest in music.

"You must show me," Tania told him. "First, though, I am to show you around the house. You did some work on the kitchen, Father says. You must be clever with your hands . . ."

And you're becoming a clever young lady in your ways, thought Pam as she watched the two young people walking side by side towards the kitchen.

Andre gave a contented sigh and smiled again. "And how have you been, my dear friend?" he asked.

Missing you terribly, she thought, but that wasn't something she could say. Being away from Andre for so long had reduced her ability to judge how intimate their conversation should be. Had they really got on so well, or had distance and her own wishful thinking charged all those memories of their time together?

"Busy. All right, I suppose, thank you. Business is good – I've had to take on someone to help. As well as Ian, that is. He's with me full time now. Much to our mother's relief!"

"And Ian himself, is he enjoying the work?"

"Yes. Yes, he is. But what about you, Andre?"

He had taken her coat, and now was hanging it in a large cupboard that Pam hadn't seen previously.

"I am trying to cope," he told her. "I have purchased this cupboard, you see. You educated me well, it is the correct period." He took her arm and led the way into the drawing room. "About other areas in life, I am less certain."

Andre paused, indicated the sofa and when Pam was seated, sat beside her. He was staring down at his hands. "I think that I am not very good with my Tania. She has become very – how do you say – 'possessive' of me? If I

195

try to have some other interest she bemoans my neglect of her. Always it is what *she* wishes to do. And I . . ."

"Haven't the heart to say no?"

"Precisely. For too long I was aching just to have her with me. Now I tell to myself that I must be satisfied. But I am not. No, I am not."

"But – what do you do? Do you still not go out very often?"

Andre shrugged. "You know how I have been. And for that time after bringing Tania to England I was afraid for her safety. That was the reason I left her with a friend in London before having her come here where people might be watching me."

Pamela hadn't understood that. "And since then – now?"

Andre was silent for long moments, gazing at her, his grey eyes so serious that she wondered what his thoughts might be.

"How can I say, and have you comprehend? You were here no longer and – and somehow it did not matter if I did nothing, if I never left the house. Forgive me, Pamela, but without you I have not been quite alive."

"But – but you didn't telephone, you did not write . . ."

"Would you – did you wish that I had?"

Pam nodded. "Yes, Andre. I wished very much that you had."

Still he did not smile. "And so, you see – I have succeeded only in mishandling yet another area of my life."

"Perhaps it's not too late now to cease wasting time." Pamela felt a massive resurgence of the impulse she'd had for so long to make up to him for whatever life had done to him. "Maybe we should make time instead for each other?"

Andre seized both of her hands in his, raised them to

196

his face and pressed his lips to her fingers. "Let us do that now. I was about to suggest that we might go out one day so that you may guide me in purchasing more furniture. But really that was a mere excuse – I wish only to be in your company."

Pamela smiled. "And so you shall! Wherever you want – if you need more furniture for Stonemoor, I'll be happy to help you choose some."

Smiling into her eyes, Andre released her hands but only to draw her close. His kiss was lingering, fervent, and continued until they heard the piano in the next room, and after a few bars' introduction, Tania's exquisite young voice.

"I did not know that your brother played the piano," said Andre as they drew apart.

"I don't think he does very often, these days, not since he's had that saxophone."

"But he does not favour classical music, I think?"

Pamela grinned. "Not our Ian, no. That's a Glenn Miller piece – *Little Brown Jug*."

"It demonstrates, I suppose, how readily Tania adapts to any kind of music. But she will always be a classicist."

"She's certainly very versatile," said Pam. And refrained from adding that the girl was only young and might be allowed to let down her hair occasionally.

Pamela was thrilled to see how lovely the house was looking when Andre took her from room to room. The weeks away had lent a certain detachment impossible to achieve while she was working here, and now she was seeing each room as she might if they were restored by someone other than herself. Her colour schemes, in their soft shades of greens and creams and peach with toning curtains, all produced the perfect background for Andre's carefully chosen furniture. The fact that the whole effect was so pleasing felt quite overwhelming. She had not remembered that she possessed the ability to recreate so much of Stonemoor's original appeal.

"You are satisfied, as I am, are you not?" Andre observed. He had been watching her expressive blue eyes and was thrilled to see how happy she was.

"I can never thank you enough for letting me have my head with what I did here," she said. "Whether or not I progress in the future, this place is what has turned me from being just another decorator into managing to achieve something rather special."

Andre smiled back at her. "What can I say – when I am the fortunate person who now possesses these constant reminders of your skill?"

Lunch was a light-hearted meal. With Tania basking in Ian's unashamed adoration, there were no barbs targeted on Pamela. And Andre seemed to relax while his daughter had no need to strive for his attention.

If I liked the girl better, I might push her and Ian together more, Pamela thought. Until Tania matured a little, however, she would not contrive to strengthen that early friendship. Even in order to free Andre of some his absorption with his daughter's demands!

Almost as if Pam had needed a reminder of the cause of her reservations about Tania, conflict resurfaced as their visit was ending.

Ian had already said goodbye and was getting into the van while Pamela and Andre were finalising arrangements for the Nortons' visit. Whether or not because the warmer relationship between herself and Andre had become evident, Pamela could not tell, but Tania rushed to her father's side and thrust an arm through his.

"I hope he's told you I am to be his hostess," the girl said, her eyes fixing Pam with an assertive stare.

"Of course," said Pamela smoothly, smiling as though she would melt Tania's assertiveness as well as reassure

Andre of her own unconcern. "I shall be glad to just come here and enjoy myself." She paused, noticing that Andre continued to appear perturbed. "In fact, your father and I have concluded that it's high time we both began enjoying life."

Tania frowned. "You do not understand. He has never been truly happy since my mother's death."

"Actually, Tania, I understand only too well. I lost someone too – my husband. And I am sure neither of them would condemn us to be miserable for the rest of our lives."

From Tania, Pam's attention had moved to Andre's face, where she read the gradual transformation of his anxiety into immense relief. She would remember that expression in his eyes; it would keep her going throughout this week, and during any future partings.

As the following Saturday approached Andre felt his emotions surging back and forth between ecstasy and despair. In so many ways, he was glad that Tania had finally decided to behave like the young mistress of his home, co-operating with Mrs Singer, and offering for his approval ideas of the food they might serve. On the other hand, however, he knew his daughter. He could not blind himself to the fact that Tania was doing all this in order to limit Pamela's role here.

I am only thankful that Pamela now seems prepared to stand up to Tania's bouts of aggression, he thought. I can hope that we may one day look forward to a more settled relationship. In the meantime, though, he would have to accept that the woman and the girl who mattered more than all the world to him did not really get on.

He had tried with Tania. As soon as Pamela and her brother were driving away, he had tackled his daughter about her attitude.

"There was absolutely no need for you to speak of your mother to Pamela Canning. She is well aware that I am a widower. I would have thought you knew me better than to suppose I should try to conceal something so significant from her."

Tania had shrugged. "But I did not know, did I? How should I, when everything you have said and done since you brought me here has emphasised how secretive you are!"

"Not with Pamela, though," he had argued.

Andre felt uncomfortable now as he recalled how far short of the truth that statement was. He had concealed a very great deal in the early days, and until last Saturday had also let Pamela remain largely in ignorance of his feelings towards her. He despised himself for his lack of courage where emotions were concerned. He had seen how Pamela had been disturbed by his failure to contact her. Comparing his recent behaviour with his openness whilst courting Anichka, he felt ashamed.

Russia had scarcely been a nation at ease with itself in 1928 when he and Anichka fell in love. Stalin's campaign against Trotsky and other Bolsheviks who did not toe his line was unnerving everyone. Security police were rounding up dissenters, and people were disappearing, into exile or worse. The rural areas like his own home village were threatened with famine, and smallholders like Anichka's father were being obliged to merge into collective farms. Despite this background and his own uncertain prospects as a musician, they had resisted opposition and married, joyously, while he was a mere twenty years old.

The passion between them had soared above all the surrounding insecurity then, and it had almost seemed that their need of security had generated his success on the concert platform. Disregarding discomfort, even

200

when eventually she was pregnant with Tania, Anichka had travelled from one city to the next, exulting in the acclaim he was receiving. Andre himself had relished public acknowledgement of his solo playing, but most of all the new-found ability to assist his family and his wife's.

There had been risks, days of terror, of never quite knowing who might betray the fact that he never could subscribe to the Communist cause. Subterfuge had seemed only to add spice to the game, providing a thrill comparable to the tension of performing before an audience. Even during the war years that followed, when he had been compelled to serve in the Red Army or risk reprisals against the people he loved, he had seen his life as a challenge. Suffering separation, obeying commands, witnessing mass slaughter, all had been endured. Because by then he possessed the vision that one day he would ensure that they were free. And now he was afraid – if not *of* his young daughter, then for her happiness.

There seemed no excuse, or none great enough to justify his conduct towards the woman whom he had grown to love whilst learning to relish this life that did not induce constant apprehension. It might be that the bullets that had ended Anichka's life and threatened his own had shocked him out of youth's perpetual spirit of expectation. He, surely, had aged by twenty years in the space of that one night. But where was the wisdom that maturity should have brought? Why did he feel he lacked the sense to reassure his daughter and at the same time shape his own life to include Pamela?

Lord, if only I could feel sure where to begin, thought Andre and paused, considering that time long ago, before oppression denied open access to the God his forefathers had acknowledged. Had his withdrawal from active belief been too protracted – or might he now return to faith in a Power which could help him?

Pamela arrived at Stonemoor House as arranged, half an hour before the Norton sisters were due. Andre greeted her at the door, and surprised her by hugging her close.

His action also surprised Tania who came through from the kitchen and stood quite still to stare as their kiss grew prolonged. The first Pamela knew of the girl's presence was the slamming of the drawing room door.

"Oh, dear," she exclaimed and sighed.

Andre's smile was rueful. "I know. I fear that Tania has a wicked ability to disturb with her opinions. I have tried speaking with her, but she seems determined to undermine everything that I do which might possibly distract me from her."

"We must be patient with her, I suppose. After all, Andre, she is bound to have felt very insecure." Although, thought Pam, someone ought perhaps to point out to the girl that she might benefit from having a more normal home life. One where her father was not solely responsible for taking care of her.

Andre insisted that Pamela should inspect each room before Sophie and Hilda Norton arrived. He was anxious that the entire house should look as perfect as it had seemed to him on the day that Pamela had completed her work here.

Their touring of every room did not go down at all well with Tania who following briskly in their wake and eventually demanded to know if Pamela was unhappy about the way Stonemoor House was kept.

Pam managed to smile at her. "On the contrary, both you and Mrs Singer as well as your father ensure that everything looks immaculate. But I'm afraid you must indulge me – this is the first really big job I tackled on my own, you know. I need repeated reassurances that it has turned out so well."

"So you say," Tania muttered. "I can't help believing that he asked you to check up on everything."

"And if I did . . ." Andre began, but Pamela restrained him with a hand on his arm. He nodded to agree that letting the subject alone might be wiser.

The Misses Norton were ecstatic when they saw the carefully restored panelling in the hall. Seeing it through their eyes and in the wintry sunlight, Pamela relished the gleam of well-polished oak.

"My, you have done well!" Sophie exclaimed, beaming towards her.

"Yes, indeed," Hilda concurred. "I'll bet this took you quite some time."

"And a lot of elbow grease," said Pam with a grin. "I'm just very thankful that the result is as good as this."

"And that she did not accede to my wishes, and paint the whole thing white!" Andre put in with a smile.

"You didn't really want white paint here, did you?" Sophie asked.

"Only as much as I wished to surround myself with white, as a sort of statement, I suppose."

"Because of being a White Russian," Tania declared, coming slowly forward to join them.

Pamela wondered if this fact would be news to the sisters, but they seemed so unmoved by it that she imagined Andre must have told them more about his background.

The Nortons' reaction to the entrance hall was repeated in every room as they were conducted through the house. They appeared to love everything that they saw, and even admitted that the place looked far better than ever it had during the years of their stay here.

"All it needs now is another family taking root," Sophie murmured dreamily.

"Sophie," her sister reproved. "It is not for us to speculate on such matters. Maybe Mr Malinowski is perfectly content here, especially now that his pretty young daughter has joined him."

"Having Tania with me certainly is good," Andre said, placing an arm about the girl's shoulders.

When lunch was served at the elegant Regency dining table Pamela was astonished by the splendid meal which seemed to be suffering none of the limitations caused by rationing. Tania finally smiled when Pam complimented her on the food.

"I did have to think very carefully," she confessed. "And Mrs Singer helped me to prepare it all. But if you could have seen some of the dreadful things we survived on at home, you would know how it is that I find meals in England more enjoyable."

Tania and her father elaborated on some of the deprivations suffered by their countrymen, and the Norton sisters contrasted this with tales of the magnificent feasts that had been served in the old days at Stonemoor House.

After Sophie and Hilda had left and she was helping Tania and her father to carry the dishes into the kitchen for Mrs Singer to tackle, Pamela felt that the house was still peopled with the Nortons and their ancestors. She might go into any one of the rooms and find it alive with the family that once had existed here.

Andre had never expressed a wish to have this become a real family home again, but she herself was aching with a need to belong at Stonemoor House. A physical ache to feel that she was a part of this place which she had helped to beautify.

Pamela reminded herself that she must never presume too much. As yet, Andre had neither done nor said anything to indicate that there was more than affectionate friendship between them. There had been no real indication that he experienced the depth of passion which he generated in her, or that he would do anything about such desire. All these emotions surging through her must remain her closely guarded secret.

While she was preparing to leave, Pamela looked all around her, almost as though she was afraid that it might be some long while before she returned. This place had become so very special, but she must be sensible about that. She could not love every home that she restored; she would have to learn to curb her feelings. And not least regarding the owner of Stonemoor House.

As if confirming this, her hopes that Andre would suggest another meeting in the near future came to nothing. You see, Pamela told herself sternly as she drove away with intense feelings of anticlimax overtaking her: that's as far as presumption will get you!

# Chapter Eleven

Christmas at Stonemoor House was among the many occasions which Pamela pictured wistfully following her last visit there, but Christmas came and passed without her hearing another word from Andre. So much for his promises about our enjoying life together, she thought, and resigned herself to disciplining any consideration of what might have been. She could imagine who had insisted that father and daughter must relish their time alone together, and she herself would hate to upset Andre by creating trouble with Tania.

She was busy, of course. Redecorating Newark House had been completed in order that the new owners could be in residence when festivities began. And since then Pam had been occupied on smaller jobs in more modest houses. Most of these were nearer to her own home, a fact which she appreciated in the heart of wintry Yorkshire with its winds and its wet even when that didn't fall as snow.

Christmas itself, with Dorothy still keeping right away and Charles in the uncommunicative mood that had persisted since her refusal to marry him, was uncomfortable. Although Pam and her mother naturally invited Elsie to join them once more and the three women made an effort for the sake of Ian and Tom, the festive spirit seemed to be absent. Tom and Ian were older now, of course, and preferred to be with their friends rather than at home with family.

Pamela noticed that Charles appeared more affection-ate with his own mother, and caught herself wishing that he would return with Elsie to her home that short distance away. As soon as the thought went through her mind, however, Pam recognised that she would do what she could, or almost anything, to remove Charlie from her conscience!

She was unprepared for the possibility of his refusing to accept that no was her final answer. When, shortly after midnight on New Year's Eve, Charles repeated his proposal, Pamela was shattered.

He began as soon as Elsie had gone home and Mildred and the lads were heading for bed.

"I've been watching you, Pam – all over Christmas I've been watching you. You're no more happy than I am, are you?"

Pamela stared at him across the living room which, despite the decorated tree and paper streamers, looked old-fashioned and rather drab.

"What makes you say that?" She had no intention of admitting to anyone else how much she was missing Andre, that every hour she was longing to know how he was and what he was doing.

"I'm not blind, lass. And I still think we could make a go of it, if only you'd give it a try. I've been saving hard, we could afford a place of our own."

"I'm sorry, Charlie, I really am." Pamela could feel her heart thundering away as alarm rose right through her. She hoped Charlie couldn't tell, he was still sitting at the far side of the table where they'd all been playing cards.

"I see. So that's it then." Charles sighed. "It's a right bugger, is this. You've taken everything away from me, haven't you? We don't even go out any more."

"It is the middle of winter," Pamela began.

"Don't give me that. There's t'pictures, isn't there?

And the repertory theatre. But I know you're avoiding me."

"I wish I didn't feel I had to, it's only that I don't want you getting any wrong ideas."

"Above my station, you mean. That's it, isn't it?"

"That it's not!" Pam contradicted hotly, springing off her chair. "And it never has been. I admire the way you've built your business up. You're a damned good plumber. Whenever we've worked on the same house anywhere, folk have always been suited with the job you've done."

Charles merely shrugged, and lowered his eyes. Pamela wished with all her heart that she could love him, but the fact remained that she did not. And marrying her cousin in those circumstances would be more unkind than leaving things as they stood.

A few days later she secured confirmation of work on the other large house that she had heard about. The decor in some of the rooms was still good, but others were shabby. The new owners also wanted one of the smaller bedrooms converting to an additional bathroom.

She immediately recommended Charlie for the job, and was thankful when he appeared pleased that she had put his name forward. By the time he had agreed prices with the owner and was ready to begin Pam had decided she could not allow the opportunity to slide away. Charles had complained about not going anywhere, hadn't he, and the disagreement between herself and Dorothy had removed Dot from his circle. If she wanted to make Charles feel any the better, she must try to put things right between her cousin and her friend.

In this house even the rooms not needing redecoration were to have new curtains and the owners were enthusiastic when Pam told them that her friend would do an excellent job making them up. Dorothy herself was less enthusiastic when Pam called round to put the idea to her.

Eventually, Dot grudgingly admitted to being prepared to give it a try. "I can't really afford not to. If I turn work down I'll never be able to give up my job at the baker's. And I suppose you and I can manage not to fall out in front of other folk."

"There won't be other folk there, actually. Mr and Mrs Hobson are having everything done before they move in."

"Lucky them! What must it be like to be able to afford to have it all made just so for you!" Despite her tart words, Dot was grinning. "Eh, Pam – it's about time we stopped fratching, isn't it? I'm glad that you've brought this job my way."

It was the best that Pamela could expect, she didn't really imagine that she and Dorothy would ever be as easy with each other as they had in the past. This was a beginning, though, and providing that Dorothy and Charles were working there at the same time it could do a great deal to make the pair of them happier.

Charles was not around when Dorothy came to the house to measure up, but she and Pamela seemed to have plenty to discuss. Dorothy had been invited to meet the new owners, but in their present home. She had taken samples of fabric and had made copious notes regarding their favoured colour schemes. Even now that they were into 1948, materials were still in short supply, making some of their ideas impractical, but Dot's knowledge of the cloth that was available was helpful. When she had calculated the yardage required for each set of curtains she was to accompany Mrs Hobson to see what could be purchased.

"I shall enjoy that," she said to Pam. "It'll be almost as good as choosing fabrics for my own place!"

From what Dorothy did not say about her private

life, Pamela gathered that no one else had superseded Charlie in her affections. This had made Pam feel even more dreadful about causing all contact between them to cease, but it also made her determined to contrive another meeting for them.

She had only just begun to feel that she might soon be happier about the whole situation when a different problem distracted her from the difficulties between Dorothy and Charles. Ian had been working with Ted Burrows who had been delayed by a bout of 'flu while trying to finish a set of offices on schedule.

Pamela arrived home from work one evening to find Ted's van in the street and Ted waiting with a scowl that would turn milk sour.

"Can I have a word?" he asked, getting out of his van as soon as Pamela had parked her own and was crossing the footpath.

"Of course, Ted. Have you got a bit of a problem? You'd better come on in . . ."

"It's more than a bit of a problem. And I'd rather we talked out here. It's about that brother of yours."

"Ian?" Pamela's heart plummeted. "Whatever's wrong?" She glanced about the lamplit street where doors were shut and lights shone through closed curtains. She was glad that none of their neighbours seemed to be around to overhear.

"I don't like telling tales. I would never have mentioned it, if it had only happened the once, but this is becoming a habit."

"Go on . . ." she prompted with a sigh. She hoped this would be something that she might keep from their mother. She couldn't bear to destroy the peace of Ian remaining in a steady job.

"The lad's been wasting time a lot. He's really got my goat, I don't mind admitting. He knows he's been put to work with me because we're behind on the job already. But somehow he won't buckle to. He's forever on the blessed telephone when he should be working."

"On the telephone?" Pamela didn't understand.

"Aye," Ted affirmed grimly. "*Their* telephone, them that own the office. It'll be running up their bill like nobody's business."

"Oh, good heavens. Well, as far as that aspect's concerned, I'll have to have a word with them, I suppose."

"I don't want none of them thinking it were me, that's one reason I had to say summat."

"I know that, Ted, I'll make it plain our Ian's responsible. If I offer to pay for the calls he's made, that should calm them down. And I'll give our Ian a talking to. I'll dock his pay if he's been shirking like this. I suppose you don't know who he was ringing up?"

Ted shook his head. "I only know it sounded like a lass on the other end. Not that I was listening in, mind."

Pamela tackled Ian later that evening, after their mother had gone to bed.

"I've had a complaint about you," she began. "Yes, from Ted – and you'll not take it out on him afterwards by going all moody, or you're finished, my lad. He tells me that you've not been working when you should. Well, you'll feel that in your pay packet at the end of this week."

"Oh, but, Pam . . ."

"Don't 'Oh but' me, it won't do you any good. You know you were sent on that job because we needed to get the work done in a hurry, there's no excuse for slacking. But what's upset me more is that you haven't been getting on because you were busy making 'phone calls – on *their* telephone."

Very briefly, a smile lit Ian's eyes and Pamela wished

212

that the resemblance to their father which this created had extended to include his integrity.

"This isn't funny, Ian, and nor is it clever. You're what – seventeen now? Old enough to know that using somebody's phone is going to cost them. Doing so without permission is a form of stealing. We shall have to tell them and . . ."

"What for?" her brother interrupted, his face scarlet.

"I'll tell you what for – because I'm not prepared to enter into your little deceits. I ought to make you confess, but I daren't trust you to admit to this. I shall tell the folk owning that office, and I shall pay for any calls that weren't theirs. And then, my lad, I shall deduct that amount from your pay."

"I'm sorry, Pam. Really, really, sorry. I didn't think."

"Yes, well. You will be really sorry if I have trouble of any sort from you again. You'll be out of a job, and I shall leave it to you to explain the reason to Mum. So think on."

Ian was silent for a minute or so, digesting the reprimand. While he was trying to think what to say, Pamela recalled something.

"Who were you telephoning, anyway? A girl?"

Her brother nodded and smiled to himself.

"So, you've got yourself a girlfriend, have you?"

"Not really, no."

"Somebody you fancy, no doubt. Does she live round here? You'd be better off taking her out, wouldn't you?"

"She doesn't live round here. And it's not like that."

"Oh? Is she spoken for?" Pamela was already foreseeing all kinds of further trouble.

"No. It's Tania, if you must know."

"Tania? Andre's Tania?"

"I don't know any other."

"Don't be so smart with me, Ian. What's going on between you two then?"

"Nothing, honest. It's just . . . well – she's interested in music, isn't she? Interested in the band. She wants to sing with us. Only she can't, not yet. Until he gets back, she can't ask permission."

"He? Andre? You mean Andre's gone away somewhere?"

Ian nodded. "I thought you'd know. He went straight after Christmas. They'd both had that 'flu that's going round over the holiday, and neither of them felt so good. Evidently, her father got to thinking that they wanted more of their own folk over here."

Pamela could feel her stomach already churning apprehensively. "Don't tell me – he hasn't gone over to Russia to try and get more of them out?"

"I don't know, Tania doesn't – not precisely where he's gone. Or when he'll be back. But she's pretty sure it's either Russia or near the borders. He's got that sister still living there, hasn't he? Any road, that's why Tania's so fed up there."

"She's not on her own at Stonemoor House, I hope? Is somebody there with her?"

"Tania could look after herself, she's as old as me. But that woman that can't talk is there. Stopping at nights as well."

"Thank goodness for that. Mrs Singer, her name is."

"I don't think she's much company for Tania," said Ian gravely.

"I don't suppose she is, poor woman. Although she does communicate, you know."

Ian nodded. "Writing notes, and that. Not the same, though, is it?"

Pamela was forced to agree. "Well, if you've helped to alleviate Tania's loneliness, that's something. But I wish

214

you hadn't used somebody else's 'phone. From now on you can ring her from home. But you'll have to be sensible about that, I'm not made of money."

"You sound just like my mother."

"You can feel grateful that I'm not your mum! You've had an easy time of it compared to the way it would feel with me for a parent."

The incident disturbed Pamela a great deal, and most of all for the revelation that Andre had left the country, and without confiding in her. And there was this sister of his – had he ever even spoken of her existence? Pam wasn't sure. For all his talk of how close he wished them to become, he remained the same Andre who would only do his own way, and without taking anyone into his confidence.

For the first time that she could recall, Pamela began to wonder what Andre's wife had been like. And what *he* had been like before the escape from Russia had resulted in Anichka's death. Had he always tended to live behind this reserve, making decisions and carrying them out, and expecting everyone to accept that he explained nothing?

I could not live with somebody like that, Pam realised, and felt as though everything that she might have hoped for was falling away, to be replaced by great sadness. She had cherished her dreams about Andre, constructing them around the possibility however far distant of their being happy together in his lovely home. Now it seemed that she had been misguided to even think that way. She remembered Jim who had been open and direct, just as she herself tried to be; any other means of living with someone seemed impossible.

Pam was nevertheless concerned about Tania. And privately pleased that Ian also was concerned for the girl. She would take him out to Stonemoor House. A bit of company ought to help Tania to get through this period without her father.

They arrived on the following Saturday after Ian had finished practising with the band. Pamela would never forget Tania's expression when she opened the door of Stonemoor House to them. Initially, sheer delight warmed the eyes which reminded Pam of Andre's, but even before they had entered the hall the girl's smile was directed to Ian and her attitude towards Pamela had chilled.

"Ian told me you were on your own here except for Mrs Singer. At least, I suppose you are still alone?" Pamela said.

"Yes."

"Have you heard from your father at all?"

Tania was gazing up at Ian and seemed to hear Pam only after a short delay. "No, but he had told me not to expect word from him. He would not take the risk of having any calls traced."

"I see." Pamela could not imagine how the girl was surviving being cut off from all news of her father like this. She could only hope that Tania did not fully comprehend how dangerous his mission could be. "And how are you, love? Are you all right here?"

Tania turned the full power of her smile on Ian. "I have one very good friend who has been talking to me often."

Mrs Singer had emerged from the kitchen and smiled and nodded in their direction as she came to hand a note to Tania.

"She says that you may have lunch here," the girl announced.

"Only if that really isn't inconvenient," Pamela insisted.

Tania was yet again looking at Ian. "I would like very much for *you* to eat with us."

The house itself felt very strange without Andre, and

216

reminded Pam of the time when he had left her in charge here. The atmosphere during their meal did little to make her feel at ease. Tania and Ian had eyes for nothing but each other, and neither of them possessed the grace to include Pam in their conversation.

Music was their main topic, chiefly Ian's band and the late Glenn Miller's special sound. Tania was listening intently while Ian explained how the trombonist bandleader had dominated swing music broadcasting during the final years of the war.

"But he had died before then, no?" said Tania.

Ian nodded. "He went missing in December 1944, somewhere above the English Channel. His orchestra had made recordings though."

"And you say he had travelled a great deal entertaining soldiers?"

"He was a marvellous chap – played in most of the war zones."

Pamela, who had heard all this before, found her mind wandering. She liked the kind of music introduced by Glenn Miller, but thought her brother's interest risked becoming obsessive. In many ways, she preferred the variety provided by traditional brass bands like the one for which Jim had played. And Roger too, of course, she thought and shuddered.

"Are you cold?" Tania asked.

Pamela shook her head and glanced towards the log fire, crackling as it blazed and emitting an agreeable smell of woodsmoke. "I'm fine, love, thanks."

Somehow, though, Pam could not get Roger Jenkins out of her mind. She still saw her misunderstanding of their friendship as one of her failures. More recently, there had been Charlie's misapprehension about their relationship, another instance of her inability to cope with her personal life. And there was Andre . . . Pamela swallowed. Now

217

that she was in his home she was more than ever aware of how keenly she felt being separated from him. Regardless of what he did.

I'm going to have to pull myself out of this mood and concentrate on work, she reflected. I can't let Andre matter so much to me when there seems so little prospect of our having a future together.

The business was certainly providing plenty of interest. As well as the Hobsons' house, Pamela was occupied with planning a major renovation far more challenging than anything she had tackled so far. She owed this contract to Ian who had given her name to the committee who administered the hall which was the one where his band performed.

Once part of a school, the site had been used by the army throughout the war and was badly in need of redecoration. Most of the rooms, including the one where concerts were held, had originally been given walls of drab brown paint. A brighter colour was requested for its rejuvenation, with a selection of pastels in the smaller rooms. Pamela was enjoying negotiating with the committee regarding shades; they had some ideas of their own but listened to her advice and seemed quite flexible.

She was itching now to finish work on the Hobsons' home in order to begin on this major task. Ian was impatient to make a start there, and seemed delighted that she had obtained the job. Their younger brother also had said that he felt proud of all that she had achieved, pleasing Pam who had been afraid that Tom might feel he was being left out now that Ian worked with her. The only person who appeared less than thrilled was their mother. This upset Pamela who would have liked to think that Mildred believed she was achieving a great deal.

218

Her mother's words had shaken her as soon as she joined in their discussion. "You've just been lucky, haven't you, Pam? You've not had to put yourself out to find these jobs, they've simply come your way."

"Mum! Surely, that's only happened because I do good work – otherwise nobody would have set me on."

"Happen so. It just seems to me that you've fallen on your feet. Some folk allus do."

Charlie had taken this up with his aunt. "Pam's worked damned hard, Auntie, you must see that. She's had to research new methods for tasks far beyond anything she'd ever tackled before the war."

"But a lot of it's common sense, isn't it?" Mildred had suggested.

Although glad that her cousin had spoken up for her in this way (a fact which seemed to indicate that he was beginning to forgive her), Pamela was distressed by Mildred's apparent failure to understand.

Eventually, she was compelled to ask her mother if there was something behind the remarks she had made. She chose a time when none of the others were at home, and was surprised that Mildred seemed close to tears when challenged.

"Eh, love – take no notice of me. Happen I'm just being daft. I'm just not happy about the way you're going on and on, taking to doing bigger places every time. In a bit you'll have got above yourself . . . You even talk different to what you used to."

"Only because I've been mixing with different people, and that started in the WAAF. But the rest is nonsense, Mother, and rather unfair. I'm not doing all this to show off, you know. I needed a job when Jim died, and for a while I was doing it for him in a way. But lately I have known that it was for me that I've been working so hard. And partly, I suppose, that's because I've nothing else."

"Ah," said Mildred, "Now we're getting somewhere. That's why I've been unhappy about the way things are turning out. I want to see you settled, lass, and there's not much sign of that, is there?"

"I know, I know. Believe me, it's something I want as well." But there was no point in burdening her mother with the massive disappointment induced by the indifference that the one man she wanted appeared to feel towards her.

Recalling how she had only so recently decided that she must bury herself in work, Pam thought ruefully that she seemed incapable of pleasing anyone. Least of all herself.

Pamela was thankful, however, for Charles's newly acquired empathy on the day that he came to work in the Hobsons' house.

"I'm glad we're still pals," she said after he had been chatting amiably while carrying in all his equipment.

"Aye – well," he said with a grin. "I've come to my senses now. I don't blame you for turning me down, and I don't suppose it was ever a very romantic proposition. It's the way I am, you see, Pam. I were allus a bit backward at coming forward with the lasses. Don't get me wrong – I'd have snapped you up like a shot if you'd been willing – but it was more that I'd reached the conclusion it was high time I were getting wed."

"I can appreciate that," Pam said seriously. "We both had life interrupted by the war."

"And we're not getting any younger," Charlie added with a grin. "Asking you was easier than plucking up courage to propose to anyone else. I shall just have to start looking round again. You'll be the first to know when I do find the right lass."

"And I'll be delighted to dance at your wedding!"

220

she told him, concealing the smile generated by his backhanded compliment. Easier than proposing to anyone else indeed!

Pamela was relieved that Charles was now scanning a wider field; she only hoped that he hadn't written off Dorothy. Or her asking Dot to choose that morning for hanging curtains would be a wasted effort.

She smiled to herself when she heard her friend's car in the drive, and prepared to explain that Charlie was present. Now that so much time had elapsed since that disastrous proposal, she could believe Dorothy would be thankful to have such an easy way of making things all right between them.

Dot came storming into the house, and searched the rooms until she located Pamela. Closing the door behind her, she stared across to where her old friend was hanging wallpaper.

"I see Charlie's van's outside. What do you think you're doing – getting me here, an' all? I thought I'd told you I didn't want to see him again, not after the way he slighted me!"

"Slighted?" Pamela began.

That was a mistake. Dorothy snorted furiously. "If you'd been passed over as not good enough, you'd know what I mean all right. But then – you've had at least two proposals that I know of. Maybe you don't see much significance in their being offered, or otherwise. Let me tell you – it hurts, it hurts like hell when the fellow you fancy goes after your best mate. Or the lass you thought was your best mate!"

"Dot, Dot, please – we've had all this out. Let's not go through it again."

Dorothy turned away. "Okay, just don't expect me to switch on the sweetness and light for your precious cousin, that's all."

Whatever Pamela might have expected, Dorothy was determined to refuse to co-operate. Her voice echoed through the house as soon as she encountered Charles.

"Excuse me, you're in my way," she began, and Pamela listened from a distance to Charles trying to say how pleased he was to see Dot again while Dot herself blatantly ignored his friendliness. "Can't you leave that for now?" her sharp tones rang out. "I can't get these curtains hung while you're mucking about under my feet."

"I shan't be a minute," Charles said gently. Pam had heard him go clomping up his stepladder which she pictured where he had set it, beneath the trapdoor leading to the loft. Unfortunately, the trapdoor was near the window where Dot was working. "And there's no need for you to be like that, Dorothy," he continued. "I've never done you any harm. I was only telling you I was glad to see you again."

Dorothy sniffed. "Well, if you can't see what's wrong, it's no use me saying. You obviously have no idea about people's feelings."

Pamela heard Charles stomping about in the loft and then an exasperated cry from Dot as he evidently prepared to descend the stepladder again.

"Oh, what is it now? I thought you were going to stop up there for a while. Can't you see you'll be coming down right where I'm standing?"

"Actually, all I want is yon lamp over there. If you can pass it up to me please, I'll stay out of your way."

"Sorry, you'll have to hang on a minute till I've moved over, then get it yourself. Sliding these hooks on this rail is very tricky."

"Forget it, I'll manage without a light," Charlie snapped and then there was silence broken only by his footsteps moving around the loft again.

Pamela sighed, thinking that she would like to bang their heads together. But mostly to give Dorothy a talking to. Couldn't she see that she was cutting off her nose to spite her face?

Pam was toying with the idea of taking Dot aside when a tremendous crashing and a heavy thud sent her haring out. Reaching the doorway of the room where Dot was working, she halted, appalled.

Charles had fallen through the ceiling a few feet from the trapdoor, but had somehow caught the ladder and was now lying on his back with his right leg twisted awkwardly between its rungs.

Dorothy had left the curtain to dangle, and was kneeling at his side, her face already paler than Charlie's.

"Now look what you've made me do!" he snapped. "If I'd had a light up there I'd never have missed my footing on that joist."

"Come on, Charlie," Dorothy began, tears welling in her eyes. "Let me give you a hand."

"Nay, it's going to take somebody a lot stronger nor you to get me on to my feet."

"Don't worry, I'm here as well," said Pam, hastening across to join them. "Let's have this stepladder out of the way first."

The instant that she tried to move the ladder, Charles yelled. "Steady on, that hurts like hell. It feels like a nasty sprain or summat."

"I dare say, love, but we'll have to disentangle you from this. You steady his leg, Dot, while I have a go at the ladder."

With Charlie gritting his teeth against the pain, and Dorothy now weeping copiously, they looked a sorry pair to Pamela as she wrestled to get the ladder away from him without inflicting further damage.

"How does it feel now?" she asked after she had

succeeded in freeing him and Charles levered himself onto one elbow, leaning forward to clutch his shin.

"Sore, but not quite so bad."

"Eh, I am sorry," Dorothy said. "It was all my fault, going on at you like that. And being that pig-headed I wouldn't break off to pass you that lamp. I were proper daft!"

"Aye, well – we all are at one time or another," said Charles. "And happen there's no real harm done."

But when the two women assisted him to his feet they found that he could put hardly any weight on the right leg.

"You'd better see a doctor, love," Dorothy said, sickened by the accident and its potential consequences. "You need it strapping up or something."

"I'll run you to the Infirmary," Pamela offered. "You'd better have it X-rayed."

Dorothy insisted that she must be the one to drive Charlie there, and after they had helped him downstairs he was settled into the passenger seat of her car.

Alone in the house once more, Pamela thought ruefully of the good intentions with which she had contrived to bring her friend and Charlie together again. If his injury was no worse than a sprain, it would still be a long time before he could forget the differences that had preceded the accident.

When Dorothy eventually returned to her, she was if anything even more wan and still barely able to control her tears.

"Whatever do you think?" she said when she located Pam: "His leg's broken! Both the tibia and fibula, they say."

"Oh, no! How long's he going to be off work then?" To someone like Charles who was self-employed that could be catastrophic.

Dot shook her head. "Eh, I don't know. They can't say; the only good thing is that they're clean breaks. They've got to keep him in, of course, for a bit."

The one happier result of the accident was that Dorothy frequently visited Charlie, initially in hospital then afterwards at home. Despite wishing it need never have occurred, Pam was thankful that the incident finally had healed the awkwardness between them.

Fortunately, although the heavy plaster cast was inhibiting, Charlie soon recovered sufficiently to work so long as it did not involve clambering up ladders.

Pamela readily let him use Ian wherever greater agility was required. She was pleased to discover that her brother had retained all the knowledge gained during that earlier period working with Charles.

"I'll have to remember this," she joked on the day when her cousin eventually had his plaster cast removed and declared that Ian could return to full-time decorating. "If ever you're not available, Charles, I can set our Ian on to do any plumbing jobs I come across!"

"Eh, not so fast!" Charles said with a grin. "I'm going to want all the work I can lay my hands on." He paused and Pam noticed that his face shone with delight. "You might as well be the first to hear – I'm getting engaged afore so long."

"Oh, Charlie, I am glad. Is it . . .?"

"Aye, it's Dot. You might say I fell for her in a big way!"

The three of them laughed, but Pamela's feelings went far beyond amusement. She couldn't have been more thankful. Whatever happened now, she should no longer feel guilty about turning down her cousin.

Pamela needed something to make her feel better. Shortly after Charlie's accident she had heard from Andre who had recently returned to England and had telephoned her one evening.

She had asked how his trip abroad had gone, but he had been his normal reticent self, revealing only that it was less successful than he had hoped. He had invited her to Stonemoor House on the following Saturday, however, and during the intervening days Pam felt her excitement soaring.

Andre had mentioned briefly the visit that she had made to Tania, and she could only think that he must have been pleased that she had thought of his beloved daughter. Perhaps at last he would be more willing to have the three of them spend time together.

He appeared a little cool with her, Pam noticed when she arrived, but she was prepared to dismiss that because of the considerable lapse of time since their last meeting. Tania, she was glad to note, was more friendly than ever in the past, and included Pamela in those first few minutes of conversation with far more grace than usual.

Andre soon interrupted to send his daughter up to her room. He still seemed rather on edge. Pam began to wonder if he could at last be struggling for the right words to broach something important. Something which would affect their future lives.

He gestured towards the sofa, and when Pam was seated went to stand before the white marble fireplace, and faced her with an expression that looked neither cordial nor content.

"As I told you, Pamela, Tania informed me that you had called here, and that Ian was with you. It felt good to know that you were sufficiently concerned to come here while I was away from home."

"It was no trouble, Andre," she said. "In fact, you've only to say the word and I'll do anything you ask me . . ."

Andre interrupted by raising a hand. "Would you hear

226

me out, please? I was about to say that appreciating your interest in Tania does not mean that I welcome your interference in her life."

Alarmed, Pamela gazed towards him. "But I don't understand."

"Do you not? Not when you have brought your brother here, and have encouraged the pair of them until she has set her heart on singing with this – this band of his."

"I didn't know it was arranged for her to sing with them."

"You didn't?" Momentarily, Andre appeared surprised. But then he shrugged. "Be that as it may, you introduced them, you must have foreseen that she, who would do anything to perform with an outfit like that, would seize the opportunity."

"But she's young enough, surely, Andre? Perhaps she only needs to be given her head for a little while, before turning to the kind of future you have in mind for her . . ."

"And ruin her voice before then, by indulging in this – this 'swing' that they are so mad about! I wish your brother had never set foot in this house!"

And I wish that I never had, thought Pamela, her throat aching so much that she could not speak. She got to her feet and rushed to find her coat, then ran out of Stonemoor House towards the van. She must get right away before she gave in to the tears that were choking her.

# Chapter Twelve

Pamela was so deeply hurt by Andre blaming her for his daughter's wish to become involved with Ian's band that she could not bring herself to talk to anyone about the way that he had reproached her. She tried (and failed) to thrust that dreadful encounter to the back of her mind, and willed herself yet again to submerge everything in work.

These repeated efforts to bury herself in her job were taking all the enjoyment out of the work she was doing. These days, she felt that she was trapped on some treadmill.

Pam was astonished when Ian chanced to mention that Tania *was* singing with the band. She had never for one second believed that Andre would have permitted such a thing to go ahead.

Ian grinned when she said as much to him. "You know what Tania's like – his life wouldn't be worth living if he forbade her. And as for Andre, he's besotted with her, isn't he? Not surprisingly, when they only have each other over here."

"And how's she been getting back and forth to all the rehearsals?" Pam enquired, wondering if Andre now had some kind of transport.

Ian smiled. "Let's just say I'm glad I bought that old car instead of a motorbike. I don't think he'd have let her ride on one of them."

Pamela began looking forward to the concert, albeit

with feelings that were mixed. She could see Andre there and, no matter how awkward the meeting, it offered the only prospect of their ever becoming reconciled. He evidently had relented towards Tania; his attitude towards herself also might have mellowed.

The band had been rehearsing for weeks now, mainly because all the individual members had never previously played in public as a group.

"It's got to be just right," Ian had emphasised seriously, and Pam was impressed by his determination that the two performances they were giving should be first rate.

The first night was a Friday in April with a repeat show on the following evening. With her mother and Tom, Pamela entered the hall and as they headed towards their seats found she was already looking around for Andre.

The concert really was extremely good, including as it did many of the pieces made famous by Glenn Miller and others popular towards the end of the war. Ian had a couple of solos and the three of them exchanged proud smiles when a tremendous wave of applause followed.

But it was Tania who, with her exquisitely clear voice, won the greatest acclaim. And when her interpretation of what should have been the final piece of the show brought the audience to their feet, Pamela felt her eyes filling with tears. For her encore the girl chose one of the hits from the new musical *Oklahoma!* and had feet tapping before the last crescendo of applause.

Expecting to find the girl exultant, Pamela was shocked by how deflated Tania seemed when she came with Ian to join them.

"Her father is not here," Ian explained. "I told her that she could share you lot with me, but . . ."

"But it's not the same," said Pamela and was surprised that Tania did not shrug her off when she put an arm round her shoulders.

Even though Tom seemed to equal his brother's admiration for the girl, gazing raptly at her when they were introduced, Tania remained subdued. Mildred Baker gave her a motherly smile while congratulating her on her voice, but Tania's answering smile was wan.

Distressed for what Andre was missing as much as for his daughter, Pamela hardly slept that night. By morning she had decided that, no matter what the outcome, she must at least make an effort to put matters right. She had learned that the band had booked another run-through of their programme for the Saturday afternoon. They were determined that this second evening's performance should be at least as good as the previous one. Andre must not be allowed to miss it.

Pamela drove up to Stonemoor House after lunch, struggling to quell the nervousness which increased each time that she recalled her last upsetting confrontation with Andre. She could only try to get him to attend the concert: relations between them were bad already, there seemed now very little that she could lose by trying. All the same, she was perturbed and caught herself wishing that she had never begun to like Andre all those many months ago.

The first sound she heard as she switched off the engine and got out of her van was his violin. Even from out here its strains sounded melancholy, eerily attuned to the day which, with its moist atmosphere and mist already drifting about the hills, appeared more autumnal than springlike.

The playing ceased only after she had rattled the doorknocker for several moments. Violin in hand, Andre opened the door to her and gasped.

"Are you going to invite me in?" Pam asked, not because he was hesitating – although he was – but to gauge his attitude towards her.

Andre smiled, and though the smile was sad it seemed

genuine enough. "Of course, Pamela. Do come in, please."

They went into the drawing room where he invited her to sit, then took a chair facing hers where he continued to hold the violin, cradling it while he weighed something in his mind.

"This is a Stradivari," Andre announced suddenly, and Pam sensed that he couldn't yet bring himself to speak of anything more personal. "It is authentic," he added and extended the instrument for her to inspect. "You may see his inscription if you look through the 'F' hole, here."

Pamela nodded, and satisfied him by looking. But she was remembering that first time when she had seen this violin, and how she had needed to know its history. Today, that seemed not to matter. So many other things between them had gone so terribly wrong.

Andre smiled slightly as he set the violin in its open case on the nearby table.

"This is the second Stradivari that I have owned, did I tell you? They were the only means of bringing any of my assets out of Russia. The other violin was sold in order to buy this house, and for me to live and provide for Tania."

"You must be very pleased that you have been able to keep one instrument."

Andre nodded. "Although – although I was thinking only now that perhaps I am just a fool who clings to an object that no longer fulfils its real function. Just as I do not."

"Because you no longer play in public?"

He shrugged, and refused to meet her eyes.

"Andre, what is stopping you now? It's nearly three years since the war ended and you came to Yorkshire. Do you really believe that someone could force you to return to live in Russia?"

"I do not know. I do not think so. Only – life there still is so difficult. You know I have tried to bring my sister over to England?"

"I knew that you were trying to get somebody out. If you weren't able to I'm very sorry."

To her consternation, Andre's eyes were awash with tears which gradually spilled down both cheeks. He made no attempt to wipe them away.

"I could have brought her out. I had everything arranged, even transport for driving us to the coast from where we would take to the boat. She refused to come."

"Oh, dear." There was nothing more for Pam to say. All she could do was sit there, and ache with the need to hold him.

"I would have accepted Irena's decision if she were married, with someone to care for her, but the only man she ever loved died at Sebastopol in 1941. Since then she has been alone, conforming rather than seeking a better life here."

Pamela could feel his hurt, but found no way to help him bear it. "At least you tried, Andre."

"I was compelled to do so. My sister is younger than I. And I promised our mother when she was dying that I would always take care of Irena."

"And you risked your own life to make that attempt."

Suddenly Andre smiled slightly. "Not entirely for her good perhaps. I believed it would be all right if I had one more person here belonging to me. But who can say if I was correct to think that? I do not know any longer. One time I believed that bringing Tania here would be more than enough."

"But she's only a girl, isn't she? And although she's your daughter it's not the same as sharing your life with someone mature. I often feel the same when I'm working

233

all day long with Ian. At times I long for conversation with a real adult. And to have a bit of relief from feeling I must always be responsible." Pamela paused for a second, and then went on: "But, of course, that isn't quite the same – I do have my mother at home. And another brother who's an absolute angel, for a lad. Ian and I aren't thrust together on our own all the time."

Andre smiled again. "You understand. And now you have said your brother's name, and I am feeling awkward and embarrassed. Because I was discourteous to you. Will you forgive me, Pamela?"

"I suppose I have, or I wouldn't be here." She smiled back at him but then found she had to take a deep breath and muster her courage. "I'd better warn you, though, that I'm likely to annoy you again today. I have a request, Andre, not for myself. And I'm afraid that you're going to remind me yet again that this is none of my business."

"Tell it to me . . ."

Pamela swallowed and then inhaled deeply before beginning. This situation was demanding a lot of careful handling. "Your Tania has a magnificent voice, I can quite see why you wish her to save it for classical pieces."

"You heard her last evening?" The breath caught in his throat while he searched her face for assurance. "Was she really good?"

"Superb. I mean that sincerely. But she needs you, Andre."

"She has her new interests now, new friends, even new music."

"She's a young girl still, who needs your approval."

"Tania did not say so, never once did she ask me to attend."

"And you had, grudgingly perhaps, consented to her appearing there? Were you never a child yourself? Did

234

you never wish you possessed a little dignity which might be maintained by trying to treat your parents with disdain?"

Andre laughed, startling her with the suddenness of his reaction, and then he shook his head at her. "You are too clever, I think, or too determined. I am never quite certain. Tell me, though, did Tania ask that you come to me with this?"

"No. And nor did I say one word to her. She was disappointed enough without having me constructing false hopes."

"She knows I do not go out for social occasions."

It was Pamela's turn to laugh, but ruefully. "I should think no one who has met you over here could be unaware of that! But if you mean to keep to the habit, I can't help thinking you're in for one hell of a dull life!"

"There have been good times," Andre began reflectively. "Going to visit the Norton sisters. Walking in snow that reached almost to the bedroom windows here . . . I seem to require some encouragement if I am to venture beyond these walls."

"The concert was extremely well done. I'm sure I should be happy to sit through it again."

The hall was quite full when they arrived, but Pam had telephoned through to have tickets saved for them. When they had found their seats, she noticed Andre was gazing all about him, and then he turned to her.

"I hear you are to renovate this place before very long. There seems no limit to your capabilities."

Pamela laughed quietly. "So far! I think you'd better reserve judgement until I've at least started on the task. I might find this is the one that proves too daunting!"

"I think not. I believe that you always consider carefully what you are about. And you satisfied me, that is no easy task."

The houselights were fading and the chatter around

them ceased as the team of young instrumentalists walked on stage to take their places.

Seeing her brother through Andre's eyes, Pam noted how smart Ian appeared in the cream-coloured suit matched by his fellow-bandsmen. He was a tall young man, and personable if not exactly handsome. Later, when he rose to give his first solo, she saw that Andre nodded approvingly. That is something, she thought, and was glad that the influence which Ian had over Tania had not turned Andre against him.

"That was very tuneful," Andre murmured to her as applause surged through the hall.

Pamela smiled, reflecting that it was easier to approve if one was not too intimately involved.

When Tania at last appeared and started to sing, though, Andre soon revealed that he could not withhold his admiration. His grey eyes gleaming with tears, he nodded to himself over her phrasing, and seemed to hold his breath each time that she reached a high note.

Conscious that he was almost too moved to speak, Pam simply waited until the clapping had ceased and the next item began. Andre reached for her hand and squeezed her fingers until they were hurting.

"Bless you for insisting that I come."

When the show ended Ian came to whisk them away to the small celebration for band members, families, and close friends. Tania hugged Pamela as well as her father, making Pam feel that her intervention had brought her more good fortune than perhaps she deserved.

There was a great deal of laughter and chattering while snacks were served on the stage itself amid all the music stands. One or two of the players gave an impromptu few bars of a piece, and then suddenly Tania crossed for a whispered conversation with one of the young men who had been playing the trumpet. She faced them all then and raised a hand until they fell silent so that she might speak.

"I could not do this earlier," she said. "Because I did not know who was here. But for me this is a special day and I have my very special person with me."

Pamela recognised the introduction to *Oh Mein Papa* as soon as the trumpet began playing. Her own eyes moist, she scarcely dared to look at Andre while his daughter's voice took up the words.

As the last note hung in the air and then vanished, Pamela felt Andre tensing beside her, struggling to contain emotion. And then he very simply raised his fingers, kissed them and tossed the kiss towards his daughter.

After a while Tania came to sit beside them. "Thank you for letting me take part in this," she told Andre. "I promise that I will sing also all the things that you wish for me."

Andre pleased Pamela by saying that now that their differences had once again been bridged they must see each other more often. This time, at last, he did not disappoint her. True to his word, he telephoned one week later to suggest that she should join him at Stonemoor House for dinner that evening.

Tania was not at home, and Pam was surprised to learn that she had gone out with the young trumpeter who had accompanied her the previous Saturday. She herself had felt sure that something was developing between Tania and Ian. But she refused to worry over this latest news. They were all young enough to change these pairings several times before settling down.

"I am glad that we are alone," said Andre during their meal. "It is like the old days, is it not, and I wish that we should recreate the ease that once was established between us."

And so do I, thought Pam, but things have not remained quite the same. On too many occasions Andre had appeared indifferent to her. She would be thirty this year, a milestone which had caused her to consider the direction her life should be taking. She could not deny that she had been attracted to Andre from the start, that he was attracting her now while he sat across the table from her, but she had matured beyond being influenced too radically by desire.

All those years ago she had loved Jim, passionately and with all the eagerness induced by the newness of loving. There had been a great understanding between them also, the quality which makes relationships endure. These days, she had discovered fresh yearnings, for a family of her own, for a home. But she also recognised that she was no longer likely to be blinded by any of these achings for fulfilment. The hurt of Jim's death had by no means been the last injury to be inflicted. It almost seemed now that it was not necessarily the fiercest pain that she might suffer. Jim had died through an accident, and while travelling to be with her. Could she not be even more distressed by someone dear to her who simply chose to detach themselves?

And detached, distanced from her was so often the way that Andre seemed to be. She had known him too long to be able to delude herself that it was otherwise.

"I mean to see you quite regularly now," he continued today, as if he could have seen into her heart and become concerned about her many misgivings. "I hope you understand that."

With anyone else, Pamela might have been tempted to suggest that he should ascertain her wishes before assuming too much! Especially when she had been considering all the shortcomings. But Andre, with his quaint English and his foreign manner, should not be judged too keenly. And he was dear to her.

"I'm happy to give it a try," she said carefully while she felt delight rocketing through her. "We used to get on, didn't we?"

"And do we no longer?" Andre asked, and she saw in his eyes that he had anticipated more enthusiasm from her.

Pamela smiled. "I'm going to be honest with you. You've perturbed me in the past, with your secrets, your disappearances, and – yes, with your refusal to trust me with the truth of what you're doing. I'm afraid I shall need some time if I am to put all that behind me."

"But we are two mature people, my dear. Life is too short."

"Ah. And what are you going to do with your life, Andre? You can't tell me you intend sitting around here for the rest of your days."

"I was coming to that. I do not quite know how, but I intend to change things. I can bear no longer to play my violin only for myself. Or even the prospect of playing it only for you!"

"Then do something about that, Andre. And meanwhile I have a lot of work ahead of me, work that's going to be demanding, as I explained. I shall be happy to see you more often, as I say, but I'm afraid I'm not ready to set everything else aside."

Less than a month afterwards Pamela was beginning to wonder if she had been unduly hard on herself as well as on Andre by refusing to make any further commitment. Dorothy and Charles were married in a church ceremony that seemed all the more meaningful for being a quiet occasion, with Pamela as Matron of Honour but no other attendants. The pair suddenly appeared so serene that

Pam couldn't avoid envying them the security of a stable relationship.

Stability seemed particularly desirable while all around the world evidence grew of countless people whose lives remained disrupted. Only the other day a group of Czech exiles had arrived at Manston airport, reminding people over here of the hardship threatening now that Prague had adopted a Soviet-style constitution. The three years that had elapsed since the end of the war could hardly be thought to have induced much feeling of true peace. Although British troops had withdrawn from Palestine earlier in May with the birth of the new state of Israel, news coming in from other areas like Korea seemed to foreshadow problems.

Knowing Andre had brought home to Pamela the value of a homeland where its citizens, despite the shortages they still faced, possessed a great deal of freedom. Today, seeing her cousin and her closest friend making each other promises, she had realised that if she herself needed a staunch partner Andre must be even more in need of someone to turn to.

And I do love him, she thought in the car taking her to the wedding reception; that love has been growing for a very long time. I just wish that I wasn't so scared now – scared perhaps of at some time in the future having too much to lose.

She might have the guts to tackle work which could have daunted a man twice her size, yet she felt afraid now of giving her heart completely. And increasingly she was finding that her habitual remedy of throwing herself into the current job was failing to blot out the areas of her life which felt so unsatisfactory.

Working now on redecorating that hall, she was employing several people along with Ted Burrows and young Ian. Their questions and the planning which she must outline to them should be occupying her fully. And they were not. Surrounded by the sounds of these men at work, and applying her brain to her own daily tasks there, still allowed too much room for her mind to stray.

Andre had already auditioned for one of the big North of England orchestras and had exclaimed to her afterwards about his great good fortune. "I cannot believe how lucky I am, Pamela. I was prepared to accept if they gave me that post of Leader of the orchestra. When they heard me play a few pieces they offered instead for me to appear as soloist in a series of touring concerts."

These were not to take place until the commencement of the winter season several months away, but being booked to appear gave Andre heart to look ahead. Frequently now when Pam approached Stonemoor House she heard his violin, its strains reaching towards her on the balmy springtime air.

Charles and Dorothy were greeting everyone today on the top floor of the Southgate Café in Halifax, a reception as small as the gathering in the church, and totally informal. Dorothy's parents, Mr and Mrs Stubbs, appeared rather bemused, as did Charlie's mother whose new summer hat and costume made her look quite unfamiliar.

Pamela was missing Andre quite severely. This was her own fault, she supposed. He had not been invited for the simple reason that she had told no one of her true feelings about him.

Towards the end of the afternoon Dorothy drew Pam aside and confided something that seemed to explain her parents' air of distraction.

"I just wanted to thank you, love, for being there for me today. And to tell you summat, because I know you'll keep it to yourself. Me and Charles brought the date forward, you know, from later in the summer. We've told folk it was because we've got a house, but it wasn't only that."

"You're not . . .?"

"Aye – a couple of months gone. I made a clean breast of it to my mother, and now I wish I hadn't. But I'm not bothered for myself. I've known Charles that long, haven't I? I couldn't expect him to be patient for ever. Any road – now you know. Just don't hang on to too many folk, will you?"

Pamela was privately amused rather than dismayed on anyone's behalf. At thirty Dot was old enough to know what she was doing, and Charlie – well, he had waited a long time.

As spring turned to summer and Dorothy's pregnancy became more evident, Pamela tried to quell the envy that she felt. It wasn't a feeling that she'd ever condoned, and being fond of both Dorothy and Charles made her even more uncomfortable about her own emotions.

They had regularly invited her to their terraced house since the day that they returned from their brief honeymoon in Bridlington, but Pam was beginning to find excuses for not seeing them. For a time she had been glad that they were determined not to exclude her from their happiness. This was a definite sign that they both had chosen to overlook past awkwardness. Now, though, watching how Dot's radiance appeared to increase with every inch of her size was unbearable.

Pamela was feeling far older than thirty and blaming the amount of work she did for her perpetual tiredness. In her heart, though, she knew that unhappiness was creating her lethargy. Even the time which she spent with Andre felt to be tainted with her own dissatisfaction. And she didn't want to be like this. The trouble was that ever since Jim's death she had been willing herself to become more self-reliant. It seemed too late now to begin confiding in an effort to obtain the comfort for which she was aching.

And unfortunately, although Andre was the only person to whom she might turn, his home situation always created more problems than Pam felt she could face. Tania was now receiving singing lessons which continued roughly where her tuition in Russia had left off. She was complying only reluctantly with this and, because he was limiting her appearances with the band, was taking out her frustration on Andre.

At one time, Pamela would have been thankful when he turned to her for understanding but, somehow, being invited to support his opinions began to weigh heavily. And add to her own problems.

"It's not for me to say, is it?" she said wearily one evening when he expected her to sympathise because Tania had flounced out of the room when told to go and practise. "She's your daughter, love, and this is something you've got to sort out between you."

"But she simply does not realise that she needs to dedicate herself, instead of merely playing at singing."

"Are you certain that isn't what *you* need her to do, rather than what Tania herself needs?" Pamela asked. She was trying to be fair to both father and daughter, and could see that the girl should still have the enjoyment of being with other young people in the band.

His grey eyes darkening, Andre gave her a look. "You feel that I am too hard on her, no?" He shrugged. "If that is so, the cause is only my concern because she already has lost so much time. The voice, as with any musical talent, must be nurtured from an early age. Tania missed a great deal during the months when I was no longer there to supervise her training. Then there has been the period since her arrival in England. Again, more time that has been wasted."

"Okay, okay," said Pam. "I agree that you have your

243

reasons, but she's the one you should be explaining this to, not me."

Andre's desperation made him sound quite angry when he responded: "Does it count for nothing with you, that I need your support? That because you are the person with whom I would choose to share my life, I wish to have your help?"

Pamela managed a smile although his words were making her uneasy. Once, she would have been delighted just because Andre wanted her with him, but his reasons seemed to be all the wrong ones. She couldn't consider such an arrangement if it were motivated purely by his requiring someone on his side while coping with his daughter. She needed to be loved for her own sake.

"Of course I'm pleased that you feel like this about me, Andre, but I'm afraid you have to face the facts as they are. Quite frankly, there's not much prospect of anyone being happy, as things stand. Tania spends most of her time resenting my existence: enlisting my aid is only likely to turn her further against your plans for her."

Andre would not agree that this was so, and somehow his refusal to accept what Pamela saw as the unhappy truth made her all the more uneasy about their possible future together. It seemed to her that Andre, despite the very real danger and suffering which he had endured, had developed a rosy notion of the life they might have.

As far as Pamela was concerned, she could only visualise the prospect of ever living at Stonemoor House as thrusting herself into a great deal of protracted conflict. And that was something with which she could not cope. Especially if she remained unsure whether Andre really loved her, or simply wanted an ally when dealing with Tania.

The redecoration of the hall on which she was working suddenly was not going particularly well either, making

Pam wish that she had turned down the opportunity to tackle so huge a job. Although the shortage of materials still continued to create difficulties, the problems were in the main centred around the people she was employing.

Now that there were other men in the team, Ted Burrows appeared to have concluded that he ought to have been promoted to being foreman. Pamela, however, had been determined to control the work herself – a decision made chiefly because of this being the first task of this nature that she had tackled. The company was hers, and she wanted not only to organise the allocation of work but also to be the person who sorted out any problems.

Tom was becoming more morose by the week, and his discontent was infecting some of the others, among them several who already had indicated that they would prefer not to be employed by a woman.

Much of the dissatisfaction festered beneath the surface. Pam was conscious that many of the men, whilst resentful of her, were prepared to accept her as the boss rather than facing unemployment. The presence of Ian in the team, however, was having a twofold effect. Aware that he was her brother, they kept giving him digs about having his sister issue all the orders, and out of loyalty to her Ian reported at home every last detail of their discontent.

Tom alone seemed to sympathise when Pamela reeled from repeated accounts of the difficulties within her firm. "I wish I knew what to say to make you feel better," he said one evening. "Our Ian relishes a bit of bother, though, he always has. Happen things aren't so bad as he makes out."

Pamela smiled slightly. "Happen not. You'll be thinking you're well out of this, won't you?"

Her youngest brother shook his head. "Not necessarily. I like what I'm doing, but there's been times when I thought Ian had dropped lucky having you set him on. That was before I got my own job, mind you."

Tom had recently begun work with a local newspaper and was being given day release to study design at the technical college.

Mildred came in from the kitchen during the conversation and immediately expressed her opinion: "What did you expect, Pamela? Taking on such a big job was only inviting trouble!"

The fact that she herself had reached this conclusion already made it no more acceptable. Feeling upset because she was being denied the sympathy that she would have appreciated from her mother, Pamela let fly. Nothing would stop her, even when Tom sprang to his feet and left them to it by striding out of the room.

"I've only done what I thought was best, Mother. The firm was all I had left, wasn't it, after Jim died. And if I'm fed up now it's at least giving jobs to them men over yonder, and to our Ian. As a matter of fact, I wasn't really grumbling just now. If Ian would keep his trap shut instead of telling me every little moan and groan from that lot, I'd be able to save my energy for sorting them out!"

"You can't expect a lad his age to keep things to himself," Mildred retorted. "And, if you can't take it, happen it's a sign you ought to sell out."

"Sell out? Sell out?" How could her mother – even knowing nothing about business – believe she could do so now that she had spent every minute since the war ended building the company up! "I shall keep it going till the day I draw my last breath."

"That's up to you, of course," her mother said with a sniff. "I just wish I believed that would bring you a bit more happiness than it seems to do at present."

"It will, naturally," Pamela asserted. "On the whole, it's all very satisfying."

"I hope you're right," said Mildred, her voice suddenly losing every ounce of sharpness. "I hope it isn't hurting

246

you as much as it hurts me while I watch you eyeing the way Dorothy's filling out wi' that bairn she's carrying. I can't help remembering that it could have been you that was looking forward to having a family."

Pamela sighed. Aye, she thought, but it would never be Charlie that I would have for the child's father.

# Chapter Thirteen

If Pamela had agonised privately while her friend was so evidently pregnant, her distress then seemed insignificant alongside the emotions which surged through her after the child was born. Charlie called in to tell his Aunt Mildred of his son's arrival one Saturday lunchtime just as Pamela came in from work.

His eyes glowing with delight, Charles seemed more animated than ever in the past, and so elated that he could hardly stop talking.

"He was born at quarter to ten this morning," he announced. "And they let me see him a few minutes later."

"And how are they both?" Pamela enquired.

"Champion, thanks. At least – Dorothy's a bit tired, like. It seemed to take her a long time. We thought the lad were going to come yesterday, but it weren't to be. Still, she's got plenty of time to take things easy now. Her mother's stopping with us, you know. I went to fetch her as soon as things started moving. And my mother's going back with me now. To have a look at the baby. She was that excited when I told her it had come. That's why I can't stay here so long, only I wanted to let you know as soon as I could. Being as how you've allus been so good to me."

"And what are you calling him?" Mildred asked. "Have you chosen a name?"

Instead of replying at once, Charles turned to Pamela. "That's what I wanted to talk to you about. We thought James, and we'd like him to be Jim – just to show we haven't, well – forgot, like."

Pamela was compelled to clear her throat before she could manage to speak. "That's nice," she said. "A nice idea." But inwardly she felt disturbed more than delighted, however touched she might be. It was good of them, of course, to wish to remember Jim in this way, but she couldn't make herself wholeheartedly pleased. Perhaps she would be, in time. At present she felt perturbed more than anything. Deeply though she had been wounded by losing her husband, it was over three years since the accident, and preserving memories in such a lasting way seemed to her to equate with considering that she had no other future.

I can't go on like this, Pamela realised that night when she lay sleepless in her bed. There's just too much wrong with my life, and I've lost the knack of even beginning to put it right. Perhaps I need to get clean away from here. In London and other cities that had been blitzed and in the new towns that were being planned, decorators who could do more than just slap on a coat of paint and a bit of wallpaper would be required. She might find that by moving on she could extend herself more – tackle more interesting work than any attempted so far. By living elsewhere she would avoid all the emotional stresses here. Maybe she owed that to herself now.

On the day that she drove over to see Dorothy's infant, Pamela felt increasingly certain that going away was what she must do. She had steeled herself to put on a smile. She was pleased for Charlie and Dot, about their marriage and now about their son. Her own yearning which gnawed into her more intensely with every week that passed would not be permitted to mar anyone else's happiness. There was no way that Pamela Canning was going to go through life spoiling things for each friend or relative in turn as they produced a baby.

The boy was lying in his crib, an elaborate affair of highly polished wood set on rockers, with yards of fragile draperies prettying it in a way that Pam suspected could prove impractical. Dark eyelashes fanning out over pink-tinged cheeks while he slept, Jim possessed a mass of brown hair which contrasted with the white broderie anglaise on which it rested.

"Isn't he a love?" Dorothy exclaimed from the high double bed where she was leaning against her pillows. "I'll be feeding him before so long, you'll have to watch. He's a right greedy little beggar. Charlie laughs at the fierce way he sucks at me."

Pamela could think of nothing she would enjoy less than witnessing her friend's joy while she was feeding the infant. But she couldn't refuse to stay, she must not deny Dorothy any part of her satisfaction. Feeling trapped, she sat beside the bed where a chair had been drawn up to the crib in order that (so she was assured) visitors should have a good look at the baby.

Worse was to follow. Mrs Stubbs had shown Pamela up to the bedroom but had remained only for a few seconds. The two friends were alone with Baby Jim when he started to cry.

Dorothy beamed. "Be a love and pass him over to me, will you? Save me getting out of bed, I'm still quite sore."

"I'll fetch your mother," Pamela began awkwardly as she sprang to her feet. "I don't know anything about babies," she added, even while she was hating her own cowardice in refusing to hold the baby.

"Rubbish!" Dot contradicted. "You used to help with both your brothers, you know you did. Your mother was always bragging to mine how capable you were."

"Were, maybe," Pamela murmured, but was obliged to turn and lean over to lift Jim from his bed.

He opened his eyes as she did so and she saw they were less blue than she expected, almost grey. So grey that she could believe Andre's son might have eyes that same colour. That did it! Pam drew in a deep shuddering breath and swallowed hard, three times, before she could face her friend with any degree of composure.

"That's right," said Dot unconcernedly. "Have a really good look at him now he's awake. We want you to be his godmother, you know. In fact, both Charles and I are going to insist on it."

They were leaving her no room to manoeuvre, she was being walled in by their determination to share their lives. They could not see that this was not something that she could endure. Hastily, Pamela handed the infant across and looked away while Dorothy adjusted his position in her arms. None of this was their fault, of course; no one had ever been told of her longing for a child of her own, any more than they had heard of her love for Andre and all the pain that was causing her.

Bereft of the tiny babe, her arms felt chilled; his warmth and his weight, although so light, had somehow impressed themselves there. Pam felt as if her arms now would feel empty for ever.

"I think I'll just go down and have a word with your mum . . ."

"Don't you dare!" Dorothy threatened with a grin. "Dearly though I love this little mite, he's not much company as yet. I get bored out of my mind when he takes his time feeding."

"I thought you said he was greedy?"

"Aye, and he is, most of the time. Just now and again he'll keep dropping off to sleep instead of sucking. It's a funny sensation, you know, feeding him. Difficult to explain really . . ."

Don't try, Pamela willed her, just don't try. There are limits to what I can take. And I'm making a disastrous mess of all this.

The visit to Dorothy plagued Pamela for days, making her feel that she had let her friend down by failing to enthuse to the degree expected of her. Already sleeping badly, she found her nights more disturbed than ever as, even when she did sleep, dreams of holding a baby of her own tormented her.

The call from Andre came as an enormous relief four days later. They had been meeting regularly for some time now, usually at Stonemoor House although they did go out from there more than they had in the past. They walked a great deal, relishing the open countryside now that summer was with them, and occasionally eating out or stopping for a drink at a wayside inn. Very rarely, Tania was pursuaded into going with them and she seemed to enjoy outings when she might appear as adult as they themselves.

Since beginning her voice-training course, Tania had developed wider interests and conversed as intelligently as her father, when she was in the right mood.

Andre had been pleased when Pam remarked that his daughter was very like him intellectually. "I hope that is so," he said with a smile. "I once was afraid that our being apart had harmed her development. She will need sense and sensibility also if she is to travel the world as we hope when she begins to perform."

Arriving at his home this time, however, Pamela found that Tania was not there, and was interested to hear that her singing tutor had taken her to Manchester where an opera company was performing.

"I'm surprised you didn't want to go as well," Pam remarked.

Andre's grin made her think of one of her brothers when they elected to make an honest admission. "Oh, I wished to go there, all right. But I was not invited. And then afterwards I came to think that perhaps, after all, this is the way that it should be. I have been trying to encourage Tania to work at creating this new life for herself. Why should I now force my presence upon her? And besides – I think that it is very good for me to savour your company without distractions."

Pam snorted ruefully. "I don't know about that, Andre. I'm not very good company, these days."

"You must let me judge that. All I will say is that I have seen how something is distressing you. Something almost as terrible as the loss of your husband which made you so sad when first we knew each other. And now I am hurting because you no longer confide in me . . ."

Shaking her head despairingly, Pamela looked at him, at the kindness in his eyes which seemed shadowed by the way that she was fending off his concern.

"Oh, Andre – I don't know where to begin."

"Perhaps with the way you feel concerning this baby that has been given to your friend and your cousin . . .?"

"You weren't supposed to say that. No one's supposed to know!" The tears were coming, and she could do nothing, nothing at all to keep them back. Spilling down her cheeks, they began dripping off her chin, splattering on to her hands.

Andre took her into his arms and let her weep. Holding her to him, he remained motionless except for the fingers that began ceaselessly to caress her hair and the back of her neck in wordless understanding.

It felt to her like hours before she was finally able to command a small degree of composure and dry away her tears. And it seemed somehow as though the time they had spent so near to each other had altered their relationship. Friendship between them had been well established, affectionate, but only today with the despatching of all barriers had she begun to believe that no one else had ever been closer to her.

Andre smiled as he released her. "Better?" he enquired gently.

Pamela nodded. "Except for feeling a fool! I ought to have got over this years since."

"Why should you have? You are young enough yet to have several children."

"But . . ."

"But you cherish your independence? Do not think that I have failed to recognise – and to admire – your ability to carve out your own career. Having babies, however, is one thing which you can not achieve alone. I think that one day you should think very carefully about the future, about what it must become for you . . ."

Although at the time Andre's words and indeed his concern for her seemed encouraging, as soon as Pamela returned to her own home she discovered they had disturbed as much as reassured her.

Andre still hadn't spoken the words that would have made everything all right. Despite his evident understanding, he had said nothing now to indicate that *he* wished to be the one to give her children. She had hoped that he might have reminded her that they could make a life together. Instead, he had carefully avoided any such suggestion. It seemed to her that he regretted ever mentioning such an idea. And now she knew beyond doubt that she would never settle for marriage to anyone else.

Pamela blamed herself. When previously discussing the future she had expressed more reservations than any man could be expected to accept. She had emphasised how

255

much she still needed to achieve. And not long ago she had hung back, still looking for some assurance of his loving her, when he had declared of his need of her assistance with Tania. She'd been a fool not to enthuse simply because the prospect seemed to fall short of being perfect. Had she still to learn that life is far from perfect, and settling for what is offered is the best option?

Throughout the summer her dread of the future persisted, until it began to spoil the occasions when they were together, creating an edginess that made Pam suspect that they were being driven apart.

At least I can be completely thankful about this evening, Pamela thought while getting ready to drive over to Manchester for Andre's first postwar public appearance.

The concert hall was already half-full when she arrived, and the anticipation in the air all around her increased her own excitement. In recent weeks while rehearsing at home Andre had refused to allow her to be present, insisting instead that he preferred to surprise her.

Privately, Pam expected to be unsurprised by his performance. She had heard how beautifully Andre played, so evocatively that even to her untrained ears his music was wonderful.

He was to perform two solos, a Tchaikovsky concerto in D Major during the first half, and in the second the Paganini concerto for violin and orchestra.

When the orchestra eventually took their places and began on the first of the two pieces that were to precede Andre's appearance, she settled into her seat and tried to force herself to concentrate on their performance. Fortunately, the entire programme was popular enough for her to appreciate its content and Pamela soon forgot how limited her knowledge of classical music was.

It was, nevertheless, for Andre that she had come here and only when he walked on to the platform did her excitement soar. His white shirt brilliant against the black of his formal clothes, Andre looked magnificent, more attractive than ever she recalled. His own sense of anticipation appeared electrical to her, evident in the way he moved and in the momentary pause before setting the violin in place. Perhaps the quality of the Stradivari contributed, but to Pam it seemed that the exquisite purity of the sound emerging was due entirely to Andre's mastery of the instrument. He conjured and cajoled music from those strings, such perfection that she felt tears springing to her eyes.

As the final notes soared above them and vanished, applause broke out on every side of her. She had needed no confirmation of her own approval of his playing, but was glad for his sake that the audience members were united in their massive acclaim.

The piece Andre performed towards the end of the programme was, if possible, even more thrilling. Pamela gazed and gazed at him, awed by the music he was creating, and knowing without the least trace of uncertainty that she loved this man and needed to be a part of him. By the time everyone around her was releasing yet another surge of clapping she was feeling quite weak from the effort of suppressing emotion.

Tania was in the audience with a group of friends. When they met at the end of the performance Pam was surprised to see her own brother among them.

"I didn't know you were coming here tonight, Ian. You never said."

"And nor did you!" he exclaimed and grinned. "I just thought I'd have you on a bit by turning up."

They talked for a while after Tania introduced her friends, most of whom were from the academy where she was being trained. Pamela was delighted that the girl was wholeheartedly appreciative of her father's performance, but was less pleased on his behalf when the youngsters were not prepared to wait and meet Andre.

"We're off to a club while we're over here," Ian confided.

"Oh, aye – and does Mum know that?" Pamela enquired.

"I don't suppose so. But I am old enough to look after myself by now."

"Well, if you're the one who's supposed to be looking after Tania, just see that you do," she warned him. "Andre's had enough to worry about in the past, there's no excuse for causing him needless anxiety now."

Anxiety seemed the very last feeling affecting Andre when he eventually met her as arranged at the stage door. Elation showed in the gleam of his eloquent grey eyes and in the liveliness of his step as he began walking at her side away from the concert hall.

"You were splendid," Pamela told him at once. "I loved every second of both pieces, and you must have realised that the entire audience loved them too."

He turned and smiled at her. "But of course I recognised that. No performer can say honestly that he is unmoved by audience response. And I have to admit that I myself felt the concertos went well."

"You've certainly every reason to be satisfied."

"Did you come here in the van?" he asked suddenly, making Pamela look curiously at him.

"Well, yes. Why do you want to know?"

Andre's smile grew wider. "I wish to travel home with you, if you agree. I came here in a hired car, and had reserved an hotel room, intending to remain in Manchester tonight. Now that I am with you I know that I shall not stay here. The hotel is only around the

258

corner a short distance from here, if we might collect my overnight things?"

They set out afterwards through Oldham as far as Denshaw where they turned off towards Milnrow in order to take the Littleborough road and head out over Blackstone Edge. The route was anything but direct but neither of them cared. Pamela was too happy for wishing the night to end, and Andre was only slowly descending from the high that had been generated that evening. He had received a rapturous approval for his return to the concert platform, success equalled only by having satisfied his own meticulous standards.

Soon after getting into the little van he had apologised for his need for quiet. "You must not think me unappreciative of all that you have done by being with me this evening. Your presence warms my heart as nothing can."

"Sometimes there aren't any words," Pam had murmured. And then had felt him grasp her arm, mute acknowledgement of her understanding.

Andre asked her to stop the van high on the moor where Yorkshire met its Lancashire neighbour and their road converged with the one leading down towards Stonemoor House.

Around them the autumn night was beautiful, spellbinding, with a moon teasing the scudding clouds, defying their efforts to conceal its light. Distant dark rocks loomed on the horizon, and each time that the moon emerged it reflected back from the nearby reservoir's surface as it was rippled by the breeze.

"We have to talk," Andre began softly. "My soul is too full for withholding my feelings for one day longer. This was not the way I intended it should be, but emotions do not always linger for the perfect situation. Indeed," he concluded, his tone wry, "it could be that no perfect situation may be found."

259

Andre paused then and reached for her hand, and drew the glove from it to begin caressing her fingers. "I love you too much, my Pamela, too much for waiting. I had it all planned. I was to apply to be naturalised . . ."

"But there's no need, Andre." She knew how much his White Russian heritage mattered to him.

"There is every need," he contradicted. "You will please hear me out. I did not wish that you should ever believe that I might have proposed marriage to you in order to remain here, in your country. And so I would have chosen to take first of all your nationality. But that ideal was conceived before I made that fruitless journey in the attempt to bring my sister over to England." Andre sighed, fell silent, but only for a moment.

"After that I knew that there would be further attempts, future occasions when I must return to Russia to try and persuade her, and try also maybe to bring others of my family to this country. If I were to surrender my own nationality it would become, I fear, yet more difficult to make such journeys. And so, my dearest love, I am asking that you accept me as I am – and swiftly, for I no longer can endure our separations. I will share with you my life, my whole self. This night has given me courage to offer that, for you have seen that – just a little – I am recovering the person who existed so long ago before the war."

"I knew tonight that we belong, Andre, that I want to be a part of you."

"And so? Did my music speak . . .?"

Pam nodded, pressed his hand to her face. "It spoke of something I barely comprehend, but it's found in beauty and peace, in hope, in reaching towards infinity."

"The hope that forces us to endure. It was all I had, you know, when I trudged for endless weeks only to be tossed ceaselessly in that wretched tiny boat until . . . until. But I did not quite give up. Just as you, my brave love, did

260

not surrender to grief. This is our new beginning, Pamela. *Our* life where, please God, I shall give you everything you want."

"I only want you. That is all, really."

"That is not quite so," he contradicted gently. "Tomorrow, you will remember. And in our future tomorrows we shall see *our* home come alive with children."

They made love that night, tenderly at first, but then with increasing passion as their yearning finally found expression. For the first time in years Pamela felt utterly contented, too happy to worry about anything.

Now that she and Andre had confirmed their love for each other, she could put up with a certain amount of conflict elsewhere. As soon as they had reached Stonemoor House she had telephoned her mother to explain that she would be staying the night there.

Mildred had been less than enthusiastic. "Oh aye? And I suppose you're alone there with him? Our Ian's just rung up to say he's stopping over in Manchester with Tania and her pals."

Is he indeed? thought Pamela. "And aren't you anxious about him?" she asked.

"Of course. I'm a mother, aren't I? But he's a lad, it's different for him."

"Oh, Mum! I'm a grown woman. Don't you think that perhaps you might give me credit for a bit of gumption? I'm not doing anything stupid, you know. You really can stop being so concerned, love. Everything's going to be all right."

Despite Mildred's misgivings, Pamela had decided that it was high time that she allowed her own heart to dictate her actions. When Andre asked her to remain at Stonemoor until Monday morning she could not refuse. Again, her mother was perturbed when Pamela rang to tell her. This time, though, it did sound as if she was developing a degree of understanding about their situation.

"Oh, well – he must be treating you right, or you'd not be wanting to spend so much time over there. Happen I've been a bit hard on you before. And I've been thinking – life can be tough on your own. I'd not want you to be left like me for ever."

Pamela was glad that she and Andre had decided that her mother should be the first to be told their news. All the way back to Halifax that Monday she was looking forward to sharing their happiness with her.

"I'm getting married, Mum," she declared the minute she walked into her old home.

Mildred left the week's washing and came to the kitchen door drying her hands. "That's good, love," she responded calmly. "When?"

Pamela laughed. "I don't know that yet! And you haven't even asked who I'm marrying."

Her mother smiled. "It had better be him, Andre What's-it. You've been fascinated with him for long enough."

As Mildred rushed to hug her, Pam grinned. "You seem to know as much about it as me!"

"Well, it's taken you so long, hasn't it? Making up your mind."

Pamela nodded. "Aye, it's not been so straightforward. But I think it's going to help now Andre's working again. But there's his daughter, you know, winning her round is not going to be easy."

"She'll be very possessive of her father, I suppose."

"You're not kidding."

"It's only to be expected, with them being separated in the past. And losing her mother like that." Mildred gave her daughter's shoulders a squeeze. "Don't let the young

262

lass spoil your happiness now, think on. You and Andre have as much right to be happy as she has. When am I going to meet him then?"

"As soon as you want. I'd certainly like to see the two of you together."

"And the girl as well, mind. I've nobbut had that brief glimpse of her, have I? She gets on with our Ian all right, doesn't she? And I couldn't help but notice young Tom was smitten as soon as he set eyes on her after the concert."

On the day that Andre had been invited to bring Tania over to Halifax, Pamela spent the morning feeling anxious. Her own home was so tiny compared with Stonemoor House, she was afraid neither Andre nor his daughter would have ever seen anywhere smaller. And if he would refrain from remarks that could hurt her mother, Tania would not. Tania would say whatever came into her mind regardless of its potential for causing harm.

Mildred was putting on a high tea, and seemed to be enjoying having a reason for creating a bit of a spread. She had spent the previous day baking buns and cakes, and today was preparing a salad and assembling an assortment of cooked meats that belied the factor of continued rationing.

Pamela's assistance had been declined, leaving her feeling restless with too little to occupy her. She could think of nothing but the hours ahead. She so wanted Andre and Tania and her own people to get on.

At last, however, Tania and her father arrived in the car that he had hired and Pam opened the door to them, feeling overwhelmed with a curious mix of delight and awkwardness in equal proportions.

Her mother beamed as she was introduced, and hugged first Andre and then his daughter. Pam smiled to herself as she noticed that Andre seemed astonished but pleased.

263

Tania smiled up at Mildred and made no attempt to ease away from her. "You remind me of my grandmother, do you know that? I thought that when I first met you. The mother of my mother, I mean. She was warm always like you, I think."

"Eh, bless you, love, that's nice!" Mildred exclaimed. "I'm right glad we're going to get on. Since our Pam grew up, I've longed to have a young lass round me again. There's too many lads in this house at times!"

"Thank you very much, Mum," Ian exclaimed, and stepped forward to greet Tania and Andre.

Tom hung back slightly, but was quickly drawn into the group and soon appeared less awed by Tania's beauty than fascinated with all that she had to say. Pamela was pleased when the young people began chatting immediately, leaving her free to ensure that Andre and her mother developed a good understanding.

Mildred clearly intended that this would be achieved right from the start. "Pam's told me a lot about you," she began, as she offered a cup of tea the minute she had invited him to be seated in one of her armchairs. "I feel as if I know you already, but there'll be gaps to fill in. You mustn't mind if I ask a lot of questions."

Pamela wondered how Andre would react. He wasn't exactly accustomed to revealing very much about himself. Andre surprised her, nevertheless, by smiling back at her mother.

"I shall tell you all that I can. I wish for you to be as happy about this marriage as I am. And, indeed, as I intend that your daughter shall be."

Mildred nodded. "I gather that your wife died, was it a long time since, love?"

"In 1945, just as the war in Europe was ending. She was shot, as we were trying to get out of Russia."

"Eh, dear – I am sorry." Mildred reflected for a few

264

moments. "Well, as you probably know, Pam lost her husband the day before VJ Day, she understands how cruel life can be. And has Tania been with you ever since?"

Andre shook his head. "No. I knew too little about where I was heading, and how I should make the journey. Bringing her out at that time was too great a risk. I left her with close friends of mine."

"You would miss each other a lot, especially after a loss like that."

It was Tania who replied, looking towards them from the table where she was sitting with Ian and Tom. "I was dreadfully afraid that my father also would be killed. I must admit that I behaved very badly, refusing to listen to anyone when they told me how he would make his way safely to England, and create a home for me here."

"That's understandable," said Pamela, and wished with all her heart that she had established a better relationship with the girl from the beginning.

Although Tania smiled in her direction, Pam remained unsure that the sympathy she was feeling now would make any substantial difference.

Andre, however, sounded optimistic when he spoke. "Now that Pamela has agreed to marry me, we shall all be happier than we believed possible. Your daughter has made Stonemoor House so beautiful . . ."

Mildred grinned as she interrupted him. "I dare say she has, I just wish she'd do summat about this place. There's an old saying, you know, about a cobbler's bairns being poorly shod. You've only to look at this room to see Pam hasn't spared any time for slapping new wallpaper on these walls!"

Pamela felt her cheeks flushing, even though Andre was merely reacting with a smile. She didn't want him to believe that she had neglected her family. "You should have said, Mum. I didn't know you wanted anything doing."

Mildred laughed. "I'm only pulling your leg, love. Take no notice."

"You don't need to bother her, not now," Ian asserted. "She's not the only person that can do decorating. Just tell me what you want, and I'll see to it."

"Listen to him!" his brother exclaimed. "You'd never think to hear him that he was the one that took ages to put his mind to a job."

"Less of that, you two," said Mildred quite sharply. "We're not having any fratching today." If discussion of Ian's earlier career continued too many uncomfortable details might emerge.

She need not have worried, Tom was far more keen to interest Tania in his own career. He had brought out his course work from the technical college, and was beginning to show her the designs that he had recently completed.

"These are very good, I think," Tania remarked, studying them closely before she turned aside to Ian. "I hope you are asking Tom to design advertising material for the band?"

"What – him?" Ian shook his head. "Happen he could do us something cheap though . . ."

The banter between the brothers continued amicably enough while Pamela, Andre and her mother began discussing arrangements for the wedding. Andre was determined that this must be soon, an idea which Pamela upheld. She was certain at last that she wanted this marriage more than anything, but she needed it to go ahead before she became daunted by any further misgivings.

Today, Tania seemed affable and ready to make everyone warm to her, but Pam had seen too much to believe the girl would become an ideal stepdaughter. I am going to have to be patient, she thought, and most of all I am

266

going to need Andre's ring on my finger before I begin to feel assured that I can make us all happy.

Even as the afternoon passed and Tania continued to put herself out to enchant her family, Pam still felt reservations preventing her from being totally relieved. The girl could behave well, but how much of that today was due to earlier warnings issued by her father?

Whatever her own reservations, Pam was delighted that her mother seemed to have taken Tania to her heart. The girl had admired Mildred's cardigan and soon was being shown patterns, and receiving promises that she would be taught to knit, a craft which her own mother had never had the opportunity to teach her.

Andre turned to Pamela and smiled. "You have a lovely family, my dearest. I am so very happy that we are all to be united."

Tea was a lively meal, with Ian and his brother vying with each other to provide Tania with every attention, while Mildred's inborn Yorkshire hospitality ensured that Andre lacked nothing. Pamela began to relax. Perhaps this rather unlikely union of theirs would be less problematic than she had feared.

While she was driving Andre and his daughter back to Stonemoor House at the end of the evening, Pam reached a decision which, she felt sure, would help to confirm her own affection for Tania. If the girl needed reassurance that she would always have a special place with them, she should have that from the start.

"I'm only having one bridesmaid, Tania love," she announced as the three of them went indoors at Stonemoor. "And I want that to be you. I hope you'll say yes."

The slightest, briefest, of smiles enhanced Tania's pretty features, and vanished. She shrugged slender shoulders.

"Perhaps," she responded coldly. "I shall have to check if I am due to perform anywhere . . ."

267

"Tania," Andre reproved her sharply, but the girl had already reached the foot of the staircase and was beginning to run from them.

Andre made as though to catch her up, but Pamela grasped his arm and shook her head.

"Let her go," she said. "She'll either be my bridesmaid willingly or I shan't have one. Either way, we're not going to have this blow up into a major difficulty."

But the trouble is, she reflected, I can think of no means of preventing the girl from becoming precisely that!

# Chapter Fourteen

Pamela had chosen her outfit for the wedding, a dress in a delicate shade of blue. The material itself was less delicate, a finely woven wool which should provide some necessary warmth for a Yorkshire day in late October. And if its longer, very full skirt was a concession to the romance of the occasion, the wrist-length sleeves and high crossover neckline contributed their own practicality. The fashionably rounded shoulders and its asymmetrical draping provided quite enough new ideas for her, especially when years of enforced economy had schooled her to consider every garment's future possibilities. In selecting shoes with peep-toes and slingbacks she had reacted against the sensible wedge heels that had been around for so long, but had made certain that they would be useful throughout the following summer.

"*You* could have something more glamorous – you'll have plenty of opportunities for wearing a beautiful gown afterwards on the concert platform," she told Tania.

Pam was trying one last time to persuade her future stepdaughter to attend her. She had gathered that Andre had tried ordering Tania to comply and then, after ordering had failed, had tried coaxing her. Neither method had succeeded, and now Pamela herself had overcome her own resolution to say nothing further on the matter. She wanted to ensure that nothing marred Andre's wholehearted happiness on the day.

"You're a lovely girl, Tania. I want you there in the church, for everyone to see that the three of us are becoming a new family. I know it can't be the same, not for any of us, and there's no way that I would even think of trying to replace your mother . . ."

Glancing across the room, she saw that Tania had turned from the window where she had been staring out at the landscape while an autumnal wind straight off the moors was lashing a deluge towards a distant farmhouse. The girl shivered. She was biting her lip and blinking rapidly, her fair head held erect with determination not to weep.

"It is – it is not that," said Tania huskily.

"Come and sit down – here, by me . . ."

To her surprise, the girl began walking towards her. Pam swiftly pushed aside lists which she had been preparing.

"What is it then, if not that you're frightened I'm intent on taking your mother's place?"

At first when Tania sat beside her she merely shrugged, but then a massive sigh emerged from the girl, a sigh which seemed to have been hauled from the very depths.

Pam laid an arm across her shoulders. "I'm not going to take your Dad away, you know. He's not going to think any less of you through making room for me in his life."

"You don't know that. Nobody can know."

"Eh, Tania love, is that what's worrying you?"

"He's all I've got, isn't he? Isn't he? The only person in all the world."

"I loved my father a very great deal as well," Pamela began softly. "And he died. I was only a young lass at the time. I thought my heart would break when I began to understand that he wouldn't be there any longer. I couldn't take it in at first, the accident in the factory. I didn't want to accept that we'd never

270

laugh together again, or sit and read a book, or go for a walk."

Tania had begun weeping, but still Pamela continued, aching and hurting while she spoke, as though the loss were recently delivered.

"We'd got on that well together, me and my father. Mum was always busy after Ian was born and Tom a couple of years afterwards. I think Dad sensed that with two brothers I could feel rather left out; he tried to make it up to me." Pamela paused, sighing. "I think if I'd had a sister I'd have got over losing my father a bit. If I had had one – a sister, I mean, she might have been like you. Very like you."

"Grumpy?"

The very English word in Tania's accent sounded odd, making Pam smile although tears were clouding her eyes.

"Come to think of it, that's just how I was for a long time after Dad died. He'd been really gentle with me, and kind with everybody."

"But your mother is the same," Tania reminded her.

"I know, I know," Pamela agreed, remembering one of the good things that had come out of introducing Tania to her family. "In those days, though, she was too busy for making a fuss of me. Tom and Ian needed a lot more of her attention. And she was taking in washing to help make ends meet . . ."

"Make ends . . .?" Tania asked, not understanding.

"Oh – you know, to bring in a bit more money. She was always a hard worker, my mother, bless her."

"I think perhaps that is why she reminds me of my grandmother. They had a tiny farm, before the state compelled them to join with others."

Tania became silent then, remembering, and Pamela felt excluded again, and perturbed. Tania and her father had left behind them such a very different life, one which she could only imagine. She felt alarmed by her own lack of ideas concerning the way that all these differences and difficulties might be bridged.

Just as she was beginning to feel terribly inadequate and inept Tania's voice interrupted her thoughts.

"Could – could I stay with your mother while you and my father go away?"

"Go away? We're not going anywhere, we'll always all three of us be here at Stonemoor House."

"No," Tania insisted. "You must go for a honeymoon, all new couples do that."

"Not always. It doesn't have to be that way. Since the war, while money's been tight, lots of folk have just gone home afterwards."

Tania shook her head. "That would feel strange, I think. But I should be happy to live with your mother for a week or more. If she will have me."

"I'm sure she'd be delighted. You could go home with her and the lads straight after the reception."

They were holding the reception here at Stonemoor House: Andre's idea which had pleased Pamela when he declared he must show off his new bride's talent as a decorator.

"What colour dress do you think I should have?"

"Tania! Oh, you little love! You shall have whichever dress you like best. And if your father says it's too extravagent, I'll foot the bill. You're going to be happy that day, I'll see to that. Now that you've delighted me by saying yes."

"You must help me choose something, I think. I do not believe my father has much knowledge of women's clothes."

They spent a whole day in Manchester, a day when Pamela might have been busy with one of her many lists. She was so afraid of getting something wrong that she had been writing lists since the day that she and Andre had fixed the date of the wedding. Mrs Singer had insisted that she would cater for the event, but needed advising on quantities of the necessary provisions. As well as noting details of those, Pam constantly was updating the list of guests and trying to write down everything that she must bring with her when moving out of her mother's home.

The visit to Manchester was fun, nevertheless, and vital in the way it introduced fresh understanding between herself and Tania. They did, indeed, seem much like sisters as they went from one large store to the next and into smaller elegant shops. Tania tried on innumerable gowns, some more suitable than the rest, but all in lovely materials. Neither she nor Pamela would accept that she must wear one of the dreary "sensible" garments that had become synonymous with the "utility" marking.

After much giggling and feverish deliberation, Tania settled for an ankle length gown of artificial silk. It was quite low cut, with tiny sleeves, but had a matching stole which rendered it more suitable for a wedding. The material was gold coloured with a scattering of flowers which predominantly were blue, and linked with the shade that Pam would be wearing. The gleam of gold emphasised Tania's glossy hair, and made her look every one of her eighteen years if not older.

"Your Dad's going to be so proud of you," Pamela told her as they hurried back to the house.

"If he notices me that day," Tania began, but grinned when Pam gave her a warning look.

Andre's emotions were barely under control when he stood in the stark interior of St Paul's church as the organ

273

began playing and he listened to the footsteps approaching. He had yearned for this day, yet had awakened to a gnawing sense of apprehension. If he could, he would have changed so much for Pamela's sake. He knew his daughter, and the malleable adult-seeming Tania accompanying them today could swiftly become the irrational young madam who so frequently infuriated him. Marriage was difficult enough, especially a second marriage, and he had no intention of seeing this one jeopardised by his daughter.

Her attitude towards Pamela often had been inexcusably awful, making him long to slap the girl whose elegant appearance regularly contrasted with unlovely behaviour. He had seen how Pamela had been hurt by her in the past, and could only imagine that future jibes would hit home all the harder.

They were nearing him now, his bride on the arm of her youngest brother. He gave them a sideways glance and felt the lump rise at his throat when he saw Pamela's eyes smiling, eyes enhanced by the blue of her gown. Behind them Tania appeared tall and erect, slender and shining, and smiling as if to convince everyone of her good intentions. Perhaps, after all, he had been right to hope for a happy outcome.

Beside him, Ian gave a tiny nudge, urging him towards the rest of the party. Ian, who had insisted that he must be his Best Man; for who else could be relied upon to see him through this strange ceremony?

Andre had been touched that the young man liked him well enough to insist, and was touched now that these warm Yorkshire folk had taken him to their hearts. He himself had not made that easy, he knew, not even easy for his bride whom he had perplexed so many times since the day that he had met her.

"Dearly beloved . . ." the service began, and Andre

274

heard those words again and again, echoing through his head while other words, those which he and Pamela had studied together, flowed around them.

He made his vows unfalteringly, surprising himself with the firmness of his own voice, for this English tongue had felt more strange today than ever since coming to England. Then Pamela was committing herself to him, promising even to obey – a curious pledge, Andre thought, while he felt that he so often was the one uncertain of what was right in this land he had adopted.

Hearing her voice, feeling her touch while placing his ring on her finger restored to him complete awareness. Through his earlier confusion of impressions she brought Andre to acute attention and a full understanding of what they were promising. And now every word was going to his heart where he knew it would be savoured for years to come.

He was no longer alone, no longer a solitary man who struggled to give a better life to his daughter, and felt for much of the time more bewildered than he dared admit. And the woman becoming his this day was the one who had recreated a soul within him. Just as she had regenerated his home – would continue to regenerate his home, and with more than exquisite embellishments.

The time came to kneel and be blessed, to have their union granted Divine approval. Andre went to his knees with a full heart, and in the certainty that his own sincere longing for renewal was ensuring that they would be given the means for preserving this joyfulness which suddenly enveloped him.

For too many years he had been denied the right to worship the God of his forefathers: on this special day he was beginning to sense that he was committing himself to more than this earthly marriage. Not only would they neither of them be alone, they would never be lacking in guidance.

Their guests were divided evenly to either side of the central aisle. As soon as they turned at the end of the ceremony Andre saw that Pamela had made sure that the absence of his own relatives and friends would not be evident. Andre smiled sideways at her, placed a hand over hers where it rested on his arm. Behind them, the organ was failing to obliterate the sound of Tania chattering to Ian. The unmistakable hiss of Mildred's reproach reached him.

Pamela turned to him and winked. "Did you hear Mum, telling them off? She wants to be thankful that Tania's turned out for us!"

"I certainly am thankful," Andre murmured seriously.

"Me and all, love, me and all!"

Pamela relished being alone with him in the Rolls Royce bearing them off towards Stonemoor House. She had thought Andre's insistence on hiring a Rolls extravagent, perhaps even ostentatious. Today, however, she was glad of the glass screen separating them from the driver. She had felt more conspicuous than she liked throughout the ceremony, beautiful though it had been. Wishing everyone to witness her total commitment to Andre hadn't been quite the same as revelling in having a large congregation. And the church had seemed astonishingly full when she began that slow walk down the aisle.

"I have a surprise for you at the house," Andre told her, the light in his grey eyes revealing that he was, for once, too elated to keep this a total secret until their arrival.

Her own eyes full of amusement as well as love, Pamela smiled back at him. "You mustn't tell me any more," she insisted. "And you don't need to. Nothing could make me happier than I am at this moment."

He kissed her then, deeply and passionately, making her wish away the hours in order to be really alone with him. But then she felt immediate guilt – this was

276

their day, each minute was to be savoured, preserved in memory to carry them into the future. And they were going away this evening, first of all up into Wharfedale, from where they would travel on to the Lake District. She had spent several hours sprucing up her little van. For weeks now she had been trying to persuade Andre to take up driving again, but although he had driven extensively in Russia he seemed unenthusiastic about tackling British roads.

The way through Cragg Vale was especially lovely with autumn sunlight enhancing the russet and gold of nearby trees and, on the slope of the meadows, the brilliant green produced by recent rain.

Stonemoor House came into view, and appeared in some way different – familiar as ever, yet strangely new because of her part-ownership. But there was no time to reflect: there, before the front steps was Andre's gift to her.

"You haven't!" she exclaimed and then: "You shouldn't have . . ."

Andre laughed. "Then *I* shall have it. I have wished always to drive such a beautiful car."

The moment their chauffeur halted Pamela opened the door and rushed out and across to admire the Wolseley that Andre had bought for her.

"Thank you, thank you!" she exclaimed and turned to hug him.

She was kissing him still when the first of their guests arrived, her mother and brothers who, after being invited to admire her bridegroom's gift, were ushered into the house.

Amid all the excitement Pamela had forgotten that this was Mildred's first visit. She was entirely unprepared for the gasp of amazement and the delight with which her mother approved her work.

"But this is beautiful, Pam love, I never dreamed it'd be anything like as grand as this!"

In a kind of daze Mildred walked through the entrance hall, gazing from side to side, until she reached the open door of the dining room. She hesitated slightly, glancing back to them. "Is it all right if I . . .?"

"Of course," Andre assured her, stepping forward to take her by the arm and conduct her into the room.

Rather bemused, Pamela followed. Her mother's smile was of someone entranced, and tears were spilling down over her cheeks. "Eh, I wish your Dad could see what you've done here. He'd be that thrilled . . ."

Pamela herself was thrilled by her mother's reaction. Nothing could have delighted her more than this unreserved admiration of her craftsmanship. This, surely, confirmed that Mildred no longer had any doubts that her daughter had been right to forge ahead with her career. But others were arriving already, headed by Tania who came rushing in to find Pamela's mother. Seeing tears on her face, she immediately misinterpreted the cause, and slipped an arm around her.

"You're not really losing Pamela very far, are you? And you have me now. I hope that my room is ready for tonight."

Tania continued to behave immaculately, pleasing both Andre and Pamela when they noticed how she helped to ensure that friends and family were made to feel welcome. Mrs Singer was being assisted by staff engaged for the day to work in the kitchen or to serve the extensive buffet meal, but Tania was keeping a watchful eye on everything. Moving from one person to the next and smiling constantly, she was offering more wine or pointing out appetising dishes for all the world as if she were an experienced hostess.

"She's a credit to you today, my love," Pamela told

Andre. "Nobody could fault her on anything." Tania couldn't have found a happier means of contributing to the occasion.

Relieved of concern regarding the catering arrangements, the pair felt relaxed and were free to wander from group to group. One introduction was closely followed by the next, as Andre met innumerable people who over the years had mattered to Pamela. If he was perturbed because of having only Tania present from his own family he gave no sign, and proved to be more gregarious than Pam had supposed he might be with strangers. And Hilda and Sophie Norton were present. They had been among the first guests to be invited, and seemed to relish all the excitement.

They themselves had created excitement with their gift which had been delivered the previous day. Both Pamela and Andre had been overwhelmed to received a longcase clock from the sisters. Today, thanking them earnestly, they began to learn something of its history.

"It's always been at Stonemoor House, and our niece said it was too big for her tiny place so it has had to be in store since we left here," Hilda confided.

"We're content that it's back in its home now," Sophie went on. "And it's a Halifax clock, by Thomas Ogden; we just know you'll always take care of it."

"We shall indeed," said Andre. "Especially now that we are learning it was made locally."

"You might be able to discover exactly how old the clock is," Hilda continued after Pam had added her appreciation to her husband's. "All we really know is that it's even older than the house."

"Thomas Ogden died in 1769," Sophie told them. "The only other thing we're sure of is that it was called a Halifax clock because it was there that makers reintroduced this moon which you see through the aperture in the arch here.

I believe that originally showing the moon like this was a Dutch idea."

"I shall find out all I can," Pamela told them, smiling. "And we will keep you up to date with anything fresh that we discover. I've always loved clocks, they seem to be alive – with the way that there's something moving all the time."

Speeches and Ian's toast to their future brought the gathering to a close, and goodbyes were said as guests began departing. Tania, still wearing her elegant gown, came over to hug them both.

"Come home safely, both of you," she said, and kissed Pam just as warmly as she kissed her father.

"And mind you think on that you'll always have a second home at our house; I shall expect you to call and see us a lot," Mildred added as she too embraced each of them in turn.

Before they could turn away, Pamela grasped Tania's hand and smiled at her again. "Thank you, love, for being my bridesmaid. And for the way you've looked after everybody here. You've made a big difference to our day."

"That is all right. I only wish that you and my father will be very happy."

Tania slid her arm into Mildred's and walked with her to the outer door. Her fingers outstretched to turn the handle, she turned and smiled towards her father and his wife.

Everything would seem different when she returned. Pamela would have her new place here, new authority, and her own father . . .? He would never be the same, would never again indulge her quite so freely, never devote so much attention to her interests. But nor would he continue as half a man, merely existing instead of living to the full. She could only be

happy that he was at last wearing that smile of fulfilment. Whatever she herself might think of Pamela, the
woman really had created something good at Stonemoor
House.